Language
and Reality in Swift's
A Tale of a Tub

Language and Reality in Swift's *A Tale of a Tub*

Frederik N. Smith

OHIO STATE UNIVERSITY PRESS : COLUMBUS

Frontispiece

Giovanni Battista Piranesi, *Le Carceri* ("The Prisons")
Plate VII, second state (ca. 1761)

Library of Congress Cataloging in Publication Data

Smith, Frederik N
1940–
Language and reality in Swift's A tale of a tub.
Bibliography: p.
Includes index.
1. Swift, Jonathan, 1667–1745. A tale of a tub.
2. Swift, Jonathan, 1667–1745—Style.
I. Title.
PR3724.T33S6 823'.5 79-15355

ISBN: 978-0-8142-5354-0

To the memory of my mother and father

Contents

Preface

The manuscript of a book may be written alone, but it is not revised without the opinions of others, nor does it reach publication without the assistance of still others.

I owe a great debt to my friends Professor William B. Piper of Rice University and Professor Robert Wallace of Case Western Reserve University, both of whom read the entire manuscript and made innumerable, invaluable comments and criticisms—the majority of which I incorporated into the final draft. I wish also to thank my friends and former colleagues Professor Louis D. Giannetti, Professor P. K. Saha, and Professor Gary Lee Stonum, as well as my former graduate students Leonard Podis and Evelyn Gajowski, all of whom read and commented on various chapters. And I owe thanks to Ms. Carol S. Sykes, my editor, who read and reread the manuscript with a thoroughness above and beyond what was required.

Beyond the gratitude expressed above, I want to take this public opportunity to express my thanks to my wife Jane, whose astute advice and endless patience are matched by a deep confidence in me.

Parts of chapter 6 appeared originally in quite different form in "The Epistemology of Fictional Failure: Swift's *Tale of a Tub* and Beckett's *Watt*," *Texas Studies in Literature and Language* 15 (Winter 1974): 649–72, published by the University of Texas Press.

All references to the *Tale* are to *A Tale of a Tub, to which is added The Battle of the Books and the Mechanical Operation of the Spirit*, ed. A. C. Guthkelch and D. Nichol Smith, 2d ed. (Oxford, 1958). For the sake of clarity I have in a few minor instances taken the liberty of silently deleting Swift's italics or reversing his italics and roman type; however, any important changes in original texts have been duly noted.

Language
and Reality in Swift's
A Tale of a Tub

Introduction

How to analyze the Tub, *was a Matter of difficulty; when after long Enquiry and Debate, the literal Meaning was preserved.*

Irvin Ehrenpreis refers to "the brilliant style which makes *A Tale of a Tub* the greatest prose satire in English."[1] Few would quibble with his judgment. But like the critics Swift condemns, we have been too often satisfied to catalogue stylistic devices or merely to cite them as examples of the Modern Author's faults. What we have failed to recognize is that the young Swift, after his early imitative, conventional odes (1690–94), was experimenting in the *Tale* (1696–97)[2] with a new tone and genre and that he was using style in this work as a way of working toward some important truths. Mark Schorer points out that for the contemporary novelist technique has become a preoccupation, a means not just of containing intellectual and moral implications but of discovering them.[3] Similarly, I think that for Swift technique in the *Tale* is a means of exploring his relationship to his mentor, Sir William Temple, his inherited literary traditions, and a wide range of seventeenth-century ideas and values.[4] And what remains constant in all his satire is his willingness to let style, rather than plot or character, carry the burden of his message.

Criticism has over the past twenty-five years made up for its earlier slighting of Swift's rhetoric. In particular, Martin Price's *Swift's Rhetorical Art* (1953), Edward W. Rosenheim, Jr.'s *Swift and the Satirist's Art* (1962), and John R. Clark's *Form and Frenzy in Swift's "Tale of a Tub"* (1970) have dealt with Swift's language at close range. But criticism, like everything else, moves in cycles, and discussion of the *Tale* seems to have entered a new phase, one that focuses less on the nature of Swift's persona and more on his own presence in the satire: I am thinking especially of studies of the *Tale* by Gardner D. Stout, Jr., John Traugott, and Cary Nelson.[5] What recent criticism has shown is that it is impossible to split the function of the author between a persona who is a modern hack and a wholly detached manipulator of that persona. In fact, the Modern Author is not a persona in the sense that Swift's other speakers are—a "style," Kathleen Williams calls him.[6] Although as a convenience I refer in the pages that follow to the "Modern" or to Swift's "persona," I intend by these terms to signify not a character but a certain identifiable style. I have accepted the rhetoric of the *Tale* as Swift's but have discovered that it everywhere pulls simultaneously in two directions, toward a convoluted verbosity and toward a concise plain-spokenness. Swift has cleverly intermingled these two styles for satiric effect.

In the *Tale* the relationship between language and reality—a critical issue in the seventeenth century—is one of Swift's most important themes as well as the basis for his unique style. Philosophers from Descartes to Locke deal with this same linguistic and philosophical issue. So too does Antoine Arnauld in *La logique ou l'art de penser,* a popular and often translated logic that Swift may have read while at Trinity College. In discussing the language of madness, philosophers and physicians such as Thomas Willis approached this same question from another angle. The Royal Society's insistence on a plain style appropriate to scientific inquiry was yet another manifestation of such concern, as was the interest in a simpler pulpit style. The search of John Wilkins and others for a universal language was likewise part of this attempt to systematize language as well as knowledge. And finally, no one denies the influence of Cervantes on Swift, and *Don Quixote,* like the *Tale,* is a satiric fiction that is very much about words and their dubious connections with things.[7] This whole period was marked by what Murray Cohen has described as "a lively struggle with the structure of language, or, more precisely, with the relationship between reality and language."[8] *A Tale of a Tub* reflects and comments on this struggle, is very much a product of its time, and could have been written in no other century, with the possible exception of our own.

The *Tale* was the first English book to take advantage of both the satirical and the philosophical possibilities inherent in this heated, contradictory debate over the relationship between language and reality. Anglican preacher and political conservative, Swift as a young man was looking for his own solution to this problem at the very time when the old structure of the universe was giving way to the new science and philosophy. In the *Tale* Swift comes across not as a gloomy skeptic but rather as a brilliant satirist and (although he would never admit it) something of a philosopher. "His Invention at the Height, and his Reading fresh in his Head" (p. 4), he self-consciously mixes fact and fiction, empiricism and rationalism, and reality and language in a way that is surely meant to reflect the confusing intellectual struggles of the prevous half century. What emerges is a paradoxical style that often contradicts itself. But such is modernism.

Throughout this study I take style to be neither the same as a writer's ideas nor the vehicle for his ideas, but rather his habitual means of arranging concepts, experiences, and implications into a significant form. As linguist Benjamin Lee Whorf says in his essay "Language, Mind, and Reality," "Thinking is most mysterious, and by far the greatest light upon it that we have is thrown by the study of language."[9] Whorf posits a connection between language and reality so intimate that the systematizations inherent in a particular language (be it English, Chinese, or Hopi) dictate the reality of a person who speaks that language, forcing certain perceptions on him, denying others, and channeling his reason.[10] Pushing Whorf's hypothesis somewhat further, we may infer a comparable link between an individual's private habits of language and his private perception of reality. If there is validity to this argument—and I think there is—then we may say that the uniqueness of a writer's style represents his personal organization of the world, his personal arrangement not merely of words but of reality itself.

Richard Ohmann, in his "Prolegomena to the Analysis of Prose Style," describes the aim of such an approach as clearly as one could want it: "If the critic is able to isolate and examine the most primitive choices which lie behind a work of prose, they can reveal to him the very roots of a writer's epistemology, the way in which he breaks up for manipulation the refractory surge of sensations which challenges all writers and all perceivers."[11] A study of a writer's style is thus no mere description of image patterns, nor a computerized table of nouns and verbs, nor a rhetorical analysis of a given passage. We can go well beyond this. In pointing up the connection between style and epistemology, Ohmann has provided a firm theoretical basis for the study of diction, syntax, and other configurations of a text. The proper study of style is very exciting and can bring together linguistics, philosophy, and psychology in a way that has been impossible since the seventeenth century.[12]

What makes this approach to style singularly appropriate for a study of Swift is his peculiar awareness of how language can inhibit or be the means of reaching an understanding of reality. To cite only the most obvious example, *Gulliver's Travels* dwells on right and wrong interpretations of experience: Gulliver delineates his reality for us in a plain, circumstantial style (he insists on this), but Swift implies that such a style is too plain and too circumstantial to bear complex, subtle interpretations of complex, subtle experiences. Gulliver views things too simply and seems incapable of accepting ambiguity. When Swift offers him the choice of being a beastly Yahoo or a reasoning Houyhnhnm, Gulliver opts for the latter and denies any resemblance he bears to the Yahoos, just as he denies any animal traits in his Houyhnhnm master. But *Gulliver's Travels* presents at least one alternative that is too subtle for its narrator: man is both a physical *and* a rational being, and neither mere Yahoo nor mere Houyhnhnm.

Swift's interest in the relationship between language and reality, however, antedates *Gulliver's Travels*. Although *A Tale of a Tub*'s broken, bathetic style is in no way an epitome of Swift's statements concerning style,[13] nor a model for his subsequent satires, it was clearly for him a pivotal work, and in it we can see him working out his ideas concerning language and its connection with understanding. What Swift does in the *Tale* (and you can feel him beginning to wrestle with these ideas in the odes) is to create a loose, flexible satire that is remarkably unassertive and that is based on the interweaving of his style with that of his Modern. If words and sentences can lead us back to a writer's epistemology, then in *A Tale of a Tub* the dichotomous configurations of style lead us back simultaneously to the Modern's and Swift's opposing epistemologies. One reason the work is so difficult is that these two outlooks are not kept clearly apart; a reading of the *Tale* uncovers no easy opposition between Swift and a fully developed persona, but a crisscrossing of two styles and two ways of knowing. Swift forces us to recognize two conflicting styles and two conflicting approaches to life, that of the aloof, intellectualized, abstracting persona as against the earthy, sensate, experience-oriented approach that he recommends.

Like a typical modern, the persona makes much of arranging

knowledge into abstracts, summaries, and compendiums—"all disposed into great Order, and reducible upon Paper" (p. 127). Swift puns here on "reducible." Without ever developing a full-fledged persona, he repeatedly undercuts his own modernistic attempts to neutralize unpleasant realities by transforming them into abstract lexical or logical items. Throughout the *Tale* he reminds himself and us of these realities, which will not be denied. The only ballast for the high-flying intellectualism of *A Tale of a Tub* is the empirical, physical reality suggested by its imagery; this explains why such things as crusts or bread, corpses, and excrement appear with such frequency. If *Gulliver's Travels* is, as Hugh Kenner says, "a satire on mindless empiricism,"[14] then Swift's earlier book is a satire on mindless rationalism, a horrifying example of empirical data *almost* overridden by mere mental functioning.

1. Irvin Ehrenpreis, *Mr. Swift and His Contemporaries*, vol. 1 of *Swift: The Man, His Works, and the Age* (Cambridge, Mass., 1962), p. 176.

2. Parts of the book were written later. For a discussion of the date of composition, see Guthkelch and Smith, pp. xlii–xlvii.

3. Mark Schorer, "Technique as Discovery," in *The Theory of the Novel*, ed. Philip Stevick (New York, 1967), p. 72.

4. For helpful background concerning these issues, see Ehrenpreis, pp. 185–203.

5. Gardner D. Stout, Jr., "Speaker and Satiric Vision in Swift's *Tale of a Tub*," *Eighteenth-Century Studies* 3 (Winter 1969): 175–99; John Traugott, "*A Tale of a Tub*," in *Focus: Swift*, ed. C. J. Rawson (London, 1971), pp. 76–120; and Cary Nelson, "Form and Claustrophobia: Intestinal Space in *A Tale of a Tub*," chap. 5 of *The Incarnate Word: Literature as Verbal Space* (Urbana, Ill., 1973).

6. Kathleen Williams, *Jonathan Swift and the Age of Compromise* (Lawrence, Kans., 1958), p. 136.

7. See Michel Foucault, *The Order of Things: An Archaeology of the Human Sciences*, trans. Richard Howard (New York, 1970), pp. 46–50.

8. Murray Cohen, "Sensible Words: Linguistic Theory in Late Seventeenth-Century England," in *Studies in Eighteenth-Century Culture*, vol. 5, ed. Ronald C. Rosbottom (Madison, Wis., 1976), p. 232.

9. Benjamin Lee Whorf, "Language, Mind, and Reality," originally published in 1942; rpt. in *Language, Thought, and Reality: Selected Writings of Benjamin Lee Whorf*, ed. John B. Carroll (Cambridge, Mass., 1956), p. 252.

10. On this whole question see "The Relation of Habitual Thought and Behavior to Language," in *Language, Thought, and Reality*, pp. 134–59, and other essays in this volume.

11. Richard Ohmann, "Prolegomena to the Analysis of Prose Style," in *Style in Prose Fiction: English Institute Essays*, ed. Harold C. Martin (New York, 1959), p. 9.

12. See Noam Chomsky, *Cartesian Linguistics: A Chapter in the History of Rationalist Thought* (New York, 1966), p. 76: "It should be borne in mind that we are dealing with a period [i.e., the seventeenth century] that antedates the divergence of linguistics, philosophy, and psychology. The insistence of each of these disciplines on 'emancipating itself' from any contamination by the other is a peculiarly modern phenomenon."

13. Perhaps the greatest impediment to a proper understanding of Swift's style is his own statements on style; his repeated emphasis on simplicity and propriety has misled readers from the eighteenth century on. See D. W. Jefferson, "An Approach to Swift," in *From Dryden to Johnson*, ed. Boris Ford (Baltimore, 1957), p. 230: "Swift's remarks on prose style, while of great interest, bear very little on the secret of his own greatness in that medium."

14. Hugh Kenner, *Flaubert, Joyce, and Beckett: The Stoic Comedians* (Boston, 1962), p. 89.

chapter one

Words and Things

Words; which are also Bodies of much Weight and Gravity, as is manifest from those deep Impressions *they make and leave upon us.*

"Words are only Names for *Things*," says Gulliver.[1] Swift would agree. But it is in *A Tale of a Tub* rather than *Gulliver's Travels* that he worked out his view of this relationship. In fact, the *Tale* is a key document in the seventeenth-century controversy over words and things.[2] Writers and thinkers of this period, reacting against the florid style of the Renaissance, sought a language more appropriate to their own scientific and philosophical reasonings and turned to the relation between words and things as a matter of great importance. Swift's wordy book about words reflects a major concern of Bacon, Hobbes, Wilkins, and Locke; it is a parody of their preoccupation with language and at the same time a young writer's fresh exploration of an inherited stylistic and philosophical question.

Although it seems to me that every author (and every speaker) has his own implicit ideas on how language relates to the real world, in the *Tale* Swift—like Sterne, Carroll, and Beckett after him—brings his thoughts about language up front, makes language one of his main themes, and proceeds quite self-consciously to work out his ideas about words and things. Even though *A Proposal for Correcting, Improving and Ascertaining the English Tongue* treats of the sociological causes and moral effects of the misuse of language, Swift, years before he wrote that politically motivated argument, had approached imaginatively the much deeper issue raised by such linguistic corruption—its distortion of the world. Written in the context of discussions of words and things such as John Wilkins's influential *Essay Towards a Real Character* (1668) and, more immediately, book 3 (entitled "Of Words") of Locke's *Essay on Human Understanding*,[3] Swift's first prose satire may be read as his personal philosophy of language. Like Wilkins and Locke, Swift urges a return to things as the proper source of knowledge; the trouble with the Modern Author is that he deals with words apart from things.

In his book *The Order of Things*, Michel Foucault argues that in Europe the general sense of language had become by Swift's day quite different from what it had been during the Renaissance: "In the seventeenth and eighteenth centuries, the peculiar existence and ancient solidity of language as a thing inscribed in the fabric of the world were dissolved in the functioning of representation; all language had value only as discourse. The art of language was a way of 'making a sign'—of simultaneously signifying something and arranging signs around that thing."[4] In an attempt to eliminate verbal ambiguity and the superficial use of language, writers and philosophers of the seventeenth century turned toward a descriptive language of signs. The accumulation of real evidence in the new philosophy and science was typically set against scholastic book knowledge.[5] And the emphasis on signs was a part of this desire to forge a new, more direct relationship between words and objects.

A peculiar but highly relevant chapter in the new emphasis on signification was the keen interest in building a universal language scheme. Believing that before Babel man had been united by a common language, linguists such as Johann Amos Komenský (Comenius), Samuel Hartlib, Francis Lodowick, Seth Ward, William Petty, George Dalgarno, and John Wilkins dreamed of a reunification of peoples and a reorganization of the world itself through the development of a universal language that might be shared once again by all men.[6] "The transition that took place in England in the middle years of the century," explains James Knowlson in his recent book on language schemes, "was thus from a character which merely *represented* things and notions by agreement, to one which *mirrored* the whole of human knowledge by means of the combination of its elements."[7] Ideally, of course, such a language not only would be an arrangement of words as signs of things but would itself *be* knowledge, since each word would provide a direct and accurate description of the thing signified.

Bishop Wilkins was a key figure in this movement. Complaining of "the Curse of Babel," he says in the *Real Character* that "besides the best way of helping Memory by natural *Method*, the *Under-*

standing likewise would be highly improved; and we should, by learning the *Character* and the *Names* of Things, be instructed likewise in their *Natures*, the knowledge of both which ought to be conjoyned." The theory itself, he goes on, "upon which such a design were to be founded, should be exactly *suted to the nature of things*."[8] In his "Epistle Dedicatory" Wilkins claims a great deal for his real character, saying that it would lead to "the improving of all Natural knowledge," "the clearing of some of our Modern differences in Religion," and even "the Universal good of Mankind."[9] Although I do not wish to argue that Swift in the *Tale* was parodying Wilkins, he had certainly read the *Essay Towards a Real Character*, he would have found such hyperbolic promises laughable, and the Modern's similar claims (on the title page and elsewhere) that his book is "Written for the Universal Improvement of Mankind" are strikingly close to Wilkins's proud projections. Swift would agree with Wilkins and others that we ought to move our words closer to the things they stand for, but he would have found Wilkins's compendium of knowledge (with its unwieldy thesaurus of elements, animals, manners, and so forth) an absurdity because paradoxically it was, in the end, so far from real things. Swift might have agreed with Wilkins's general goal, but he could have accepted neither his universal claims for his project nor his encyclopedic methods.[10]

Despite the Modern Author's attempts to organize all knowledge for us, he lets slip in the final paragraph of *A Tale of a Tub* that he has "thought fit to make *Invention* the *Master*, and to give *Method* and *Reason*, the Office of *Lacquays*" (p. 209). But Swift has been undermining his attempts all along. Multiple introductions, digressions, and the "scenic" or anecdotal style of the *Tale* blur its potentially neat profile. Swift breaks things down even further, however. His emphasis on the individual word—an arrangement of the typesetter's twenty-six pieces—is part of his unrelenting fragmentation of his persona's ideas. One thing that makes *A Tale of a Tub* unique is that in it words tend to jump out of the text and out of their context, to take on meanings or values in their own right, apart from their larger meanings or values within the sentences in which they appear. "It *often* happens that *men*," says Locke, "even when they would apply themselves to an attentive consideration, *do set their thoughts more on words than things*."[11] He could be describing Swift's Modern.

Hugh Kenner cites the *Tale* as the first book that admits openly (and over and over) to being Herr Gutenberg's progeny.[12] Capital letters, asterisks, chapter divisions, parentheses, italics, footnotes, marginalia, even blank spaces in the text—everywhere Swift draws attention to the technological parts of the book in our hands. Like the carcass of human nature, *A Tale of a Tub* is anatomized before our very eyes: "They tell us, that the Fashion of jumbling fifty Things together in a Dish, was at first introduced in Compliance to a depraved and *debauched Appetite*, as well as to a *crazy Constitution*; And to see a Man hunting thro' an *Ollio*, after the *Head* and *Brains* of a *Goose*, a *Wigeon*, or a *Woodcock*, is a Sign, he wants a Stomach and Digestion for more substantial Victuals" (p. 144). The ingredients of the *Tale* flash in every spoonful. And the ignorant eater mentioned here is the ignorant reader, who picks through this olio in search of the head or brains of the Modern's panegyric without understanding that the man really responsible is Jonathan Swift.

For example, italics in the *Tale* draw our attention repeatedly to the typographical existence of words. "Whatever word or Sentence is Printed in a different Character," says the Modern, "shall be judged to contain something extraordinary either of *Wit* or *Sublime*" (pp. 46–47). Yet italicizing the words "Wit" and "Sublime" makes them in no way extraordinary; as a matter of fact, the italics in this case emphasize the lack of any special meaning in those words.[13] Swift knows—although the Modern does not—that it is not the printer's type but the way an author uses language that lends a statement its significance or force.

Thus Swift's italics often work ironically, drawing our attention to the Modern's fine-sounding but quite empty words. At the same time, the italicization of words—usually of nouns, by the way[14]—repeatedly compels us to focus our eyes on an odd word or a word used in an odd way, sometimes sets up a parallelism between two key words in a sentence, and, beyond this, makes us dig for the real meaning that Swift has concealed within the Modern's pedantic vocabulary. The italics in this passage work one way for the Modern and another for Swift:

> I have one Word to say upon the Subject of *Profound Writers*, who are grown very numerous of late; And, I know very well, the judicious World is resolved to list me in that Number. I conceive therefore, as to the Business of being *Profound*, that it is with *Writers*, as with *Wells*; A

> Person with good Eyes may see to the Bottom of the deepest, provided any *Water* be there; and, that often, when there is nothing in the World at the Bottom, besides *Dryness* and *Dirt*, tho' it be but a Yard and half under Ground, it shall pass, however, for wondrous *Deep*, upon no wiser Reason than because it is wondrous *Dark*. (Pp. 207–8)

Of course, the Modern has a good deal more than "one Word" to say on this or any other subject! In this paragraph there are ten italicized words, six nouns and four adjectives. Although Swift might have italicized any of the twelve other nouns and five other adjectives, he has drawn our attention to the words that are, from his point of view, most important. If this were really the proud Modern speaking, the one word that he would certainly italicize would be the "me" in "I know very well, the judicious World is resolved to list me in that Number." But Swift chooses rather to stress the paradox of a literal and a figurative profundity, of darkness that passes for depth. He italicizes "Profound Writers," then splits the two words in order to use "Profound" to modify "Writers" and "Wells," thus setting up analogies between literary works and wells, readers and those who stare into wells. By the time we get to the end of the paragraph, Swift has us thinking both at once as we read "Dryness" and "Dirt" (which expresses his contempt for bad writing) and "Deep" and "Dark" (which is essentially the paradox he is playing with). Swift is, of course, ridiculing the shallowness of the Modern's *Tale of a Tub* at the same time that he is encouraging us to plumb the very real depths of his own *Tale of a Tub*. The effect of all this is that we pay a disproportionate amount of attention to the meaning of individual words.

Both the numerous footnotes (which were added to the fifth edition)[15] and the marginal notes (which appeared in the first and all subsequent editions) refer often to single words within the text proper—defining a word, interpreting it, or questioning its use. The *Tale* keeps the reader looking simultaneously at the body of the text, at the bottom of the page, and at the margin. In a theoretical way we ought to observe that an author who uses such notes is on the one hand underlining the purely typographical nature of his book, since we do not use notes in speaking, but on the other hand refusing to let his book stand still, since notes offer alternate or fuller readings. When the Modern says that Peter sets his papal bulls roaring in order to frighten "Naughty Boys" (p. 112), and when Swift adds at the bottom of the page, "That is Kings who incurr his Displeasure," then we are forced to accept "Naughty Boys" both as youths who pester Lord Peter the fop *and* as the royal enemies of the Pope in Rome. "Ventriloqual gadget," Kenner calls the footnote.[16] Swift's footnotes are necessary to the multilevel effect of *A Tale of a Tub*.

Like the italics and footnotes, the marginal notes focus our attention on individual words or phrases, if only in forcing us to slow down or interrupt our left-to-right reading. Beyond this, many of the notes explain or define words used in the text proper. "Three Pence" is said to be "A Lawyer's Coach-hire" (p. 176). "True illuminated" is "A Name of the Rosycrucians" (p. 186). "Husks and their Harlots" is "Virtuoso Experiments, and Modern Comedies" (p. 65). And sometimes it is difficult to know what validity one of these readings has over another. "Husks and their Harlots," for example, would seem to suggest simply "dried-up old fops and their women"; the equation with "Virtuoso Experiments, and Modern Comedies" would occur to no one but the Modern Author. As usual, the Modern is compromised: although he condemns hieroglyphic writing, Swift shows him consistently writing that way himself.

Less obvious, perhaps, is what we might call the "glossary style" of *A Tale of a Tub*.[17] The Modern frequently uses synonymous pairs of words to get his meaning across, a device characteristic of Bacon, Browne, Milton, and other seventeenth-century writers. The *Tale* is full of such doublets: "Cant, or Jargon" (p. 28), "Transposal or Misapplication" (p. 43), "Briguing and Caballing" (p. 65), "Thought and Application of Mind" (p. 71), "Dispositions and Opinions" (p. 81), "Errors and Defects" (p. 92), "Tyros's or junior Scholars" (p. 101), and so on. What is obvious from this list is that whereas a few terms are usefully joined, the second term helping to define the first (e.g., "Briguing and Caballing"), most of these pairs are redundant, the second term merely echoing the first (e.g., "Errors and Defects").[18] And Swift on occasion toys ironically with this rhetorical construction, as in "the Dross and Grossness" (p. 62) and "the most Illustrious and Epidemick" (p. 142). The Modern believes mistakenly that a multiplicity of words guarantees meaning; on the other hand, Swift intends for us to read his *Tale of a Tub* on one level as a parody of such seventeenth-century redundancy, as is clear from the following absurdity: "Now this Physico-logical Scheme of Oratorical Receptacles or Machines, contains a great Mystery, being a Type, a Sign, an Emblem, a Shadow, a Symbol, bearing Analogy to the Spacious Commonwealth of Writers" (p. 61). It is significant that in the *Tale* the italics, the footnotes and marginal notes, and the Modern's glossary style all play up the synonymy of language. But the Modern's use of words and more words betrays everywhere the authority of his categorical statements.

Another aspect of Swift's fascination with individual words is his emphasis on proper names. In the "Apology" he denies the charge that he has borrowed the names of the three brothers (p. 13). In section 2 the brothers go without names, although the Modern promises to supply them later (p. 84). In section 4 "the learned brother" becomes "Peter," Swift stressing Peter's insistence on a proper title: "He told his Brothers, he would have them to know, that he was their Elder, and consequently his Father's sole Heir; Nay, a while after, he would not allow them to call Him, *Brother*, but Mr. *PETER*; And then he must be styl'd, *Father PETER*; and sometimes, *My Lord PETER*" (p. 105). True to religious history, Swift delays naming the other brothers until section 6, when they are baptized "Martin" and "Jack" (p. 134). Names or titles are clearly important to Peter in a way that they are not to Swift. Peter's assumption of progressively more formal titles shows Swift's contempt of papal aloofness; by insisting on such artificial respect, Peter indeed *becomes* these titles, and nothing more.

Jack likewise travels under various labels. It is typical that Peter should *demand* his titles whereas Jack *is given* his nicknames: "And now the little Boys in the Streets began to salute him with several Names. Sometimes they would call Him, *Jack the Bald*; sometimes, *Jack with a Lanthorn*; sometimes, *Dutch Jack*; sometimes, *French Hugh*; sometimes, *Tom the Beggar*; and sometimes, *Knocking Jack of the North*. And it was under one, or some, or all of these Appellations (which I leave the Learned Reader to determine) that he hath given Rise to the most Illustrious and Epidemick Sect of *Aeolists*" (pp. 141–42). The italicization of each nickname and Swift's footnote on each draw attention to the names proper. But to push further, if we assume that one's name is his most personal possession, then the multiplicity of names here implies a multiplicity of identities. And I take Swift seriously when he leaves it up to the reader to decide which name or names (and thus which identity or identities) Jack deserves. Names in *A Tale of a Tub* tend to shift, to be loosely, not absolutely, applied to people.[19]

So what's in a name? The most obvious explanation for the instability of proper names is that Swift intends to satirize both

Catholics and Protestants into stereotypes, suggesting that whatever you call them they are all the same. But Swift is seldom so easy. The several names for Calvin—"Jack the Bald," "Jack with a Lanthorn," "Dutch Jack," and so on—suggest that Calvinism is not one movement but different movements in different countries, as it was. Swift plays loose with Calvinism by playing loose with John Calvin's name; but he likewise knocks the Modern for making so much of mere nicknames. Like the alternate readings forced on us elsewhere, the multiplication of names in the *Tale* is part of Swift's simultaneous objection to and delight in alternate explanations of things. Throughout his writings, and in *A Tale of a Tub* in particular, Swift plays on the fluidity of language, forces his reader to juggle alternate expressions, and generally condemns yet exploits the multifarious meanings of words. He has it both ways: while making fun of Peter's insistence on a proper title and Jack's numerous nicknames, he raises the quite serious problem of naming and suggests that agreement is essentially a matter of propriety and convenience. Interestingly, the Modern Author does not have a name, and Jonathan Swift attached his own name to only one of his literary works.

Swift's emphasis on naming is only part of his keen interest in words. The Modern is explicit about the plight of words in the Restoration theater (pp. 60–61), the various definitions of the word "Critic" (pp. 92–93), and other matters of diction. And clauses like these are common: "a damn'd Kick on the Mouth, which hath ever since been call'd a *Salute*" (p. 115); "which we commonly suppose to be a Distemper, and call by the Name of *Madness* or *Phrenzy*" (p. 162); "the whole Operation of Preaching is to this very Day among their Professors, styled by the Phrase of *Holding forth*" (p. 202). In the *Tale* Swift uses words so self-consciously that we sometimes get entangled in his language at the expense of his meaning.

But for all his verbal pyrotechnics, Swift intends to bring up (without necessarily resolving) some crucial questions about the nature of language. He jokes poignantly about the whole words-and-things controversy. In one passage he seems to satirize the thinking behind the Royal Society's insistence on "so many *things*, almost in an equal number of *words*":[20] "Air being a heavy Body, and therefore (according to the System of *Epicurus*) continually descending, must needs be more so, when loaden and press'd down by Words; which are also Bodies of much Weight and Gravity, as it is manifest from those deep *Impressions* they make and leave upon us" (p. 60). The pseudoserious argument of course pivots on the ironic pun on "Impressions," which Swift forces us to take in its physical as well as its figurative sense.[21] He reduces the Royal Society's honest desire to bring words and things closer together to an absurdity: words are themselves things. Correspondingly, "Words are but Wind" (p. 153) is a gross perversion of Bacon's "Wordes are but the Images of matter."[22] Swift here takes Bacon's (and Locke's) warning that words do not stand for things but for the ideas of things and reduces it to another absurdity: words have no relation whatever to things. Thus Swift brings the whole seventeenth-century debate over words and things down to the ridiculous opposition between words as things and words as hot air.

This matter of the signification of words comes up time and time again. After a series of crack-brained equations ("Is not Religion a *Cloak* . . . "), the Modern argues that "those Beings which the World calls improperly *Suits of Cloathes*, are in Reality the most refined Species of Animals, or to proceed higher, that they are Rational Creatures, or Men" (p. 78). Then, narrowing his focus, he says that people "do according to certain Compositions receive different Appellations" and gives a couple of examples: "If certain Ermins and Furs be placed in a certain Position, we stile them a *Judge*, and so, an apt Conjunction of Lawn and black Sattin, we intitle a *Bishop*" (p.79).[23] These few pages are reminiscent of Locke's extended discussion "Of General Terms," in which he shows how quickly the human mind fits particulars into the pigeonholes of genus and species.[24] This process has to do not with real essences but only with what Locke calls "nominal essences" and is just another kind of naming: "Men, making abstract *ideas* and settling them in their minds with names annexed to them, do thereby enable themselves to consider things and discourse of them, as it were in bundles, for the easier and readier improvement and communication of their knowledge, which would advance but slowly were words and thoughts confined only to particulars."[25] Locke considers what several accidents are required to name a thing "gold," "horse," or "man." In light of Locke's commentary, what the Modern says does not sound foolish at all but seems rather like Swift's humorous account of the agreements we make among ourselves that the presence of a couple of accidents is sufficient for labeling a person "man" and a few more for labeling him "judge," "bishop," or something else. Our dictionaries are collections of such agreed-upon signs for things.[26]

Disputing the value of the judge's "bench," the Modern advises us to look into the "Etymology of the Name, which in the *Phoenician* Tongue is a Word of great Signification, importing, if literally interpreted, *The Place of Sleep*; but in common Acceptation, *A Seat well bolster'd and cushion'd, for the Repose of old and gouty Limbs: Senes ut in otia tuta recedant*" (p. 57). Here again the tongue-in-cheek tone should not be allowed to obscure Swift's fascination with words and their histories; in this case he is making a rather clear separation between a word's etymology, its literal denotation, and its popular connotation. No matter that the reference to the Phoenician origin of the word is malarkey. No matter either that in the end the common implication of the word is undercut by a learned quotation from Horace. At least the subject was for Swift a most serious one. The words "Signification" (that which is signified by a word) and "Acceptation" (the sense in which a word is accepted or received) are both common in seventeenth-century discussions of language and are found elsewhere in the *Tale*, as well as in book 3 of *An Essay Concerning Human Understanding*.[27]

Behind the Modern's misguided explanation of the word "Zeal" is an ironic consideration of a topic treated quite seriously by others: "For this Meddly of Humor, he made a Shift to find a very plausible Name, honoring it with the Title of *Zeal*; which is, perhaps, the most significant Word that hath been ever yet produced in any Language; As, I think, I have fully proved in my excellent *Analytical* Discourse upon that Subject; wherein I have deduced a *Histori-theo-physilogical* Account of *Zeal*, shewing how it first proceeded from a *Notion* into a *Word*, and from thence in a hot Summer, ripned into a *tangible Substance*" (p. 137).[28] The hyperbolic diction and proud tone (one is responsible for the other), plus the absurdity of the closing metaphor, serve to repel us from the content of the Modern's lingusitics. The terms "Analytical Discourse," "physilogical Account," and "tangible Substance" lend an air of parody to the passage. Our immediate response is to guess that Swift would take exception to everything the Modern says here.

But look again. The subtlety of the linguistic pun on "*sign*ificant Word" suggests that Swift may be saying something on that topic worth listening to. In fact, the three key terms in seventeenth-century linguistics are here—"Notion," "Word," and "tangible Substance." Swift would agree with the Modern that a sign for a complex idea stands for a "Meddly of Humor." And Swift would undoubtedly agree with the point that Locke hammers home ad nauseum: "We should have a great many fewer disputes in the world if words were taken for what they are, the signs of our *ideas* only and not for things themselves."[29] Thus although Swift would say (with the Modern) that the notion or idea spawns its sign,[30] he would certainly add (against the Modern) that the word could not possibly spawn the thing itself. That the Modern should put "Notion" and "Word" ahead of "tangible Substance" is an indication of his inverted priorities.

The story of the three brothers and their manipulation of their father's will is itself an example of the gradual abasement of the meaning of words. And in telling that story, Swift has borrowed a favorite trick of the Modern's—taking a metaphor in its literal sense[31]—and has ingeniously spun a book out of it. "Words are the clothing of our thoughts" was a seventeenth-century cliché.[32] Swift uses it in his *Thoughts on Various Subjects*: "Common Speakers have only one set of Ideas, and one set of Words to clothe them in."[33] It appears also in his quite serious *Tatler* contribution on linguistic degeneracy: "In this last Point, the usual Pretence is, that they spell as they speak: A noble Standard for Language! To depend upon the Caprice of every Coxcomb; who, because Words are the Clothing of our Thoughts, cuts them out, and shapes them as he pleases, and changes them oftener than his Dress."[34]

That Swift had this cliché in mind as he was writing *A Tale of a Tub* is clear from his absurd equation of language with clothing in section 2, the first part of the allegory: "To this System of Religion were tagged several subaltern Doctrines, which were entertained with great Vogue: as particularly, the Faculties of the Mind were deduced by the Learned among them in this manner: *Embroidery*, was *Sheer wit; Gold Fringe* was *agreeable Conversation, Gold Lace* was *Repartee*, a huge long *Periwig* was *Humor*, and a *Coat full of Powder* was very good *Raillery*: All which required abundance of *Finesse* and *Delicatesse* to manage with Advantage, as well as a strict Observance after Times and Fashions" (p. 80). Thus Swift is using his story of the three brothers as an allegory of corruption not only in the Church but also in language and style. Like clothing and religion, language degenerates when one insists upon "a strict

Observance after Times and Fashions." And a moment later writing and clothing are confused in a pun, as the Modern Author says, "And so leaving these broken Ends, I carefully gather up the chief Thread of my Story, and proceed" (p. 81).[35] Looked at this way, the *Tale* assumes a satisfying wholeness (if we insist on such a thing!), the story proper giving us an allegory of linguistic degeneracy, the digressions a series of bad examples of degenerated language. The Modern Author's style is fashionable all right, but it bears little or no relation to what men with common sense regard as real, moral, or human.

In a passage that is in effect a little essay on words, Swift implies that the source of such decadence is a cavalier use of language.

> However, after some Pause the Brother so often mentioned for his Erudition, who was well Skill'd in Criticisms, had found in a certain Author, which he said should be nameless, that the same Word which in the Will is called *Fringe*, does also signifie a *Broom-stick*; and doubtless ought to have the same Interpretation in this Paragraph. This, another of the Brothers disliked, because of that Epithet, *Silver*, which could not, he humbly conceived, in Propriety of Speech be reasonably applied to a *Broom-stick*: but it was replied upon him, that this Epithet was understood in a *Mythological*, and *Allegorical* Sense. However, he objected again, why their Father should forbid them to wear *Broom-stick* on their Coats, a Caution that seemed unnatural and impertinent; upon which he was taken up short, as one that spoke irreverently of a *Mystery*, which doubtless was very useful and significant, but ought not to be over-curiously pryed into, or nicely reasoned upon. And in short, their Father's Authority being now considerably sunk, this Expedient was allowed to serve as a lawful Dispensation, for wearing their full Proportion of *Silver Fringe*. (P. 88)

Just beyond the edge of the page, Swift listens intently while the three brothers bicker over the rules of signification. To the attentive reader, the verbal in-jokes "signifie" and "significant," plus the irony of a "nameless" author, point to Swift's presence. The question would seem to be not simply whether the father's will can be wrenched this way, but also whether words in general can be torn loose from their accepted referents. May one person (or even three) decide that the word "Fringe" signifies what others customarily call a "Broom-stick"? Swift typically buries his point of view within a passage; here the one commonsensical brother thinks the "Mystery" of signification *ought* to be pried into, and at least he asks the right questions. The passage implies that to switch referents on the basis of what is momentarily expedient is to destroy the "Authority" of linguistic convention.

What leaves words open to such private redefinition—Swift elsewhere equates linguistic change with linguistic corruption[36]—is the imperfection of language itself. As Locke says, "Thus we may conceive how *words*, which were by nature so well adapted to that purpose, came to be made use of by men as *the signs* of their *ideas*: not by any natural connexion that there is between particular articulate sounds and certain *ideas*, for then there would be but one language amongst all men; but by a voluntary imposition whereby such a word is made arbitrarily the mark of such an *idea*."[37] Swift would agree, regretfully. Because the connection between a word and an idea of a thing is based only on convention, the three brothers may, if they want, decide that "Fringe" means "Broomstick." But to abandon linguistic convention is to abandon the possibility of communication with others. If you say "toe-*may*-toe" and I say "toe-*mah*-toe," we may get on one another's nerves; but if you say "Fringe" and I say "Broom-stick," how can we understand one another?

The consequences of linguistic distortion go further. Swift deals most memorably with the problem in his three-page dramatization of Peter's mutton dinner.

> *Come Brothers*, said *Peter, fall to, and spare not; here is excellent good Mutton; or hold, now my Hand is in, I'll help you*. At which word, in much Ceremony, with Fork and Knife, he carves out two good Slices of the Loaf, and presents each on a Plate to his Brothers. The Elder of the two not suddenly entring into *Lord Peter*'s Conceit, began with very civil Language to examine the Mystery. *My Lord*, said he, *I doubt, with great Submission, there may be some Mistake. What*, says *Peter, you are pleasant; Come then, let us hear this Jest, your Head is so big with. None in the World, my Lord; but unless I am very much deceived, your Lordship was pleased a while ago, to let fall a Word about Mutton, and I would be glad to see it with all my Heart. How*, said *Peter*, appearing in great Surprise, *I do not comprehend this at all*—Upon which, the younger interposing, to set the Business right; *My Lord*, said he, *My Brother, I suppose is hungry, and longs for the Mutton, your Lordship hath promised us to Dinner*. (Pp. 116–17)

Swift is, of course, joking about transubstantiation. But also at issue here is the source of linguistic authority.[38] What we have is a sort of emperor's-new-clothes situation. Peter had earlier "let fall a Word about Mutton," but the brothers say they "would be glad to see it."

And Peter speaks of "excellent good Mutton," but Swift (not the imperceptive Modern here) speaks of a "Loaf" of bread. In this context I find "Conceit" an interesting word: it signifies Peter's mad fancy and at the same time (referring to the rhetorical device) suggests his linguistic trickery.

The question is, Is this thing before us a "shoulder of Mutton" or a "Crust of Bread"? What name do we give it?

> *Pray*, said Peter, *take me along with you, either you are both mad, or disposed to be merrier than I approve of; If* You *there, do not like your Piece, I will carve you another, tho' I should take that to be the choice Bit of the whole Shoulder. What then, my Lord*, replied the first, *it seems this is a shoulder of Mutton all this while. Pray Sir*, says *Peter, eat your Vittles, and leave off your Impertinence, if you please, for I am not disposed to relish it at present*: But the other could not forbear, being over-provoked at the affected Seriousness of *Peter's* Countenance. *By G—, My Lord*, said he, *I can only say, that to my Eyes, and Fingers, and Teeth, and Nose, it seems to be nothing but a Crust of Bread*. Upon which, the second put in his Word: *I never saw a Piece of Mutton in my Life, so nearly resembling a Slice from a Twelve-peny Loaf. Look ye, Gentlemen*, cries *Peter* in a Rage, *to convince you, what a couple of blind, positive, ignorant, wilful Puppies you are, I will use but this plain Argument; By G—, it is true, good, natural Mutton as any in* Leaden-Hall *Market; and G— confound you both eternally, if you offer to believe otherwise*. Such a thundring Proof as this, left no farther Room for Objection. (Pp. 117–18)

The struggle is between dictation of meaning and empirical testing for meaning. Between "*By G—, it is true, good, natural Mutton as any in* Leaden-Hall *Market*" and "*I can only say, that to my Eyes, and Fingers, and Teeth, and Nose, it seems to be nothing but a Crust of Bread*," Peter reminds me of Humpty Dumpty in *Through the Looking Glass*: "'When *I* use a word,' Humpty Dumpty said, 'it means just what I choose it to mean—neither more nor less.'"[39] Because Peter's *proof* "left no farther room for Objection," it precludes the world of the senses and is to Swift as unreal as Wilkins's arbitrary scheme. The error is linguistic as well as theological. Of course, as in the "Broom-stick" passage, the wrong opinion wins out; Martin and Jack eventually surrender to Peter's dogma. But not before Swift has made his point: to set aside the conventionality of language is to set aside communicable reality, or rather, what we conventionally call reality.

The point Swift makes here about words and things is precisely that made by Locke: "For words, being sounds, can produce in us no other simple *ideas* than those very sounds, nor excite in us but by that voluntary connexion which is known to be between them and those simple *ideas* which common use has made them signs of. He that thinks otherwise, let him try if any words can give him the taste of a pineapple and make him have the true *idea* of the relish of that celebrated delicious fruit."[40] The word "pineapple" is no more the same as my relish in eating a real pineapple than the word "mutton" is the same as my relish in eating a real leg of mutton. To confuse one with the other is to mistake language for reality. *A Tale of a Tub* implies a culture in which language has become the art of sign-making. Yet the Modern's myriad signs often seem to be signs without referents. Swift admits that sign-making is critical; he also suggests that mere sign-making is not enough and that it can degenerate into sign-collecting.

Johnson notwithstanding, Swift never, even in *The Conduct of the Allies*, relies on "strong facts" alone for his effects.[41] In the *Tale* he toys with language and draws attention to the linguistic process of naming things; but whereas the Modern treats language as the art of making signs, Swift insists that making signs is only one of its functions. Although he is never again the philosopher of language that he is in the *Tale*, Swift here explores the signification of words while simultaneously demonstrating their deep resonances. He uses language not just for signifying but also for implying, reminding, and insinuating. A great deal of the force of this and Swift's later satires depends upon his extraordinary sensitivity to the signification as well as the multiple connotations of individual words.

1. *Gulliver's Travels*, ed. Herbert Davis (Oxford, 1965), p. 185.

2. For a summary of the debate, see A. C. Howell, "*Res et Verba*: Words and Things," *ELH* 13, no. 2 (1946): 131–42. Howell's essay is conveniently reprinted in *Seventeenth-Century Prose: Modern Essays in Criticism*, ed. Stanley E. Fish (Oxford, 1971), pp. 187–99. That words and things was a subject not limited to the philosophers is shown by Wycherley's fascination with their relationship in *The Country Wife*: in that play the word "sign" is endlessly toyed with.

3. On the matter of Swift's relation to Locke, see W. B. Carnochan, "Gulliver and the Human Understanding," chap. 4 of *Lemuel Gulliver's Mirror for Man* (Berkeley, 1968), and Denis Donoghue, "Words," chap. 4 of *Jonathan Swift: A Critical Introduction* (Cambridge, 1969). Although the evidence is admittedly inconclusive, in my opinion Carnochan and Donoghue wrongly insist that Swift is anti-Lockean. A helpful analysis of Locke's relation to seventeenth-century discussion of language is to be found in John W. Yolton, "Signs and Signification," chap. 9 of *Locke and the*

Compass of Human Understanding (Cambridge, 1970). Ricardo Quintana's *Two Augustans: John Locke, Jonathan Swift* (Madison, 1978) has been published only recently.

4. Michel Foucault, *The Order of Things: An Archaeology of the Human Sciences*, trans. Richard Howard (New York, 1970), p. 43.

5. I echo James Knowlson, *Universal Language Schemes in England and France, 1600–1800* (Toronto, 1975), p. 34; Knowlson's book is a welcome addition to the study of language in this period. Murray Cohen's *Sensible Words: Linguistic Practice in England, 1640–1785* (Baltimore, 1977) has appeared since I completed this study.

6. Knowlson, pp. 10–15. The universal language movement in England and its multiple causes are described succinctly in Vivian Salmon, "Language-Planning in Seventeenth-Century England: Its Context and Aims," in *In Memory of J. R. Firth*, ed. C. E. Bazell et al. (London, 1966), pp. 370–97.

7. Knowlson, p. 74.

8. John Wilkins, *An Essay Towards a Real Character, and a Philosophical Language*, ed. R. C. Alston (1668; facsimile rpt., Menston, England, 1968), p. 21.

9. Ibid., n.p.

10. Swift parallels Wilkins also in his reference to the antiquity of the Phoenician tongue (p. 57; cf. *A Real Character*, p. 11) and his discussion of hieroglyphics (pp. 98–99; cf. *A Real Character*, p. 12).

11. John Locke, *An Essay Concerning Human Understanding*, ed. John W. Yolton, 2 vols. (1690; rpt. New York, 1961), 3. 2. 7.

12. Hugh Kenner, *Flaubert, Joyce, and Beckett: The Stoic Comedians* (Boston, 1962), p. 39. On Swift's involvement in the printing of the fifth edition of 1710, see Guthkelch and Smith, pp. xix–xxviii.

13. Cf. Swift's joke about capital letters used to no purpose: "Upon the Covers of these Papers, I casually observed written in large Letters, the two following Words, *DETUR DIGNISSIMO*; which, for ought I knew, might contain some important Meaning" (p. 23).

14. On page 69 the following words are italicized: "inneundo," "W-tt-n," "Notions," "Looks," "Dreams," "Visions," "Distortion," "Modernists," "Enthusiasms," "troubled," "muddy," "Vapour," "Madness," "Conquests," "Systems," "Postulatum," "Vapour," "Angles," and "Species." Of the nineteen words, sixteen are nouns, two are adjectives, and one is a proper name. The percentages are typical and suggest the strongly nominal quality of Swift's prose. It is interesting that the italicized words manage to catch perfectly the flavor of this passage from "A Digression on Madness."

15. For a discussion of the notes, see Guthkelch and Smith, pp. xxii–xxv.

16. Kenner, p. 40.

17. I have borrowed the term from W. K. Wimsatt, who uses it in *Philosophic Words: A Study of Style and Meaning in the "Rambler" and "Dictionary" of Samuel Johnson* (New Haven, 1948), p. 7.

18. Cf. Wilkins, p. 19 ("defects and imperfections") and p. 20 ("Defects or Imperfections"). *A Real Character* is replete with such redundancy, even when Wilkins is complaining about such a thing: "The chief Difficulty and Labour will be so to contrive the Enumeration of things and notions, as that they may be full and *adequate*, without any *Redundancy* or *Deficiency* as to the Number of them, and regular as to their Place and Order" (p. 20).

19. Cf. the discussion of the multiplicity of "godfathers" for books (pp. 71–72) and

Swift's note on "Bumbastus": "This is one of the Names of *Paracelsus*: He was call'd *Christophorus, Theophrastus, Paracelsus, and Bumbastus*" (p. 152).

20. Thomas Sprat, *History of the Royal Society* (London, 1667), p. 113.

21. And he even puns on its double usage in a physical sense: the word means both the mark left by a heavy body or a blow and the characters made by printing from type.

22. Francis Bacon, *The Advancement of Learning*, ed. William Wright (Oxford, 1920), p. 30.

23. Swift may also be toying with the seventeenth century's use of phrases like "the fabricke of man," as in Sir Thomas Browne, *Religio Medici and Other Works*, ed. F. C. Martin (Oxford, 1964), p. 36. Similar phraseology appears elsewhere in Browne.

24. Cf. the Modern's references to "*Genus* and *Species*" (p. 57), "Classis" (p. 63), and "Specie" (p. 100).

25. Locke, 3. 3. 20.

26. Wilkins claims in his "Epistle Dedicatory" to be doing far more than mere dictionary-making, his goal "*being as much to be preferred before that, as* things *are better than* words, *as* real knowledge *is beyond* elegancy of speech, *as the* general good of mankind, *is beyond that of any* particular Countrey *or* Nation."

27. Cf. "Acceptation" (p. 96) and Swift's several puns on "Sign" (e.g., pp. 61, 144, 196).

28. The inspiration for this passage may have been Henry More's discussion of the etymology of "Zeal" in *Enthusiasmus Triumphatus* (1662), Augustan Reprint Society, no. 118 (Los Angeles, 1966), p. 12.

29. Locke, 3. 10. 15.

30. Cf. Locke's discussions of this matter, 3. 4. 11 and 3. 5. 15.

31. See Maurice J. Quinlan, "Swift's Use of Literalization as a Rhetorical Device," *PMLA* 82 (December 1967): 516–21.

32. As examples see Ben Jonson, *Timber, or Discoveries* (1641; rpt. Oxford, 1947), 7:625: "For that which is high and lofty, declaring excellent matter, becomes vast and tumorous, speaking of petty and inferior things: so that which was even, and apt in a meane and plaine subject, will appeare most poore and humble in a high Argument. Would you not laugh, to meet a great Counsellor of state in a flat cap, with his trunck hose, and a hobby-horse Cloake, his Gloves under his girdle, and yon Haberdasher in a velvet Gowne, furr'd with sables?"; Thomas Sprat, *History of the Royal Society* (London, 1667), p. 111: "They were at first, no doubt, an admirable Instrument in the hands of *Wise Men*, when they were onely employ'd to describe *Goodness, Honesty, Obedience*, in larger, fairer, and more moving Images; to represent *Truth*, cloth'd with Bodies"; and John Dryden, "Preface to the Translation of Ovid's Epistles," in *The Poems of John Dryden* (Oxford, 1958), 1:185: "For thought, if it be Translated truly, cannot be lost in another Language, but the words that convey it to our apprehension (which are the Image and Ornament of that thought) may be so ill chosen as to make it appear in an unhandsome dress, and rob it of its native Lustre."

33. In *A Proposal for Correcting the English Tongue, Polite Conversation, etc.*, ed. Herbert Davis and Louis Landa (Oxford, 1964), p. 244. Cf. Swift's sermon *Upon Sleeping in Church*, in *Irish Tracts and Sermons*, ed. Herbert Davis (Oxford, 1948), p. 213. Elsewhere in his works Swift speaks of "thread-bare phrases" and phrases "worn to rags."

34. *Tatler*, no. 230 (28 September 1710), in *The Bickerstaff Papers and Pamphlets on the Church*, ed. Herbert Davis (Oxford, 1966), p. 176.

35. This seems to be a common formula, as in Sir William Temple, "Of Poetry," in *The Works of Sir William Temple*, ed. Jonathan Swift (1702; rpt. London, 1770), 4:427: "But to spin off this thread, which is already grown too long. . . . " Up to his usual tricks, Swift a few lines below uses "Thread" to refer specifically to clothing.

36. Throughout *A Proposal for Correcting, Improving and Ascertaining the English Tongue*.

37. Locke, 3. 2. 1.

38. It is perhaps significant that in 1662 Antoine Arnauld, in his *Port-Royal Logic*, discussed rather extensively the linguistic problems raised by Christ's words "This is my body." See the most recent translation by James Dickoff and Patricia James, *The Art of Thinking* (New York, 1964), pp. 95–98; the potential influence of the *Logic* on Swift is taken up in chap. 5.

39. Lewis Carroll, *Alice in Wonderland*, ed. Donald J. Gray (New York, 1971), p. 163.

40. Locke, 3. 4. 11.

41. Boswell records Johnson's objection to Swift's mere factuality in the *Life of Johnson*, ed. G. Birkbeck Hill, rev. L. F. Powell (Oxford, 1934), 2:65. Alan T. McKenzie, in "Proper Words in Proper Places: Syntax and Substantive in *The Conduct of the Allies*," *Eighteenth-Century Studies* 1 (Spring 1968): 253–60, takes issue with Johnson's criticism.

chapter two

Wordplay

In order to allure them, he gave a Liberty to his Pen, which might not suit with maturer Years, or graver Characters.

It should not surprise us that the age of Descartes, Charles II, the Royal Society, and the periwig would have spawned *A Tale of a Tub*, a work that sums up the serious play that is so characteristic of the period.[1] Swift comes at the end of that generation. The man who wrote the *Tale* is the man who corresponded with Stella in a private language and with his friend Sheridan in a highly esoteric Anglo-Latin. Swift is everywhere a lover of words, but nowhere more than in his first prose satire. In the *Tale* he toys with hard words, archaisms, neologisms, puns, proverbs, foreign terms, clichés, slang, and every sort of verbal nonsense. What is odd is that despite his objection in principle to many of these things, in the *Tale* he surrenders to them. Verbal ingenuity is characteristic of all of Swift's satire, but in the *Tale* he seems to enjoy such ingenuity for itself, and its frequency implies a downright playful attitude toward language.[2]

Regarding his collation of the drafts of *An Enquiry into the Behavior of the Queen's Last Ministry*, Irvin Ehrenpreis says that Swift "was struggling against a tendency to write in just the way he disliked."[3] I think an analogous struggle exists in *A Tale of a Tub*. If Swift despises neologisms and puns, for example, then why is he responsible for so many himself? His decision to write as a modern hack author allows him to play loose with the language in a way he could not otherwise have done. To view the style of the *Tale* simply as a parody of modernism's abasement of language is to overlook the *joie de mot* at its heart. What comes clear in the reading is that the stylistic gusto of *A Tale of a Tub* belongs to Swift as much as that similar gusto of *Tristram Shandy* belongs to Sterne—or that of *Ulysses* to Joyce. Swift in 1696–97 may have been worrying about the corruption of English, but in the *Tale* he loves corrupting it; this is one of the paradoxes that make the satire so difficult.

Amazingly little has been written on the lexical inventiveness of Swift.[4] Talk of his linguistic conservatism has kept us from acknowledging many of his linguistic games in the *Tale* and elsewhere. One critic goes so far as to tell us that "the chief characteristic of Swift's style is that it has little use for the recesses of language."[5] Nothing could be further from the truth. Mocking stillborn language schemes like Wilkins's *Essay Towards a Real Character*, Swift demonstrates over and over what *can* be done with words when an author brings them to life. It is significant, for example, that according to one calculation, the first volume of Johnson's two-volume *Dictionary* contains some 1,761 references to Swift, a total that among prose writers puts him third behind Addison (2,439) and the Authorized Version (2,270).[6] Similarly, the frequency with which he is mentioned in *The Oxford English Dictionary* is an indication of Swift's use of words in rare, old-fashioned, new, or peculiar ways.[7] A sort of amateur lexicographer himself, Swift throughout his life seems to have recorded in his notebooks instances of proverbs, clichés, and odd usages he came across in books or conversation, and many of these found their way into his published satires. In the *Tale* the Modern's allusions to his use of a commonplace book may be a hint of Swift's actual practice, even at this early date.[8]

Swift is extraordinarily sensitive to language, and in *A Tale of a Tub* he plays untiringly on the multiple connotations of words and their recent or antiquated meanings. *A Discourse to Prove the Antiquity of the English Tongue* is a series of ridiculous jokes about etymology (e.g., Achilles = A Kill-ease), a subject Swift took very seriously in the *Tale*. In this work he likewise uses words in unconventional senses, coins words of his own, and puns continually. Swift is a "linguistic conservative" in that he feared the corruption of English and in that he was a master of the plain style; but his idea for an academy (which was not new) and his plain style (which is never as plain as it looks) are only one side of the coin. We ought to remember that although his style is indeed plain by comparison with Browne's or Milton's, by comparison with Defoe's, or even Addison's, it is subtle and complex. Outside of a couple of pieces like the "Apology" to the *Tale* or *The Conduct of the Allies* (and there are exceptions in both), Swift seldom says *merely* what he means. "Poetry," writes Winifred Nowottny, "is language at full stretch, bringing into maximal interplay the various potentialities afforded by linguistic forms in artistic structures."[9] One could say exactly the same of *A Tale of a Tub*.

One clear sign of Swift's delight in words is the frequent use of neologisms in the *Tale*. In *A Proposal for Correcting, Improving and Ascertaining the English Tongue* he hits at "new conceited Words,"[10] and in his *Tatler* essay on language he says:

> It is manifest, that all new affected Modes of Speech, whether borrowed from the Court, the Town, or the Theatre, are the first perishing Parts in any Language; and, as I could prove by many Hundred Instances, have been so in ours. The Writings of *Hooker*, who was a Country Clergyman, and of *Parsons* the Jesuit, both in the Reign of Queen *Elizabeth*; are in a Style that, with very few Allowances, would not offend any present Reader; much more clear and intelligible than those of Sir *H. Wooton*, Sir *Robert Naunton, Osborn, Daniel* the Historian, and several others who writ later; but being Men of the Court, and affecting the Phrases then in Fashion; they are often either not to be understood, or appear perfectly ridiculous.[11]

But that neologisms make a language unintelligible to subsequent generations is not Swift's only objection. Surely he would agree with Locke: "These, for the most part, the several *sects* of philosophy and religion have introduced. For their authors or promoters, either affecting something singular and out of the way of common apprehensions, or to support some strange opinions or cover some weakness of their hypothesis, seldom fail to *coin* new words and such as when they come to be examined, may justly be called *insignificant terms*."[12] Neologisms are dangerous because the ambiguity of their referents makes their meanings entirely personal and therefore incommunicable. And in Swift's mind there is always a connection between linguistic corruption and moral corruption.[13] Although in the *Tale* the Modern complains of "the Narrowness of our Mother-Tongue" (p. 167),[14] and although we may infer Swift's opposite theoretical position, his coining of words in the *Tale*, not entirely parodic, controverts his theory. "Lilliput," "Yahoo," and "Houyhnhnm," to cite only the most obvious examples from *Gulliver's Travels*, show that he was not averse to inventing new words for new realities.

Swift's reference in the *Tatler* to the dated modernisms of Sir

Henry Wotton and others suggests we look to them for the sort of newfangledness he objected to. Wotton's uncompleted *Philosophical Survey of Education, or Moral Architecture* (1639), published posthumously by Izaak Walton in *Reliquiae Wottonianae* (1651), offers a number of bad examples. Short as the *Survey* is (eighteen pages in the most recent edition), six of Wotton's words are listed in *The Oxford English Dictionary* as first uses:

unquietude (only use recorded)
manurement
washy
serenetude (only use)
insinuant
proditorius[15]

Compared with Swift's, as we shall see, Wotton's coinages are rather uninventive, formed as they are by the simple addition of a suffix to an old word. At any rate, there are in the *Survey* a number of other words current in Wotton's day but out of use by 1710, the date of the *Tatler* essay.[16] On this evidence Swift's fear for contemporary English sounds real enough. By 1710 much of Wotton's diction would indeed have appeared difficult and even ridiculous.

Yet in *A Tale of a Tub* the Modern's coinages, recent words, and odd usages make him far more difficult and ridiculous than Wotton, although Swift cheats by putting in the Modern's mouth a number of words already out of vogue, or nearly so, by 1704: for example, "annihilate" (pp. 35, 43), used as an adjective, was being replaced by the past participle; an instance of "Expedition" (p. 145), in the sense of the action of expediting, last occurs in 1649; and Swift's use of "flesht" (p. 101), meaning "to initiate," is the last recorded use of this word.[17] "What I am going to say," promises the Modern, "is literally true this Minute I am writing" (p. 36). He may be overestimating.

The Oxford English Dictionary lists over forty words in *A Tale of a Tub* that I take to be Swift's coinages.[18] In addition, a surprising number of words are of quite recent origin, and he uses them too with an awareness of their novelty.[19] Swift possesses a remarkable sensitivity to the age of words and is aware when an old word feels archaic, just as when a very recent word, or a neologism, has the feel of newness about it. "If any *English* man should now write or speak as our forefathers did about six or seven hundred years past," says

Wilkins, "We should as little understand him as if he were a foreiner." Bentley goes further, asking in his *Dissertation upon Phalaris*: "For what Englishman does not think himself able from the very turn and fashion of the style, to distinguish a fresh English composition from another a hundred years old?"[20] The pervasive concern in the second half of the seventeenth century for the relative antiquity of words[21] meant that Swift could count on his reader's sensitivity in this regard, and in the *Tale* he intentionally uses new words, or constructs his own, for ironic effect. "Neologisms are dangerous," warns a recent critic, "because they may produce an illusion, that of being reality when only being 'terms.' "[22] I suppose this is true. But given a subtle satirist and a responsive reader, neologisms can be both a way of parodying an overly inventive persona and an apt proof of the real author's real inventiveness with words.

The paragraph in the *Tale* on the structure of Restoration theaters shows how Swift's Modern uses a decidedly modern vocabulary in talking about a modern subject. After each seventeenth-century coinage or new usage I insert the date of its first citation in *The Oxford English Dictionary*:

> I confess, there is something yet more refined in the Contrivance [1695] and Structure of our Modern Theatres. For, First; the Pit [1649] is sunk below the Stage with due regard to the Institution above-deduced; that whatever *weighty* Matter shall be delivered thence (whether it be *Lead* or *Gold*) may fall plum into the Jaws of certain *Criticks* (as I think they are called) which stand ready open to devour them. Then, the Boxes [1609] are built round, and raised to a Level with the Scene [1638], in deference [1660] to the Ladies, because, That large Portion of Wit laid out in raising Pruriences [1688] and Protuberances [1646], is observ'd to run much upon a Line, and ever in a Circle. The whining Passions, and little starved Conceits, are gently wafted [1704] up by their own extreme Levity [1704], to the middle Region [1626], and there fix [1626] and are frozen by the frigid [1643] Understandings of the Inhabitants. Bombastry [1704] and Buffoonry [1621], by Nature lofty and light, soar highest of all, and would be lost in the Roof, if the prudent Architect had not with much Foresight contrived for them a fourth Place, called *the Twelve-Peny Gallery* [1690], and there planted a suitable Colony, who greedily intercept them in their Passage. (P. 61)

Some of these words deserve special comment. "Pit," "Box," and "Scene" are relatively recent names for parts of the typical Restoration theater. As recently as 1690 playwright John Crowne had introduced the term "Gallery" in the phrase "eighteen-penny gallery."[23] And the word "Contrivance" was apparently first used in the sense of the adaptation of a means to an end in John Woodward's *Natural History of the Earth* (1695), where the author speaks of "Proofs of Contrivance in the Structure of the Globe,"[24] a phrase Swift seems to echo. But even more interesting are Swift's two neologisms: "Bombastry,"[25] perhaps an echo of "pedantry," is developed from the earlier "bombast" and is reminiscent of "Bumbastus," which Swift cites elsewhere (p. 152) as a humorous nickname for Paracelsus; "Levity," a term from physics that signifies an inherent property of a body that causes it to rise,[26] is used here for the first time in a figurative sense. In addition, although "deference" goes back to 1660, Swift may be one of the first writers to employ "in deference to," for *The Oxford English Dictionary* records no incidence of the phrase before the mid nineteenth century. And the transitive verb "waft," although dating back to the previous century, began about this time to mean to carry a thing (especially a sound, scent, or something similar) through space, as in Pope's pastoral to "Summer" ("And Winds shall waft it to the Pow'rs above"), a sense Swift bends to his own ironic purpose.[27] The important thing here is to observe in a general way that many of Swift's words are chosen self-consciously from the previous fifty years or so. The Modern has an authentic modern vocabulary.

In the pages that follow I shall discuss the morphology of neologisms and unique or original usages in the *Tale*, their satirical effect, and what they tell us about Swift's attitude toward language. These words fall into a wide range of types: (1) a few seem to have been borrowed from nonliterary vocabularies; (2) a number are foreign (usually Latin) words used in an English text for the first time; (3) a number are compounds formed by the combination of two or more extant words; (4) a few are old words used in a new sense; and (5) a great many are new words formed by the addition of a prefix or (usually) a suffix to an existing root. The transformations are familiar, although their variety is remarkable, especially when compared with Wotton's simple addition of suffixes. But whatever transformation lies behind Swift's forty plus neologisms, what stands out is his fascination with etymology. His coinage "Liftings" (p. 129), for example, is probably his colloquial equivalent to the Latinate "exhaltation," as elsewhere "Flowings" (p. 128) is substituted for the Latin "*effluvia*." On the other hand, Swift's lexical masterpiece—"Reincrudation" (p. 68)—is a high-sounding Latinism for the low process of being made crude again; although built on the recent and very rare (single instances only) "reincrudate" and "reincrudescence," this new word refers ironically to a manner of writing and may also be a blasphemous allusion to the Incarnation. Swift's conglomerate is a full-blown parody of seventeenth-century virtuosos who could take anything, no matter how foul, and lexicalize it into a more sanitary abstraction. (Recall Wotton's "manurement.") To uncover the etymology of a Swiftian neologism is often to uncover a humor and satire that extend well beyond the word itself.

The simpler neologisms are much less interesting to us and less useful to Swift than the more complex types. In the first group, "separate Maintenance" (p. 121), a legal term, and "good for nothing" (p. 173) are both listed in *The Oxford English Dictionary* as first instances, although they are simply terms that Swift may have been responsible for importing from nonliterary sources.[28] In the second group, terms such as "*Opus magnum*" (pp. 127, 187), "*bonae notae*" (p. 68), and "Amorphy" (p. 124) are foreign words that Swift first brought into English. In a couple of these cases he cannot resist the irony of using the term outside its usual context: "separate Maintenance" he employs in reference to the "Divorce" of the three brothers, and "*Opus magnum*," an alchemical term meaning "the conversion of baser metals into gold," in reference to the best way to read *A Tale of a Tub*!

In the third group, Swift's interest in etymology leads him into parodies of certain characteristic seventeenth-century word formations. With "Monster-mongers" (p. 131) he has taken an apparently fading sense of "monster," meaning a prodigy or a marvel, and combined it with an old word for "merchant"; the model is not new (cf. "fly-monger," "water-monger," and so forth), and *The Oxford English Dictionary* suggests that from the middle of the sixteenth century these compounds had discreditable connotations. Similarly, "Physico-logical" (p. 61) is based on a popular seventeenth-century model for scientific terms (cf. "physico-chemical," "physico-mathematical," and so on); Swift mocks this series of compounds,[29] but at the same time his own compound has peculiar significance in the *Tale*, where the Modern's overblown *logical* arguments are consistently deflated by Swift's heavy *physical* imagery. Finally, the most satirically poignant neologism (it is also a pun) in the *Tale* is "Micro-Coat" (p. 78), a comical takeoff on "Microcosm";[30] in reducing the Renaissance "microcosm" to the Restoration "Micro-Coat," Swift has polarized the difference between the two periods, a difference between man as little world and man as clothes. Swift's compounds force us to pay attention to their constituent elements, and those elements clash ironically with each other (e.g., "Physico-" versus "-logical") or with something else (e.g., "-Coat" versus "- cosm"). The dichotomies are simultaneously playful and serious.

In the fourth group of neologisms, Swift uses an old word in a new way, either employing it for the first time in a figurative sense or reviving its dead metaphor. "Abortion" (p. 206), which originated in its medical sense in the sixteenth century, was first used by Swift to mean "a failure of an aim or promise"; but notice how the sexual imagery of the previous section, plus the puns in this very sentence ("Going too short," "Labors of the Brain") keep us aware of the earlier medical meaning at the same time. Similarly, "astride" (p. 171) is used by Swift for the first time in a figurative sense, although again his irony insists upon our recalling the word's physical meaning—Fancy astride of Reason *like a horse*. Swift does just the opposite with the word "Protrusions" (p. 202), employing it in a more concrete sense than it had been employed before; whereas Browne and Boyle use it to mean the action of protruding, Swift uses it to mean that which protrudes, although here it is "Zeal" that protrudes! Swift makes fun of his own usage.

In two other cases he may for the first time be punning on a heretofore unknown physical sense of an old word: namely, "Bottom" (p. 190), where he seems to be implying the posteriors, although in *The Oxford English Dictionary* 1794 is the earliest citation in this sense; and "Intercourse" (p. 60), where he seems to be implying sexual congress (cf. "Engine," "erected," and "Seminary" above), although 1798 is the earliest citation. But whether we accept these last two new usages or not, we ought to recognize that although Swift often gives words new meanings for satiric effect, he also seems to push literal senses into figurative, and figurative into literal, simply because he enjoys the richness of language. He seems driven to keep every old sense of a word alive while cultivating new ones.

The most frequent and most satirical transformation among Swift's neologisms is the addition of a suffix to an extant word. He is responsible for first turning the action "claim" into the person "Claim*ant*" (p. 21), the adjective "sedate" into the superlative "seda*test*" (p. 138),[31] and the noun "pederasty" into the adjective "Pederas*tick*" (p. 41). As in this last example, Swift ordinarily uses suffixes in an ironic sense in order to heighten the derogatory tone of the root word. Thus in transforming "Banter," a word he disliked,[32] into "Bant*ring*" (p. 19), Swift suggests that this banter is of indefinite duration, and his elision (he hated contractions)[33] is a sort of bantering of his own. In transforming "modern," which first appeared in this sense in 1670, into "Modern*ists*" (p. 169), Swift personifies (a Modernist = one who practices modernism) that seventeenth-century bias he wrote the *Tale* to condemn. In transforming "yeoman" into "Yeoman*try*" (p. 181), Swift cheats a little on the conventional spelling ("-try" instead of "-ry") in order to establish an ironic echo of "Gentry"[34]—the parallel lexically elevating yeomen to the level of gentlemen. "Sparge*faction*" (p. 110), built on the Latinate verb "sparge," meaning to sprinkle, follows the model of seventeenth-century coinages such as "rarefaction," "torrefaction," and "petrifaction"; but Swift's earlier equation of sprinkling and pickling, combined with the political sense of "faction," yields something like "pickling faction" (i.e., Catholics). And "Fastidio*sity*" (p. 124), one of the *Tale*'s finest coinages, follows the transformation "curious" → "curiosity," the suffix used to convert an adjective into a noun indicating state or condition; Swift's neologism, itself a wee satire, echoes recent seventeenth-century concoctions such as "spirituosity," "virtuosity," and "coxcombity." Neologisms of this type mock what Swift viewed as the century's linguistically unsound practice of multiplying words by the addition of suffixes. But beyond this, the above neologisms show Swift using suffixes to imply an unfavorable attitude toward root words; his dislike for certain word formations, that is, often shows his dislike for the things those words stand for.

Swift's problem in the *Tale* is to create a persona who relies heavily on faddish words and his own coinages, while keeping that persona from compromising his own position. He succeeds brilliantly. Although he uses enough neologisms and relatively new words to give the feel of modernism to his work, the frequency and quality of those words very quickly prove the Modern a pedant. In fact, some of Swift's coinages are themselves little parodies of modernism's cut-and-paste jobs. And to Swift the building of new words out of the scraps of old ones involves the destruction of old truths. "Reincrudation" is such an abomination because it attempts to conceal reality, because it is a made-up word that attempts to escape the inescapable filth at its center.[35] Like "Micro-Coat" and "Fastidiosity," but more obviously, "Rein*crud*ation" can be viewed as a sort of symbol of the struggle in the *Tale* between the unreality of the Modern and the reality of Swift, between the attempt to create a word world apart from experience and the attempt to use words to get back to the experiential world. The paradox is that while neologisms in the *Tale* parody the distortion of lexical wizardry, they likewise demonstrate what a lexical wizard can do. Swift simply never separates himself categorically from his persona, and, like his Modern, he shows a certain relish for neologisms and odd usages, as he does for puns.

It is difficult to explain our prejudice against puns. Herbert Davis speaks of "that dangerous practice," Denis Donoghue of "this subversive game."[36] Swift himself ridicules puns in *A Modest Defence of Punning* ("We sit up at *Supper Late* in the *Eve*ning, which is false in the *Supperlative* Degree") and teases Stella for slipping into unwanted puns.[37] We all knock the pun for its cheapness while delighting in its ingenuity. Although some of Swift's puns undercut the Modern or modernism or something else, and are important to his satire, others have no clear purpose, or simply make us groan.[38] In fact, many would not be caught on a first reading. I think Swift wrote the *Tale* in one of those rare moods we have all experienced at some time or other—when every word looms a potential pun. They average better than one per page. And Swift's open lexical form keeps his readers always attentive to possible puns and perhaps allows them to contribute a few of their own.

Arthur Koestler defines the pun as "two strings of thought tied by an acoustic knot."[39] As such, the pun is an apt satirical device for Swift, who can use it to combine in a single word a thought of his own with a thought of the Modern's. Puns in *A Tale of a Tub* are of several types: (1) a few are based on a confusion between a name and the thing itself; (2) a large number are based on the inherent double meaning of a word; (3) a smaller number originate in the etymology of a word, the pun in this case dwelling in one syllable; and finally, (4) a special kind is the double entendre, a neutral word that takes on sexual connotation from its sexually charged context. Of course, context is what makes all puns, for the two strings of thought must in each case be supported and encouraged by other words in the immediate vicinity. I shall discuss examples of each type of pun, tracing their morphology and pointing to their local effects, satiric purpose, and implications concerning Swift's attitude toward language.

Puns based on a confusion between a name and the thing itself are relatively rare in the *Tale*, although this sort of confusion is not, being closely related to Swift's habitual literalization of metaphor.[40] The most important example of this type is in that beautifully ironic sentence, "But to return to *Madness*" (p. 174).[41] Coming as it does after the central paragraph of the *Tale*, Swift's transition means two things: while the Modern casually informs us that he is returning to the *subject* of madness, he unwittingly suggests that he is returning to the *condition* of madness. But the irony here gives rise to further irony, as we ask ourselves, Has the Modern ever really left madness?

The second type of pun, that based on the inherent double meaning of a word, is by far the most common in *A Tale of a Tub*. Such is the nature of the puns on "Dark" (pp. 128, 208), meaning both profound and dim; "Revolutions" (p. 189), meaning complete changes and spinning; "Gravity" (p. 60), meaning seriousness and heaviness; "Hemp" (p. 101), meaning hashish and the hangman's rope;[42] "Caballing" (p. 65), meaning a plotting and the mystery of the cabala; "Sheer wit" (p. 80), meaning absolute wit and transparent wit; "Vessel" (pp. 153, 156), meaning the human body and a large cask or barrel; "Inspiration" (pp. 154, 155, 159), meaning divine influence and flatulation; "Bulls" (p. 110), meaning papal documents and horned animals with hooves; and "knotty Point" (p. 170), meaning a difficult problem in philosophy and mere tangled laces. Another such pun is that on "Vision" (p. 171), meaning the action of seeing with the bodily eye, but also, as Swift defines the term in his *Thoughts on Various Subjects*, "the Art of seeing Things invisible."[43] An especially outrageous pun of this sort—"all Mankind appeared *closed up* in Bars of Gold Lace" (p. 84)—shows Swift playing on the pronunciation of a word.[44] There seem also to be a couple of puns that rely on the reader's awareness of contemporary slang, namely, "Cackling" (p. 66), meaning both the chittering of a hen and farting, and "Academy" (p. 166), meaning both a university and a brothel.[45] In addition, there are other possible puns, like "Naturals" (p. 29), meaning in an unimproved condition, but perhaps hinting at "natural," a current word for a half-witted person; "Occasion" (p. 191), meaning simply situation, but perhaps suggesting "occasions," meaning the necessities of nature, a sense first used in 1698; and "Remains" (p. 70), meaning remainder, but perhaps ironically implying a corpse, a sense first found in Dryden in 1700.[46]

In each of the above cases the first meaning, usually the more appropriate in an intellectual context, is the Modern's, and the second, usually the literal or less complimentary meaning, is Swift's. And in every instance the second meaning serves to drag the Modern's high-flying intellectualism back to earth. By reviving the dead metaphors in these words, Swift forces us to see them in their usually older, more physical senses. As with the word "Dark," for example, while the persona in the *Tale* brags that moderns write profound books, Swift whispers that they write dim books, and so on. Swift's puns are often little doors into his thoughts on the Modern's various subjects.

For example, one of the most significant labels in the *Tale*—"Modern"—may well contain a powerful pun on an apparently obsolete sense of the word (frequent in Shakespeare) meaning everyday, ordinary, or commonplace.[47] Similarly, when the Modern defines "Happiness" as "a perpetual *Possession* of being well Deceived" (p. 171), we are meant to see that "Possession" can be taken in two ways. Whereas the Modern says that happiness is to be continuously deceived, Swift says that to be deceived is to be possessed, and possession is madness.[48] A comparable pun occurs at the end of the "Digression on Madness," where, after introducing his grand scheme for utilizing insanity, the Modern says: "which, perhaps, the gentle, courteous, and candid Reader, brimful of that Modern Charity and Tenderness, usually annexed to his Office, will be very hardly persuaded to believe" (p. 180). The tentative syntax, the melodramatic compliment to the reader, and that Beckettian "perhaps"—all weaken what the Modern has just said. But the final blow is landed by the quite casual pun on "hardly," which the Modern uses to mean "emphatically" and Swift to mean scarcely."[49] You can hardly believe, warns Swift, this stuff the Modern just told you!

A third, more arcane and less prevalent kind of pun is that in which Swift uses the etymology of a word to set up a double meaning for just one syllable. Such is the pun "*Rag*ousts" (p. 143), which immediately follows a reference to modern foods "drest up in various compounds." Other even more subtle puns are "*Top*ography" (p. 35), which alludes to the shapes of clouds in the sky; "*pen*etrating" (p. 39), which leads into a discussion of pens as weapons; and "*Rota*tion" (p. 40), which refers to the Rota Club, a political club founded in 1659 to advocate rotation in government offices. Although some few of these etymological puns mock the thing the word names, Swift seems in this group mainly to be sporting with language, playing games his reader may not even notice.

The double entendre, the fourth type of pun in the *Tale*, depends upon a sexually charged context to turn ordinarily innocent words into obscene insinuations.[50] In such contexts Swift's words "Engine" (pp. 59, 164), "Machine" (p. 164), "Tongue" (p. 195), "Ear" (pp. 195, 200, 203), "Nose" (p. 201), "Sprout" (p. 202), and "Handle" (p. 203) are all Freudian jokes on "penis."[51] But to get the full effect of Swift's double entendres we must look not at single words but at a whole passage. At the end of a paragraph full of words such as "propagate," "Loppings," and "Protuberancy," we get this:

> Lastly, the devouter Sisters, who lookt upon all extraordinary Dilatations of that Member, as Protrusions of Zeal, or spiritual Excrescencies, were sure to honor every Head they say upon, as if they had been *Marks of Grace*; but, especially, that of the Preacher, whose *Ears* were usually of the prime Magnitude; which upon that Account, he was very frequent and exact in exposing with all Advantages to the People: in his Rhetorical *Paroxysms*, turning sometimes to *hold forth* the one, and sometimes to *hold forth* the other: From which Custom, the whole Operation of Preaching is to this very Day among their Professors, styled by the Phrase of *Holding forth*. (P. 202)

Although Swift's subject is Puritan preachers and their effect on their congregations, he forces us to recognize the sexual connotations of this relationship, so that by the end of the paragraph, "Rhetorical Paroxysms" and "Holding forth" have both come to mean orgasm. Of course, the equation is never absolute, and Swift throughout pretends to be talking only about the language of these preachers; but the ambiguity of his own language is enough to damn the religious practices of the Puritans by associating their services with orgies. Yet we cannot escape paradoxes: Swift satirizes the seductive rhetoric of dissenting preachers, but it is the seductiveness of his own rhetoric that makes that satire possible; at the same time, it takes two to have rhetorical intercourse, and in a double entendre it is the reader himself who gives a perfectly clean word its dirty meaning. Since words are like seeds, those scattered on a fruitful ground "will multiply far beyond either the Hopes or Imagination of the Sower" (p. 186). Swift's puns turn a good reader into an irresponsible one. Thus *we* end up guilty of overreading while Swift, like Sterne in *Tristram Shandy*, may pretend to a transparent innocence.

Some puns have no satiric purpose whatsoever. Here Swift plays on the double meaning of a word: anxious to try his dedication, the Modern climbed "a prodigious Number of dark, winding *Stairs*; But found them all in the same *Story*, both of your Lordship and themselves" (p. 24). Here he fools with the etymology of a word: giving Cicero's advice concerning English hackney-*coach*men, the Modern goes on, "For, to speak a bold Truth, it is a fatal Mis*carriage* . . . " (p. 168). And here he makes a double pun on the etymology of a word and an old superstition: discoursing on the gallows *ladder*, the Modern says, "'Tis observed by Foreigners themselves, to the Honor of our Country, that we excel all Nations in our Practice and *Understanding* of this Machine" (pp. 58–59). Swift is out to have fun, and this is proved finally by that single pun in the "Apology" in which he accuses Wotton of "going out of his way to be *waggish*, to tell us of a Cow that prickt up her *Tail*" (p. 19). Daringly, Swift in this instance breaks into his serious argument with a joke, taking the chance he may appear as waggish as Wotton. It is as if, having held his own waggishness in check through the entire "Apology," Swift on the last page cannot hold any longer and slips for a moment into a parodic style more appropriate to the body of the *Tale*.[52]

As Swift says in the Introduction to *Polite Conversation*, puns "break, or very much entangle the Thread of Discourse."[53] His view here is comparable to Freud's in *Jokes and Their Relation to the Unconscious*: "the diversion of a train of thought, the displacement of the psychical emphasis onto a topic other than the opening one."[54] But who in *A Tale of a Tub* keeps derailing us, the Modern or Swift? To say that puns in the *Tale* are always serious ironies is to say that Swift's relation to his persona is always antagonistic, which clearly it is not. It is perhaps possible to say that the Modern moves always in an elaborative, expansive direction, whereas Swift moves in the opposite direction, achieving an explosive compression of ideas in few words.[55] But the neatness of such a juxtaposition is quite un-Swiftian. I think it is truer to our experience in reading the *Tale* to say simply that its style pulls simultaneously in two directions, in general toward a belabored wordiness, and in many particular instances toward an incisive brevity. When Swift packs his words close, what results are oxymorons like "oracular Belches" (p. 156) and, with even greater compression, neologisms like "Rein-crudation" or puns like "Possession" or "Paroxysms." These terms are abstract and physical, serious and comic, exemplary and parodic at the same time. Both the Modern and Swift are in each of them.

Wordplay in *A Tale of a Tub* may suggest the Modern's verbal irresponsibility, but it is likewise one of Swift's most important and subtle ways of communicating to his reader. Thus while the surface ideas in the following passage are the persona's, the deeper effects are not. Complaining first of "a superficial Vein among many Readers of the present Age," the Modern goes on to argue that

> *Wisdom* is a *Fox*, who after long hunting, will at last cost you the Pains to dig out: 'Tis a *Cheese*, which by how much the richer, has the thicker, the homelier, and the courser Coat; and whereof to a judicious Palate, the *Maggots* are the best. 'Tis a *Sack-Posset*, wherein the deeper you go, you will find it the sweeter. *Wisdom* is a *Hen*, whose *Cackling* we must value and consider, because it is attended with an *Egg*; But then, lastly, 'tis a *Nut*, which unless you chuse with Judgment, may cost you a Tooth, and pay you with nothing but a *Worm*. In consequence of these momentous Truths, the *Grubaean* Sages have always chosen to convey their Precepts and their Arts, shut up within the Vehicles of Types and Fables, which having been perhaps more careful and curious in adorning, than was altogether necessary, it has fared with these Vehicles after the usual Fate of Coaches over-finely painted and gilt; that the transitory Gazers have so dazzled their Eyes, and fill'd their Imaginations with the outward Lustre, as neither to regard or consider, the Person or the Parts of the Owner within. A Misfortune we undergo with somewhat less Reluctancy, because it has been common to us with *Pythagoras*, *Aesop*, *Socrates*, and other of our Predecessors. (P. 66)

Swift's characteristic slippages of meaning are the essence of the humor and satire in this passage. "Grubaean," a brilliant coinage, generally echoes the corruption of the whole passage, and more particularly offers a pun on "Worms," which ends the preceding sentence, and "Maggots," which occurs a few lines above.[56] Swift's transformation is worth tracing:

Maggot
↓
Worm
↓
Grub
↓
Grub-Street
↓
Grubaean
↓
Grubaean Sages[57]

To realize all of Swift's wit, the reader must dig out this transformation in reverse order. If he does, he finds that what began for the Modern as the kernel of wisdom has become for Swift the filthy Grub-Street parasite who feeds on the wisdom of others. Moreover, Swift does not leave it at this, but develops another pun on "Vehicle," meaning both a literary form and a gentleman's coach; in this context the words "convey," "shut up within," and "transitory" all assume double meanings.[58] At any rate, Swift finally works his way back to the problem of the reader, who may be so "dazzled" by the outside of *A Tale of a Tub*'s vehicle that he will be unable to consider the owner within. Swift has by the end of the paragraph made an extremely complex analogy—

Nut : Coach : Fable :: Worm : Gentlemen : Wisdom

—and thus the *Tale* itself, like a nut, may break a tooth, or like a gilt coach, blind our eyes to what is inside. What is at the start of the paragraph the Modern's criticism of the superficiality of modern readers has been transformed by the end into Swift's criticism of the superficiality of modern writers, of whom the Modern Author himself is the prime example. The situation is even more complicated than this, however, for the Modern professes a depth that he cannot deliver on, although Swift does, and thus in a sense fulfills his persona's unwitting claims.

Swift's characteristic handling of words permits him to twist the Modern's point of view into his own. The coinage "Grubaean," the pun on "Vehicle," and what we might call the bleeding of meaning throughout the whole passage—all this forces on us at least two points of view and a discomforting density of meaning.[59] While theoretically turning over the paragraph to his persona, Swift's verbal ingenuity carries it well beyond him. Swift objects here to shutting up ideas in types and fables, and despite his metaphors, he avoids that; he writes about ideas in an altogether different way, allowing connotation to beget connotation to beget connotation. Words in the *Tale* never come as mere static, explicit, ahistorical entities. Of course, Swift's powerfully resonant use of words, plus his apparent ease in the face of compounded ambiguity, put tremendous responsibility on his reader: "Unless you chuse with Judgment," he warns us. A reader must be able to spy Swift inside this gilt vehicle.

"Let us ask ourselves," says Wittgenstein, "why do we feel a grammatical joke to be *deep*?"[60] In *A Tale of a Tub* neologisms and puns demonstrate the paradox that while the Modern engages in a kind of anticreation, a kind of writing that destroys reality, Swift himself is truly creating, using the Modern's words in order to rub our noses in reality. Neologisms and puns both challenge the stricter boundaries of language, and in that sense can be dangerously destructive of it and the world it mirrors; yet in the very process of breaking language down, neologisms and puns force a reconsideration of words and their relation to reality. Thus while the Modern is turning reality into cool lexical abstraction, Swift, simultaneously, is destroying that lexical abstraction in order to reconstitute language on another, more direct, more realistic basis. Destruction in the *Tale* becomes a kind of creation.

1. For a brief discussion of the sense of serious play in the seventeenth and eighteenth centuries, see Johan Huizinga, *Homo Ludens: A Study of the Play-Element in Culture* (1950; rpt. Boston, 1955), pp. 182–89.

2. Martin Price, *Swift's Rhetorical Art: A Study in Structure and Meaning* (1953; rpt. London, 1963), p. 55, speaks of Swift's "verbal play" but does not develop the notion in much detail.

3. Irvin Ehrenpreis, ed., *An Enquiry into the Behavior of the Queen's Last Ministry* (Bloomington, Ind., 1956), p. xxi.

4. See J. H. Neumann, "Jonathan Swift and the Vocabulary of English," *Modern Language Quarterly* 4 (1943): 191–204; and Lois M. Scott-Thomas, "The Vocabulary of Jonathan Swift," *Dalhousie Review* 25 (1946): 442–47. See especially Barbara Strang, "Swift and the English Language: A Study in Principles and Practice," in *To Honor Roman Jakobson: Essays on the Occasion of His Seventieth Birthday* (The Hague, 1967), pp. 1947–59.

5. Denis Donoghue, *Jonathan Swift: A Critical Introduction* (Cambridge, 1969), p. 21. Cf. Strang, p. 1948: "For Swift the central linguistic issue was not how the language could and should be extended, but how the writer could make use of its resources; for him, questions about language and style have, in this sense, almost coalesced."

6. These figures are drawn from Lewis M. Freed's Cornell doctoral dissertation entitled "The Sources of Johnson's Dictionary" (1930). See W. K. Wimsatt, *Philosophic Words: A Study of Style and Meaning in the "Rambler" and "Dictionary" of Samuel Johnson* (New Haven, 1948), p. 34 n. 17.

7. I echo the directions to the *Dictionary*'s researchers, who were told in 1879 to "Make a quotation for *every* word that strikes you as rare, obsolete, old-fashioned, new, or used in a peculiar way" and to pay special attention to what might be first or last uses. See "Historical Introduction" (Oxford, 1884), 1:xi. References to Swift are by no means confined to *A Tale of a Tub*: for example, check the words "cephalagic," "debellator," "eludible," "modernism," "prize-fighting," "Provincial," "tritical," "triumfeminate," "truism," and "trumpery."

8. Guthkelch and Smith, p. lv. For a summary of Swift's practice, see David Hamilton, "Swift, Wagstaff, and the Composition of *Polite Conversation*," *Huntington Library Quarterly* 30 (August 1967): 281–95.

9. Winifred Nowottny, *The Language Poets Use* (1962; rpt. London, 1965), p. 123.

10. *A Proposal for Correcting the English Tongue, Polite Conversation, etc.*, ed. Herbert Davis and Louis Landa (Oxford, 1964), p. 10.

11. In *Bickerstaff Papers and Pamphlets on the Church*, ed. Herbert Davis (Oxford, 1966), p. 177.

12. John Locke, *An Essay Concerning Human Understanding*, ed. John W. Yolton, 2 vols. (1690; rpt. New York, 1961), 3. 10. 2.

13. See, for example, how Swift conflates Steele's writing with his moral character in *The Importance of the "Guardian" Considered*, in *Political Tracts 1713–1719*, ed. Herbert Davis and Irvin Ehrenpreis (Oxford, 1964).

14. Cf. p. 99, where Swift speaks ironically of critics who "invented other Terms instead thereof that were more cautious and mystical."

15. Sir Henry Wotton, *A Philosophical Survey of Education, or Moral Architecture* (London, 1938), pp. 5, 7, 11, 11, 11, and 14. "Manurement" is a polite word modeled on "excrement."

16. According to the *OED*, these words from the *Survey* were by 1710 no longer in use: "Resultance," "bewray," "Inurement," "roomage," "disauthorize," "disordinate," "at Suddains," and "Surprizals."

17. In addition, Swift deliberately introduces older spellings of words, as "Lanthorn" (pp. 36, 192), "Fasion" (p. 76), and "Rarieties" (p. 110). See Glossary under "Fasion."

18. See Glossary for a complete listing. I have attempted to verify the dates for the first usages by checking the words in seventeenth-century dictionaries.

19. The following words had entered the vocabulary of English within the ten years preceding the publication of *A Tale of a Tub*: "bigotted" (p. 122), "Briguing" (p. 65), "Chocolate-Houses" (p. 74), "cleanlily" (p. 192), "Critick" (p. 209), "Delicatesse" (p. 80), "Exchange-Women" (p. 140), "Inclemencies" (p. 56), "Innuendo" (pp. 114, 169, 186), "Spunging-house" (p. 204), and "Transposal" (p. 43). Since Swift seems to have written the bulk of the *Tale* in 1696 and 1697, this list represents words that were apparently no more than three years old when Swift was at work on his satire. See Glossary.

20. John Wilkins, *An Essay Towards a Real Character, and a Philosophical Language*, ed. R. C. Alston (1668; facsimile ed., Menston, England, 1968), p. 6; Richard Bentley, *The Works of Richard Bentley*, ed. Alexander Dyce (1697; rpt. London, 1836), 2:164.

21. Compare the introductory remarks in the dictionaries of Thomas Blount and Edward Phillips. Blount, "To the Reader," *Glossographia* (London, 1656), n.p.: "By this new world of Words, I found we were slipt into that condition which Seneca complains of in his time; When mens minds once begin to enure themselves to dislike, whatever is usual is disdained: They affect novelty in speech, they recal oreworn and uncouth words, they forge new phrases, and that which is newest is best liked; there is presumptuous, and far fetching of words." Phillips, Preface, *The New World of English Words* (London, 1658), n.p.: "Whether this innovation of words, deprave, or enrich our *English* Tongue, is a consideration that admits of various censures, according to the different fancies of men. Certainly, as by an invasion of strangers, many of the Old Inhabitants must needs to be either slain, or forced to fly the Land; so it happens in the introducing of strange words, the old ones, in whose room they come, must needs in time be forgotten, and grow obsolete."

22. Julian Marias, "Philosophic Truth and the Metaphoric System," in *Interpretation: The Poetry of Meaning*, ed. Stanley R. Hopper and David L. Miller (New York, 1967), p. 45.

23. John Crowne, *The English Friar*, 4:1. See *The Dramatic Works of John Crowne* (Edinburgh, 1874), 4:84. Crowne's phrase is likewise a derogatory remark about the people who sit in the gallery.

24. John Woodward, *The Natural History of the Earth*, 3. 1. See the *OED* under "Contrivance."

25. Counter to Guthkelch and Smith, I have restored the reading of the fifth edition. See Glossary.

26. Cf. "fix," an alchemical term, and the seventeenth-century commonplace of line and circle.

27. Alexander Pope, "Summer," line 80. Pope wrote and circulated his poem in 1704. Cf. "gently wafted to and fro" (p. 156).

28. See Glossary.

29. Cf. "Histori-theo-physilogical" (p. 137).

30. Swift's footnote will not let us escape the irony: "Alluding to the Word Microcosm, or a little World, as Man hath been called by Philosophers." For a fine discussion of the clothes metaphor in the eighteenth century, see Paul Fussell, "The Wardrobe of the Imagination," chap. 9 of *The Rhetorical World of Augustan Humanism* (Oxford, 1965). "It is easy to forget now," says Fussell, "that eighteenth-century costume is conceived with a powerful symbolic dimension" (p. 211).

31. Cf. "sedate" (p. 139), a word used first by Locke in 1693.

32. But he uses it on p. 207.

33. See Swift's *Tatler*, no. 230. Cf. "thundring" (p. 118) and "fatning" (p. 169).

34. See Glossary under "Yeomantry."

35. Note, too, that "Reincrudation" *sounds* like a lexical enhancement of "crud," just as "Fastidiosity" *sounds* like an extreme fastidiousness.

36. Davis and Landa, *A Proposal*, p. v, and Donoghue, p. 125.

37. Of Swift's collecting for *A Modest Defence* and other pieces, Herbert Davis says: "We may well consider these activities as the natural occupation of one who had just finished diverting himself with *A Tale of a Tub*. For there he had shown all the

dangerous possibilities of indulgence in verbal wit, parodying and imitating the extravagances of the previous age, almost allowing the same devils to possess him for a moment in order to rid himself of them for ever; but perhaps not quite succeeding" (*A Proposal*, p. xl).

38. William Empson, *Seven Types of Ambiguity*, 3d ed. (Norfolk, Conn., 1953), pp. 106–9, argues that in the seventeenth century the pun was a less conscious, less refined affair than it was in the eighteenth century. Swift's punning may have a connection with Wilkins's theory of language; see Hugh Kenner, "Pope's Reasonable Rhymes," *ELH* 40 (Spring 1974): 74–88.

39. Arthur Koestler, *The Act of Creation* (New York, 1964), p. 65.

40. See Maurice J. Quinlan, "Swift's Use of Literalization as a Rhetorical Device," *PMLA* 82 (December 1967): 516–21.

41. Cf. "But, to return" (p. 42). "To return to the rheumatism," had written the physician Thomas Sydenham a few years before in *Epistle I: Epidemic Diseases*, in *The Works of Thomas Sydenham*, trans. R. G. Latham (London, 1848), 2:27.

42. Cf. p. 95, where Swift puns on "Altitude" in the same two senses.

43. The whole sentence is: "For, Cant and Vision are to the Ear and Eye, the same that Tickling is to the Touch." Thus if "Vision" is the art of seeing something where there is nothing to see, then "Cant" must be the art of speaking when there is nothing to say.

44. And on its orthography; in his poem "The Grand Question Debated," Swift contracts the word "clothes" to "clo'es" (line 136).

45. See Glossary.

46. See Glossary.

47. For this suggestion I am indebted to my former colleague, Professor William McCollom, Department of English, Case Western Reserve University, Cleveland, Ohio.

48. Thomas Willis in the *Practice of Physick, Being the Whole Works of that Renowned and Famous Physician*, trans. S. Pordage (London, 1684), p. 202, speaks of madmen who are "as it were Demoniacks or possessed with the Devil."

49. See *OED*. Both senses were alive in 1704. Cf. "hardly" (pp. 172, 173) and "hard-mouthed" immediately above. And cf. "scarcely to be believed" in Swift's sermon *On the Trinity*, in *Irish Tracts and Sermons*, ed. Herbert Davis (Oxford, 1948), p. 233.

50. In the "Apology" Swift defends his use of double entendres in a religious context.

51. On a couple of occasions Swift may be playing on the etymological association between "pen" and "penis," as with "Quill" and "Pith" (p. 70) and "Point" and "Feather" (p. 169). In *The Merchant of Venice*, 5. 1. 237, Shakespeare makes such a joke.

52. Another possible but far less obvious pun in the "Apology" occurs in the sentence used as the epigraph for this chapter: in "graver Characters" (p. 4; cf. p. 11) Swift seems to be punning on several meanings of "characters"—in the sense of his own or his readers' distinguishing "characteristic," and also in the sense of printed letters of the alphabet (with an additional pun on "graver"). He may also be making a subtle joke at the expense of Wilkins's *Essay Towards a Real Character*: at one point Wilkins says, "The *Hebrew* Character, as to the shape of it, though it appear solemn and grave. . . . " Unlike "waggish," however, this kind of supersubtle pun hardly ripples the serious surface of Swift's argument in the "Apology."

53. *Polite Conversation*, in Davis and Landa, *A Proposal*, p. 109.

54. Sigmund Freud, *Jokes and Their Relation to the Unconscious*, trans. James Strachey (London, 1960), p. 51.

55. Cf. Morris W. Croll, "The Baroque Style in Prose" (1929), rpt. in *Style, Rhetoric, and Rhythm: Essays by Morris W. Croll*, ed. J. Max Patrick and Robert O. Evans (Princeton, 1966), p. 230, who speaks of "two sides of the seventeenth-century mind: its sententiousness, its penetrating wit, its stoic intensity, on the one hand, and its dislike of formalism, its roving and self-exploring curiosity, in brief, its skeptical tendency, on the other."

56. Cary Nelson, "Form and Claustrophobia: Intestinal Space in *A Tale of a Tub*," chap. 5 of *The Incarnate Word: Literature as Verbal Space* (Urbana, 1973), p. 115, notes that "maggots" was also an eighteenth-century image for "crazy schemes." One definition in the *OED* is "a whimsical or perverse fancy."

57. An oxymoron like "oracular Belches." Swift may be thinking here of "grubby," meaning stunted or dwarfish, a word that first appeared some hundred years earlier. He may also be punning on "Grubaean's Ages."

58. Swift seems especially to be enjoying the ambiguity of the word "transitory," which is used also earlier in the paragraph and which here refers both to a moving vehicle and to the evanescence of those watching the vehicle.

59. Cf. Glossary under "Cackling," a word that appears immediately above. The general effect of neologisms and puns in the *Tale* is close to what Leo Spitzer calls "Linguistic Perspectivism in the *Don Quijote*," in *Linguistics and Literary History: Essays in Stylistics* (Princeton, 1948), pp. 41–85.

60. Ludwig Wittgenstein, *Philosophical Investigations*, trans. G. E. M. Anscombe (New York, 1953), p. 47.

chapter three

Lexical Fields

I was laughed to scorn, for a Clown *and a* Pedant, *without all Taste and Refinement.*

The seventeenth century was the age of the dictionary, and the emphasis on "hard words" in the dictionaries of Blount (1656), Coles (1676), and others, plus the publication of specialized dictionaries, like Blount's *Nomo-Lexicon: A Law Dictionary* (1670) and B. E.'s *New Dictionary of the Terms Ancient and Modern of the Canting Crew* (1690), points to a special interest in the usages of certain professional groups or levels of society. *A Tale of a Tub* in prose, like *Hudibras* in verse, reflects the linguistic fragmentation of its time.[1] As Wotton suggested in 1705, the style of the *Tale* is a shocking juxtaposition of high and low, literary and colloquial, proper and vulgar.[2] And though in the "Apology" Swift ridicules Wotton's own improprieties,[3] he himself scrambles vocabularies—but to ironic effect.

In particular, the *Tale* echoes a century-long theoretical and practical struggle between a Latinate, polysyllabic diction and an Anglo-Saxon, colloquial diction. For ironic purposes—and because he enjoyed language in all its reaches—Swift wrote his first prose work in a unique, bastardized style that jams Latinisms and colloquialisms up against one another. Even more than Donne, Burton, or Browne, he capitalized on the Romance and Germanic contradictions inherent in our language.[4] Swift delights in parodying the jargons peculiar to religion, law, criticism, medicine, and philosophy, and in peppering these specialized, pedantic vocabularies with down-home colloquialisms. Much of his success in the *Tale* and elsewhere depends upon his keen sensitivity to what I call "lexical field"[5]—a word's complex of related words, level of usage, and aura of tone and value. Shifting lexical fields is one of Swift's chief devices for humor and satire.[6]

What Wimsatt calls "philosophic words" were appropriate to seventeenth-century philosophers, scientists, and others because they imply a belief in the unity and systematization of knowledge and an intellectual control of real phenomena, and because these attitudes were conveyed in an assured tone. "The scientific authority, the deliberation and certainty," says Wimsatt, "is backed up by a thump on the table."[7] Browne's *Vulgar Errors,* which Swift surely had in mind as he wrote the *Tale,*[8] is an extreme instance of this philosophic style. In this passage Browne takes up the popular belief that chameleons feed on air: "Whatsoever properly nourisheth before its assimulation, by the action of natural heat it receiveth a corpulency or incrassation progressional unto its conversion; which notwithstanding cannot be effected upon air; for the action of heat doth not condense but rarifie that body, and by attenuation, rather then for nutrition, disposeth it for expulsion."[9] The Anglo-Latin "assimulation," "action" (twice), "corpulency," "incrassation," "progressional," "conversion," "condense," "rarifie," "attenuation," "nutrition," and "expulsion"—all suggest the order of scientific abstraction. "By their very removal from the ordinary," says Wimsatt, "the Latin words suggest the principles of things—a reason or an explanation."[10] In this passage Browne's philosophic words are based on the intellectual concepts of cause and effect, increase and decrease, analogy and antithesis. Although his ideas about chameleons may be wrong, his language, at any rate, lends his argument credibility.

But if the seventeenth century fostered a Browne, it also fostered a Bunyan; and in *A Letter to a Young Gentleman* Swift cites *The Pilgrim's Progress* as a paragon of stylistic simplicity. Surely he would have admired a passage like the following: "And with that, a great darkness and horror fell upon Christian, so that he could not see before him; also here he in great measure lost his senses, so that he could neither remember nor orderly talk of any of those sweet refreshments that he had met with in the way of his pilgrimage. But all the words that he spake still tended to discover that he had horror of mind and hearty fears that he should die in that River, and never obtain entrance in at the Gate."[11] Swift admits that he has been better entertained and informed by Bunyan than by many preachers of university erudition who "are apt to fill their Sermons with philosophical Terms, and Notions of the metaphysical or abstracted kind."[12] In the passage from Bunyan there is not a word that could not be understood readily by a man of small education and ordinary intelligence. Whereas in the single sentence from Browne there are 26 polysyllables out of a total of 52 words (50 percent), in the two sentences from Bunyan there are only 19 polysyllables out of 89 words (21 percent). And whereas in the passage from Browne there are 17 words of three or more syllables (33 percent), in the passage from Bunyan there are only 5 three-syllable words (6 percent). No principles of things here. Browne writes *about* the superstitions of the common people in a highly academic prose, whereas Bunyan writes *for* the common people in a direct, unadorned prose reminiscent of the Authorized Version. In *A Tale of a Tub* Swift embraced both styles simultaneously.

Hard words crowd every page of the *Tale*.[13] The Modern wants to impress us with his learning, and he parades that learning in a difficult vocabulary. Erudite, polysyllabic, Latinate words from this lexical field lend the book its philosophical air:

Anatomy (pp. 123, 174)
Approbation (p. 182)
capacitate (p. 44)
Celestial (p. 79)
Circumfusion (p. 79)
Contexture (p. 123)
dilucidate (p. 68)
disembogue (pp. 153, 156)
Epidemical (p. 124)
Eructation (pp. 108, 160)
Evomition (p. 108)
Exantlation (p. 67)
Excresencies (p. 202)
Exhalations (pp. 163, 166)
Oscitation (p. 124)
Paroxysms (pp. 196, 202)
Perspiration (pp. 107, 185)
Pretermission (p. 96)
Suffocations (p. 101)
Superficies (pp. 76, 103, 174)

The *Tale* has about it the musty smell of university and laboratory. But the Modern's big words expose him; he uses them mechanically, like a poet who has just discovered Roget. He shuffles fat Latinisms not as symbols for ideas but in lieu of ideas.

Then there is that "other" diction of *A Tale of a Tub*, those words more common to speech than to writing, more appropriate in the mouths of farmers, tradesmen, and fishwives than of scholars, preachers, and philosophers.[14] Here is a sampling of words from the *Tale* that are found also in B. E.'s *New Dictionary of the Canting Crew*, the first dictionary of English slang:[15]

bilkt (p. 75)
Bully (pp. 19, 165)
Jade (p. 188)
Jakes (pp. 36, 163)

Cackling (p. 66)
Cant (p. 171)
Chops (p. 115)[16]
Claps (p. 75)
Coxcomb (p. 122)
Curs (p. 189)
Hell (pp. 76, 102)
Hob-Nails (p. 63)
Noddle (p. 198)
paumed (p. 138)
Rabble (pp. 45, 46, 54)
Raree-Shows (p. 109)
Snivel (p. 112)
Spunging-house (p. 204)
Thwack (p. 197)
waggish (p. 19)

And there are innumerable other low words not in B. E., such as "Fart" (p. 112), "Gear" (p. 195), "grunting" (p. 203), "jog" (p. 188), "pop" (p. 181), and "Spittle" (p. 129). Words from this lexical field are mostly of Anglo-Saxon etymology, are of one or two syllables, and are dominated by abrupt consonants;[17] some, like "snivel" and "Thwack," are onomatopoetic. Although the *Tale* is composed for the most part in a highly literate, bookish vocabulary, its many colloquialisms mean that we are always brought back, if fitfully, to ordinary speech.

Swift achieves the same effect with his clichés. Although in *A Letter to a Young Gentlemen* he warns against "old threadbare Phrases,"[18] he employs them throughout *A Tale of a Tub*:

> Time which has lain heavy upon my Hands (p. 30)
> the breadth of a Hair (pp. 43, 81)
> as good Luck would have it (p. 87)
> time out of Mind (p. 121)
> kickt out of Doors (pp. 122, 138, 171)
> when the Fulness of time is come (p. 148)
> stifled, or hid under a Bushel (p. 153)
> the Reason is just at our Elbow (p. 172)
> left him in the lurch (p. 204)
> it would run like Wild-Fire (p. 207)

Again the words are primarily monosyllabic and of Anglo-Saxon origin and are familiar to all of us. Clichés in the *Tale* introduce elements of spontaneous, everyday talk into the Modern's style; but coupled with his highly self-conscious, learned vocabularly, they seem essentially like unwitting slips of the tongue. Just as the Modern literally goes blank at the heights of some of his most abstruse arguments, so he drops into clichés in the midst of his predominantly intellectual phraseology.[19] Swift means for us to realize that a speaker who uses clichés is not only falling back on everyone else's words but also on everyone else's ideas. On the other hand, it is difficult to pin Swift down, for on several occasions he himself—surely not the Modern—toys humorously with a cliché, as in "ought to be understood *cum grano Salis*" (p. 89) and "[Nature] put her best Furniture forward" (p. 173). And that Swift's clichés are not simply an ironic device is shown by their frequency in his correspondence, especially the *Journal to Stella*.

The following paragraph demonstrates the *Tale*'s characteristic word-heaviness and its effect on the reader:

> Tho' I have been hitherto as cautious as I could, upon all Occasions, most nicely to follow the Rules and Methods of Writing, laid down by the Example of our illustrious *Moderns*; yet has the unhappy shortness of my Memory led me into an Error, from which I must immediately extricate my self, before I can decently pursue my Principal Subject. I confess with Shame, it was an unpardonable Omission to proceed so far as I have already done, before I had performed the due Discourses, Expostulatory, Supplicatory, or Deprecatory with my *good Lords* the *Criticks*. Towards some Atonement for this grevious Neglect, I do here make humbly bold to present them with a short Account of themselves and their *Art*, by looking into the Original and Pedigree of the Word, as it is generally understood among us, and very briefly considering the antient and present State thereof. (P. 92)

Notice the words "Occasions," "cautious," "illustrious," "extricate," "Omission," "Discourses," "Expostulatory," "Supplicatory," "Deprecatory," and "Original." Swift is having fun here with Latinisms, most obviously in his string of "-tory" adjectives, which concludes, tellingly, with a word used in this sense for the first time in English.[20] The sheer multiplication of words (especially adjectives and adverbs), plus the melodramatic parody of authorial apologia ("I confess with Shame") and ironic meticulousness ("Tho' I have been hitherto as cautious as I could")—all this gives the passage its superformal tone. Of course, Swift's real attitude everywhere shows through the bowing and scraping. "Our illustrious *Moderns*" and "my *good Lords* the *Criticks*" drip with sarcasm. And the contradictions inherent in the whole paragraph are caught in the Modern's unintentional (Swift's intentional) oxymoron: "I do here make humbly bold."

In the *Tale* Swift chooses to use his colloquial style sparingly, mostly for jarring loose some particularly offensive pedantry with a well-placed word or phrase. But on a couple of occasions he quits his Latinisms altogether.

> A Mountebank in *Leicester-Fields*, had drawn a huge Assembly about him. Among the rest, a fat unweildy Fellow, half stifled in the Press, would be every fit crying out, Lord! what a filthy Crowd is here; Pray, good People, give way a little, Bless me! what a Devil has rak'd this Rabble together: Z---ds, what squeezing is this! Honest Friend, remove your Elbow. At last, a *Weaver* that stood next him could hold no longer: A Plague confound you (*said he*) for an over-grown Sloven; and who (in the Devil's Name) I wonder, helps to make up the Crowd half so much as your self? Don't you consider (with a Pox) that you take up more room with that Carkass than any five here? Is not the Place as free for us as for you? Bring your own Guts to a reasonable Compass (and be d--n'd) and then I'll engage we shall have room enough for us all. (P. 46)

The distance between this passage and the passage on critics is as great as the distance between Browne and Bunyan. The sense of real speech is caught here in expletives like "Z---ds," "Bless me," and "with a Pox." And there are colloquialisms such as "filthy," "rak'd," "Rabble," "Sloven," and "Guts." The difference between the two passages can be measured: whereas polysyllables comprise 37 percent of the words in the passage on critics, here they comprise only 24 percent; and whereas in the first some 16 percent of the words are of three or more syllables, here a mere 4 percent are. The real difference, however, is in the *quality* of the diction. Both paragraphs set up a verbal relationship between people, but whereas the Modern treats the critics with a polysyllabic sycophancy (Swift's true feelings held under tenuous lexical control), the lowly weaver curses the blathering fat man (saying precisely what someone in that situation would feel like saying). The difference is crucial, for all of Swift's satire depends upon our being able to sense when his language is being used to mask ignorance and when it is being used as a means to understanding. One guideline we have is that polysyllabic, Latinate diction ordinarily represents Swift's satire of his speaker, whereas colloquial diction suggests that Swift is sincere.

Swift's definition of good style—"Proper Words in proper Places"[21]—suggests the importance he put on *context* in the use of words. Yet his own satirical style could be more aptly described as proper words in improper places, or better, as improper words in proper places. A good example of Swift's sensitivity to context is to be found in one of his best-known sentences: "For, if we take an Examination of what is generally understood by *Happiness*, as it has Respect, either to the Understanding of the Senses, we shall find all its Properties and Adjuncts will herd under this short Definition: That, *it is a perpetual Possession of being well Deceived*" (p. 171). The terms "Examination," "Properties," "Adjuncts," "Definition," and "Possession" were all picked from the same lexical barrel—one labeled *Polysyllabic Hard Words.* "Herd," on the other hand, was picked from another barrel—one labeled *Monosyllabic Low Words.* Although Swift reaches into another lexical field for just one word, the colloquial tone and animal connotations of that word are enough to shake the credibility of the Modern's pseudointellectualism.[22] How different the effect if we substitute a synonym like "assemble"! Of course, "herd" does not work alone: its tone echoes words like "Tickling" and phrases like "Dupe and play the Wag with," which appear immediately above; and in the definition that follows, we are expected to catch the pun on "Possession." But the full force of this particular sentence depends on our responsiveness to Swift's quite intentional use of an improper word in a proper place. It is as if Swift means to show that the pedantic Modern is a farm boy underneath, a new London dandy (like the three brothers) with the smell of cow dung still clinging to his shoes.

That Swift was aware of lexical field is shown not only by his remarks on language in *A Letter to a Young Gentleman* and *A Proposal for Correcting, Improving and Ascertaining the English Tongue*[23] but also by some things he says in *A Tale of a Tub* itself. At one point he objects to "the Cant, or Jargon of the Trade" (p. 28),[24] and elsewhere he uses formulas such as "which are vulgarly called" (p. 79), "to speak in Form" (p. 155), and "as the common Phrase is" (p. 192).[25] In the preface he complains about the tenderness of modern wit, which "has its Walks and Purlieus, out of which it may not stray the breadth of a Hair" (p. 43). And in the "Apology," his etymology of the word "Banter" demonstrates his serious attentiveness to level of usage: "This Polite Word of theirs was first borrowed from the Bullies in *White-Fryars,* then fell among the Footmen, and at last retired to the Pedants, by whom it is applied as properly to the Productions of Wit, as if I should apply it to Sir *Isaac Newton*'s Mathematicks" (p. 19). "Banter" is of unknown etymology, and in 1690 Locke uses it as an example of the formation of a new word: "He that first brought the word *sham, wheedle,* or *banter* in use, put together as he thought fit those *ideas* he made it stand for."[26] Swift's etymology, though humorous, may well be correct in suggesting that the word originated as a slang term, only gradually working its way up from vulgar to polite society. Every word has its proper lexical field, and although "banter" is appropriate in the company of other slang—low words like "sham" or "wheedle," for instance—it is inappropriate amidst more polite, learned, or literary words. Yet while Swift the philologist objects to the incongruous use of colloquialisms, Swift the satirist saw here an opportunity for powerful ironic effect.

In each of the following passages one or more colloquial words or phrases serve momentarily to rip away the Modern's learned rhetoric and let us hear Swift. I have eliminated the original italics and have italicized these colloquial words and phrases.

> Nor have my Endeavours been wanting to second so useful an Example: But it seems, there is an unhappy Expence usually annexed to the Calling of a God-Father, which was clearly out of my Head, as it is very reasonable to believe. *Where the Pinch lay*, I cannot certainly affirm. (P. 72)

> But Heroick Virtue it self hath not been exempt from the Obloquy of Evil Tongues. For it hath been objected, that those Antient Heroes, famous for their Combating so many Giants, and Dragons, and *Robbers*, were in their own Persons a greater *Nuisance* to Mankind, than any of those Monsters they subdued. (P. 94)

> Martin had still proceeded as gravely as he began; and doubtless, would have delivered an admirable Lecture of Morality, which might have exceedingly contributed to my Reader's Repose, both of Body and Mind: (the true ultimate End of Ethicks;) But Jack was already gone a *Flight-shot* beyond his Patience. (Pp. 139–40)

> For, I have observed, that from a laborious Collection of Seven Hundred Thirty Eight Flowers, and shining Hints of the best Modern Authors, digested with great Reading, into my Book of Common-places; I have not been able after five Years to draw, *hook*, or force into common Conversation, any more than a Dozen. (Pp. 209–10)

The colloquialisms are in each case out of key with the accompanying words and phrases. The result is a sort of stylistic cacophony that exposes the Modern's pretentious intellectualization. Swift is never willing to surrender authorship totally to his persona, and these heavy, at least partially imagistic, socially low words yank us suddenly back to his point of view. When we come upon one of Swift's colloquialisms, we are forced to reevaluate what we have just read, put it into a more sensible perspective, and perceive that though words can be used to talk about reality, they are no substitute for it. Swift's sympathies are not with the Modern's rationalizations but with everyday things such as pinches, robbers, arrows, and hooks.

The stylistic satire in the *Tale* is directed less at particular authors or works than it is at certain types of diction and the wrongheadedness they imply. Critics have in this sense been misled by Swift's own reference in the "Apology" to places "where the Author personates the Style and Manner of other Writers, whom he has a mind to expose" (p. 7). We must keep in mind that Swift is pointing here only to some few passages (he makes this clear), and that he is answering Wotton and Bentley, not offering a reader's guide to *A Tale of a Tub*. True enough, Cervantes, Browne, Marvell, Dryden, Rabelais, Lucretius, Shakespeare, Descartes, Milton, Wotton, Bentley, and the Authorized Version are all echoed in the *Tale*; but Swift's method is inclusive, he was writing (as he put it) when his reading was fresh in his head, and, surely, to track down his allusions and parodies would be the work of seven years, and then some. His satire is typically directed at groups rather than individuals: looking back from his letter to Pope of 29 September 1725 concerning *Gulliver's Travels*, I think it is wiser to say that even thirty years earlier Swift's ire was raised not by Counselor Such-a-One or Physician Such-a-One, but by the whole tribe of lawyers or physicians.[27]

Swift objects to the exclusiveness of the jargon of law, religion, medicine, criticism, science, philosophy, and the occult. Cleverly, he compels us to face this problem by flooding the *Tale* with specialized terms peculiar to each of these professions: from lawyers we get "Fee-Simple" (p. 47), "Codicil annexed" (p. 87), and "Heirs general" (p. 90); from preachers and theologians "Antitype" (p. 40), "Vessel" (pp. 58, 153), and "Circumfusion" (p. 79); from physicians "Fistula" (p. 166), "Diureticks" (p. 185), and "Pilgrim's Salve" (p. 196); from scientists "annihilate" (p. 35), "Mechanick" (p. 101), and "Hermetically" (p. 126); from philosophers "Signification" (p. 57), "*Forma informans*" (p. 151), and "Vortex" (p. 167); from critics "Emblem" (p. 61), "Hieroglyph" (p. 98), and "*Observanda's*" (p. 148); and from the Dark Authors "*Verè adepti*" (p. 114), "*Arcanum*" (pp. 114, 127), and "*Opus magnum*" (pp. 127, 187).

Although these different types of jargon are sprinkled throughout the *Tale*, Swift at certain points concentrates on parodying the style of a single profession. And it is in such passages that his sensitivity to language stands out; in them he establishes a credible jargon for a profession while simultaneously undercutting that jargon with a few earthy colloquialisms of his own. And by satirizing the cant of a profession, Swift satirizes the profession itself—its methods, practitioners, and basic assumptions. Particularly apt are his parodies of the language of lawyers and the law, of theological discourse, and of contemporary medical treatises.

When Gulliver is asked by his Houyhnhnm master to explain something of English law, the question opens Swift's spleen. Interestingly, he levels much of his criticism at the language of lawyers, who practice "the Art of proving by Words multiplied for the Purpose, that *White* is *Black*, and *Black* is *White*, according as they are paid":[28] "It is likewise to be observed, that this Society hath a peculiar Cant and Jargon of their own, that no other Mortal can understand, and wherein all their Laws are written, which they take special Care to multiply; whereby they have wholly confounded the very Essence of Truth and Falsehood, of Right and Wrong; so that it will take Thirty Years to decide whether the Field, left me by my Ancestors for six Generations, belong to me, or to a Stranger three Hundred Miles off."[29] It is the prolixity and ambiguity of legal style that rankle Swift most, and this is precisely what he had opposed years before in *A Tale of a Tub*. Even then he had seen the connection between lexical irresponsibility and moral irresponsibility.

Of course, the special accomplishment of the *Tale* is Swift's neat way of sliding into a demonstration of the kind of thing he objects to.

> For, as to the *Bar*, tho' it be compounded of the same Matter, and designed for the same Use, it cannot however be well allowed the Honor of a fourth, by reason of its level or inferior Situation, exposing it to perpetual Interruption from Collaterals. Neither can the *Bench* it self, tho raised to a proper Eminency, put in a better Claim, whatever its Advocates insist on. For if they please to look into the original Design of its Erection, and the Circumstances or Adjuncts subservient to that Design, they will soon acknowledge the present Practice exactly correspondent to the Primitive Institution, and both to answer the Etymology of the Name, which in the *Phoenician* Tongue is a Word of great Signification, importing, if literally interpreted, *The Place of Sleep*; but in common Acceptation, *A Seat well bolster'd and cushion'd, for the Repose of old and gouty Limbs: Senes ut in otia tuta recedant*. Fortune being indebted to them this Part of Retaliation, that, as formerly, they have long *Talkt*, whilst others *Slept*, so now they may *Sleep* as long whilst others *Talk*. (Pp. 56–57)

The Modern is speaking here of the court, and so Swift throws in a number of legal terms: "Collaterals," "Claim," "Advocates," and so forth. But his parody goes beyond this, and he manages to give the passage much of the formality, redundancy, and circumlocution common to legal documents in his (or our) period.

Swift's objection in *Gulliver's Travels* to the jargon "wherein all their Laws are written" suggests that we look there for the target of his parody.[30] Compare, for example, the style of the above excerpt from the *Tale* with this from *The Statutes of the Realm* for the year 1677, the sort of legal document Swift would have had easy access to while at Moor Park.

> That all and every Judgment Order and Decree to be made as aforesaid shall be good and effectuall both in Law and Equity to all intents and purposes and shall be obeyed by all persons concerned therein and shall binde and conclude all persons Bodyes Corporate or Politicke notwithstanding any disability matter or thing to the contrary. And all such Builders and persons interessed shall hold and enjoy their Estates Termes and Interests soe decreed according to the tenour of such Order and Decree notwithstanding any other Estate Right Title or Interest in Law or Equity Trust Charge or other Incumbrance whatsoever, and that noe Writt or Error or Certiorari shall be admitted or allowed for the reversall or removeall of the same.[31]

Note the run-on syntax, redundant doublets, and pervasive abstraction. Swift catches all of this. The sponginess of "Law and Equity to all intents and purposes and shall be obeyed by all persons concerned therein" is aptly parodied in "Circumstances and Adjuncts subservient to that Design, they will soon acknowledge the present Practice exactly correspondent."

Much of the ironic formality of the *Tale* derives from the Modern's meticulous legalese. Swift is familiar with the terms "Right of Presentation" (p. 47), "*Scandalum Magnatum*" (p. 53), "Wills . . . Nuncupatory" (p. 85), "Innuendo" (pp. 114, 169, 186), and "separate Maintenance" (p. 121)—all of which he could have picked up while a student of divinity.[32] But these rather specialized terms are padded out with quasi-legal words and phrases like "Claimant" (p. 21), "form aforesaid" (p. 47), "positive Precept" (pp. 85, 87), "sufficient Warrant" (p. 113), "pursuant to which" (p. 121), and numerous "whereofs," "thereins," and "whereases." Of course, we are meant always to look past the Modern's wordy, circumlocutious style; in the bench passage, for example, the sheer weight of his words (to use a Swiftian metaphor) drags him down into nonsense.

Swift's point of view is likewise implied in the word "gouty," from another lexical field, and in the colloquial, monosyllabic analogy at the close of the paragraph. It is interesting that in this instance Swift and the Modern are both criticizing the law; but in addition Swift cleverly turns the Modern's style into a bad example of the style of documents of that profession. Yet somehow we are not bothered by the inconsistency. The effect is what Swift is after: the Modern says that lawyers and judges use courtrooms to catch up on their sleep—and his language shows why they do. Although the satire of *A Tale of a Tub* is not everywhere directed at the law, its pervasively formal, quasi-legal style is one of Swift's important satiric techniques.

In *A Letter to a Young Gentleman* Swift objects to the comparably dense style of some preachers. "I am apt to put my self in the Place of the Vulgar," he says, typically, "and think many Words difficult or obscure, which the Preacher will not allow to be so, because those words are obvious to Schollars."[33] Swift's populist bias is apparent here: he is against polysyllables because they sail over the heads of vulgar (Swift uses the word in its unprejudicial sense) congregations. Although he lists many words he finds too "philosophical" or "metaphysical," a couple of them—"Ubiquity" (p. 154) and "Phoenomenon" (pp. 60, 165, 167)—he himself uses in the *Tale*. Indeed, much of the *Tale* is a prime example of the sort of aloof, pseudointellectual style the *Letter* demolishes point by point.

In a manner analogous to the passage on the bench, Swift in what follows is speaking of religious practices, and so echoes the language of religious discourse:

> It is from this Custom of the Priests, that some Authors maintain these *Aeolists*, to have been very antient in the World. Because, the Delivery of their Mysteries, which I have just now mention'd, appears exactly the same with that of other antient Oracles, whose Inspirations were owing to certain subterraneous *Effluviums* of *Wind*, delivered with the *same* Pain to the Priest, and much about the *same* Influence on the People. It is true indeed, that these were frequently managed and directed by *Female* Officers, whose Organs were understood to be better disposed for the Admission of those Oracular *Gusts*, as entring and passing up thro' a Receptacle of greater Capacity, and causing also a Pruriency by the Way, such as with due Management, hath been refined from a Carnal, into a Spiritual Extasie. And to strengthen this profound Conjecture, it is farther insisted, that this Custom of *Female* Priests is kept up still in certain refined Colleges of our *Modern Aeolists*, who are agreed to receive their Inspiration, derived thro' the Receptacle aforesaid, like their Ancestors, the *Sibyls*. (Pp. 156–57)

Note the terms "Aeolists" (twice), "Inspiration" (twice), "subterraneous," "Effluviums," "Admission," "Oracular," "Receptacle" (twice), "Capacity," "Pruriency," "Carnal," "Spiritual," "Extasie," and "Conjecture."[34] These Latinisms, along with academic formulas like "some Authors maintain," "which I have just now mention'd," and "it is farther insisted," give the paragraph its learned air. But within this group of words the religious terms are undermined by other terms that have scientific, even bodily connotations: "subterraneous," meaning in this context not beneath the surface of the earth but within a man's bowels (found in Browne); "Effluviums," meaning "flatulation" (found in Browne and Boyle); "Admission," meaning the fact of being admitted into a human body (as opposed to a society or position); "Receptacle," used here as a euphemism for "rump," but hinting at "vagina" (cf. "receive" and its various religious connotations); and "Pruriency," meaning the quality of itching, but also lascivious desire (seems not to have been used in this latter sense before Swift). Finally, in this learned context the word "Gusts" functions as an earthy synonym for "Effluviums" (the irony heightened by the epithet "Oracular")[35] and is a good example of Swift's subtle qualification of the Modern's rhetoric through a momentary shift in lexical field. As a matter of fact, in these few pages Swift toys unrelentingly with lexical field, locating synonyms for the word "Wind" in classical mythology ("Aeolus"), in religious enthusiasm ("Inspiration," "Spirit," and "Breath"), in scientific abstraction ("Effluvium"), in poetic diction ("Tempest"), and in low colloquialism ("Gusts" and "Belches"). By assembling so many hard words, Swift allows the Modern to masquerade as a seventeenth-century thinker; but by intermixing religious and decidedly nonreligious hard words, and by sliding irreverently from lexical field to lexical field, Swift manages to turn the mystery of belief into the smell of a fart and the excitement of an orgasm. The words "Inspiration" and "Extasie" carry all three connotations. So does Swift's Latinate coinage "Aeolist."

Although Wotton accuses the author of the *Tale* of a blasphemous "Game at Leap-Frog between Flesh and Spirit,"[36] Swift has only exaggerated a tendency quite apparent in the religious style of his day. In fact, examples can be found on every page of Bentley's eight sermons delivered as part of the Boyle lectures at Cambridge in 1692.

> Now, mutual gravitation or attraction, in our present acception of the words, is the same thing with this; 'tis an operation, or virtue, or

> influence of distant bodies upon each other through an empty interval, without any *effluvia*, or exhalations, or other corporeal medium to convey and transmit it. This power, therefore, cannot be innate and essential to matter: and if it be not essential, it is consequently most manifest, since it doth not depend upon motion or rest, or figure or position of parts, which are all the ways that matter can diversify itself, that it could never supervene to it, unless impressed and infused into it by an immaterial and divine power.[37]

Answering the arguments of atheists, Bentley uses the principle of gravitation as a proof for the existence of God. In fact, both the Modern ("Mysteries") and Bentley ("divine power") are groping to explain an immaterial, apparently unexplainable force, and in so doing turn to the material, explainable operations and Latinate diction of contemporary science. Of course, whereas Bentley at least intends his physical analogy to document the power of God, the Modern (like the Aeolists) himself descends into the physical. Yet in a sense we may say that both passages debase the spiritual by mingling it with the material. The difference is only one of degree: even in Bentley one can find such terms as "attraction," "bodies," "corporeal," "motion," and "position"; Swift merely permits the potential physicality of such words from the religious writing of his time to flower into damning double entendres.[38] His synonym for "Effluviums" is not "exhalations," as in Bentley, but "Gusts." Swift is mocking here not only the style of the dissenting preachers, but also the absurd conflation of religious argument with the physics of Boyle.[39] And he satirizes the contradiction of disciplines through the juxtaposition of religious and scientific vocabularies.

As a final example of Swift's device of shifting lexical fields, let us turn to what is unquestionably the most famous passage in *A Tale of a Tub*. I have eliminated Swift's original italics and instead have italicized those words that stand out because of their decidedly colloquial connotations.

> Whereof I have been farther convinced from some late Experiments. Last Week I saw a Woman *flay'd*, and you will hardly believe, how much it altered her Person for the worse. Yesterday I ordered the *Carcass* of a Beau *to be stript* in my Presence; when we were all amazed to find so many unsuspected Faults under one Suit of Cloaths: Then I *laid open* his Brain, his Heart, and his Spleen; But, I plainly perceived at every Operation, that the farther we proceeded, we found the Defects encrease upon us in Number and Bulk: from all which, I justly formed this Conclusion to my self; That whatever Philosopher or Projector can find out an Art *to sodder and patch up* the Flaws and Imperfections of Nature,

> will deserve much better of Mankind, and teach us a more useful Science, than that so much in present Esteem, of *widening* and exposing them (like him who held Anatomy to be the ultimate End of Physick.) And he, whose Fortunes and Dispositions have placed him in a convenient Station to enjoy the Fruits of this noble Art; He that can with Epicurus content his Ideas with the Films and Images that *fly off* upon his Senses from the Superficies of Things; Such a Man truly wise, *creams off* Nature, leaving *the Sower and the Dregs*, for Philosophy and Reason *to lap up*. This is the sublime and refined Point of Felicity, called, the *Possession* of being well deceived; The Serene Peaceful State of being *a Fool among Knaves*. (Pp. 173–74)

Swift imitates here the manner of late seventeenth century writings on anatomy. The following excerpt from Thomas Willis's *Of the Soul of Brutes* bears an especially close resemblance to the passage from the *Tale*.

> Anatomical observations plainly prove the contrary. Some time since, dissecting the dead Carcase of a Maid, dying of a sudden Leipothymy or swooning away, we found in the fleshy part of the Diaphragma a great Imposthume, with a bag full of filthy matter, and watery little bladders; yet she was not troubled ever with a Delirium or Phrensie. Some time since also when we had made an Anatomical Inspection of a Gentleman of the University, (of whome we have made mention in a late Tract) who dyed of a long spurious Pleurisie, it manifestly appeared, that a great Imposthume being ripened in the Pleura, and the intercostal Muscles, and broke inwardly, that a vast plenty of matter had flowed forth into the cavity of the Thorax, which gnawing the Diaphragma lying under, had made a great hole in it; nor was this man however in all his sickness Delirious, or Frantick. Wherefore, I think this Distemper scarce ever to be produced from such a cause: but that opinion seems to arise from hence, because often-times in a true Phrensie, together with a continual raving, the motion of the Diaphragma is wont to be hindred or perverted.[40]

We must realize that Willis is writing not for laymen but for other physicians, and that what may seem shockingly insensitive to us would have seemed simply matter-of-fact to those interested in anatomy. We would be as shocked today by the tone of an article in a medical journal.[41] But Swift too was responding as a layman, and he recognizes the awful incongruity of talking about the dissection of a human being in such cool Latinisms as "Leipothymy," "Diaphragma," and "Imposthume." Does not "Leipothymy," after all, which Willis defines as "swooning away," mean in this case a sudden, unexplained death? And does not "Anatomical Inspection of a Gentleman" mean cutting up the corpse of a man and analyzing the pieces? Willis's diction tends to keep his cadavers at a distance, as does his academic allusion to "a late Tract" and his argumentative method, which manages to transform a medical confusion into a rhetorical assertion.

In recounting his experiences with human dissection, the Modern, like Willis, tries to keep real phenomena under control of mind. He uses big words and a sterile tone in order to desensitize our consciences along with his own. And in the first part of the paragraph he does pretty well, piling up abstractions like "Proportion," "Wisdom," "Qualities," "Degree," and "Corporeal Beings." But as soon as the Modern turns to his real examples, these rationalizations give way to diseased cadavers. The generalized time frame becomes "Last Week" and "Yesterday." "Fallen under my Cognizance" is replaced by "I saw," "I ordered," and "I plainly perceived." And "most Corporeal Beings" turns into "a Woman flay'd" and "a Carcass of a Beau." Swift documents this switch from the abstract to the particular in part by sliding into a more personal tone (the greater frequency of the pronoun "I"), and also by moving his emphasis from the safe, fixed noun to the not-so-safe, active verb and its intensifying preposition ("fly off," "creams off," and "lap up").[42] But the chief sign of Swift's attitude toward the Modern's intellectualizations is to be found in his momentary shifts from polysyllabic Latinisms to monosyllabic colloquialisms. Such shifts set up ironies: the colloquialisms describe less dignified things ("the Sower and the Dregs") and less prestigious activities ("to sodder and patch up"), and clash mightily with the prevailing tone of the other words. The word "Carcass," used both by Willis and Swift, points up the difference between the two passages: Willis uses it in its neutral sense to mean simply the dead body of a man or beast; Swift uses it in this sense also, but with more than a side glance at its contemptuousness when applied to the human body.[43] He wants us to catch the animalism in his use of the word "Carcass," and so he echoes it in the verbs "flay'd" and "lap up." In this passage Swift's low words undermine the Modern's attempts to gloss over unpleasant reality and divert a moral response to that reality. When in the last lines the Modern unwittingly acknowledges that he is a fool possessed, we have been prepared to agree with him.

But let us not overlook Willis's several shifts in lexical field. Amidst all the polysyllabic Latinisms, "ripened" and "gnawing" seem oddly out of place. So too the plain, literal phrases "bag full of filthy matter," "watery little bladders," and "had made a great hole in it." Yet we should remember that Willis was writing prior to a time when the language of science had clearly and irrevocably split off from the language of everyday discourse, and his few Anglo-Saxonisms would not have struck other scientists as inconsistent. Swift, on the other hand, would have perceived in the incongruity of Willis's diction a horrifying insensitivity to human life. Indeed, I would guess that he would have seen how the casual literalisms only make the cold Latinisms more horrifying. Thus what Swift does is to assume the disparities he found in seventheenth-century English into his own style and then to heighten these disparities so as to draw attention to them. Swift's more frequent and more radical shifts of lexical field—and, typically, their self-consciousness—force upon us an awareness of the incompatible vocabulary as well as the incompatible views of what it is to be human. For Swift the incongruity of diction in the English of his day was a moral as well as a lexical problem. Conveniently, of course, that inherited lexical diversity provided him with one of his most powerful satiric weapons in the war against the immoralities he saw everywhere.

"The vulgar dialect," Lord Orrery tells us, "was not only a fund of humor for Swift, but I verily believe was acceptable to his nature."[44] In *A Letter to a Young Gentleman* Swift explicitly opposes the exclusiveness of professional jargon to the direct communicableness of everyday speech: "I know not how it comes to pass, that Professors in most Arts and Sciences are generally the worst qualified to explain their Meanings to those who are not of their Tribe: A common Farmer shall make you understand in three Words, *that his Foot is out of Joint, or his Collar-bone broken*; wherein a *Surgeon*, after a hundred Terms of Art, if you are not a Scholar, shall leave you to seek. It is frequently the same Case in Law, Physick, and even many of the meaner Arts."[45] It is clear where Swift stands. He thinks of the speech of the common people as a kind of norm, a kind of practical touchstone against which one can measure the language of scholars. Language is not a matter of big words or rhetorical polish, but success of communication; and communication is more likely in the mouth of a farmer than in the mouth of a lawyer, a preacher, or a physician. Swift, who once admitted trying out his poems on his servants,[46] acknowledges not only the clarity and directness of the speech of the common people, but also their assumptions about life.

Swift's words are values. The Latinate polysyllables that almost run away with *A Tale of a Tub* imply a desire to subsume particulars under abstractions, an absolute faith in reason, and a moral insensitivity to human activities. Swift will have none of this. His proportionally sparse colloquialisms are enough to offer us an alternate perception of things, and they imply the significance of particulars, the danger of overrationalization, and the moral importance of every human activity. Swift's readers have been confused by the scarcity of positive values in his satire; but if nowhere else, those values are to be looked for in his use of colloquial English, which for him contains certain assumptions about what is good or worthwhile. The cultured few must never elevate themselves too far above the uncultured many, for in them, as in their language, is an earthy common sense.

1. Ian Jack, *Augustan Satire: Intention and Idiom in English Poetry, 1660–1750* (Oxford, 1952), p. 27, says that *Hudibras* "has a greater variety of idiom than any other poem in the language."

2. William Wotton, *A Defense of the Reflections Upon Ancient and Modern Learning*, in Guthkelch and Smith, p. 326: "This too is described in the Language of the Stews, which with now and then a Scripture-Expression, composes this Writer's Stile." Cf. John Oldmixon, *Reflections on Dr. Swift's Letter to Harley* (1712), Augustan Reprint Society, no. 15 (Ann Arbor, 1948), p. 29, who applies La Bruyère's comments on Rabelais to the *Tale*: "This a Monstrous Collection of Political and Ingenious Morality, with a Mixture of Beastliness; where 'tis bad 'tis abominable, and fit for the Diversion of the Rabble, and where 'tis good 'tis exquisite, and may entertain the most delicate."

3. "To instance only in the Answerer mentioned; it is grievous to see him in some of his Writings at every turn going out of his way to be waggish, to tell us of *a Cow that prickt up her Tail*, and in his answer to this Discourse, he says *it is all a Farce and a Ladle*: With other Passages equally shining" (p. 19).

4. W. B. C. Watkins, *Perilous Balance: The Tragic Genius of Swift, Johnson, and Sterne* (Princeton, 1939), p. 7, says that Swift "knew the effectiveness of mingling unusual and simple words." Hugh Sykes Davies, "Milton and the Vocabulary of Verse and Prose," in *Literary English Since Shakespeare*, ed. George Watson (Oxford, 1970), pp. 175–93, does a good job of describing the split in English between the older Germanic and newer Romance elements. In the seventeenth century, says Davies, "the tendency to segregation is suddenly intensified" (p. 192). Cf. Ian Watt, "The Ironic Voice," in *The Augustan Age*, ed. Ian Watt (New York, 1968), p. 102: "To say that the Augustans invented the dichotomy of the elite and the mob would obviously be exaggerated; but they certainly conceptualized the distinction and applied it more unrelentingly than ever before. The distinction almost defines the way they looked at themselves as writers."

5. I have borrowed the term from Stephen Ullmann, *Language and Style* (New York, 1966), p. 12, who uses it in a somewhat less restrictive sense: "A lexical field is a closely organized sector of the vocabulary, whose elements fit together and delimit

each other like pieces in a mosaic. In each field some sphere of experience is analyzed, divided up and classified in a unique way. In this sense, the vocabulary of every language embodies a peculiar vision of the universe; it implies a definite philosophy of life and hierarchy of values which is handed down from one generation to another." Winifred Nowottny, *The Language Poets Use* (London, 1962), p. 39, seems to mean much the same thing by her term "linguistic field."

6. Ronald Paulson, *Theme and Structure in Swift's "Tale of a Tub"* (New Haven, 1960), is the one critic to have discussed this technique in Swift. "The usual practice in the *Tale*," he says, "is for a respectable context to be set up, and one word placed in it which, reasserting its normal meaning, completely alters the significance of its context" (p. 60). I carry my analysis beyond Paulson's.

7. W. K. Wimsatt, *The Prose Style of Samuel Johnson* (New Haven, 1941), p. 60.

8. On Browne's influence, see Guthkelch and Smith, p. lix.

9. Thomas Browne, *Pseudodoxia Epidemica* (its real title), in *The Works of Sir Thomas Browne*, ed. Geoffrey Keynes (Chicago, 1964), 2:228. Swift's reference in the *Tale* to "the *Camelion*, sworn foe to *Inspiration*" (p. 159), may have been prompted by this passage in Browne.

10. W. K. Wimsatt, *Philosophic Words: A Study of Style and Meaning in the "Rambler" and "Dictionary" of Samuel Johnson* (New Haven, 1948), p. 12.

11. John Bunyan, *The Pilgrim's Progress*, ed. Roger Sharrock (Baltimore, 1965), p. 198.

12. *A Letter to a Young Gentleman*, in *Irish Tracts 1720–1723 and Sermons*, ed. Herbert Davis (Oxford, 1968), p. 77.

13. Cf. Hugh Blair, *Lectures on Rhetoric and Belles Lettres* (1783), ed. Harold F. Harding (Carbondale, Ill., 1965), 1:481–82: "It is very remarkable, how few Latinized words Dean Swift employs. No writer, in our language, is so purely English as he is, or borrows so little assistance from words of foreign derivation." Blair must have been thinking of *Gulliver's Travels* rather than *A Tale of a Tub*.

14. James Sutherland, *On English Prose* (Toronto, 1957), p. 76, speaks of the "colloquial ease" of Swift. But in the *Tale*, at least, this side of Swift's style is almost overthrown.

15. The title of this book is itself a classic: *A New Dictionary of the Terms Ancient and Modern of the Canting Crew, In its several Tribes, of Gypsies, Beggars, Thieves, Cheats, &c. With an Addition of some Proverbs, Phrases, Figurative Speeches, &c. Useful for all sorts of People, (especially Foreigners) to secure their Money and preserve their Lives; besides Diverting and Entertaining, being wholly New* (1690; rpt. London, 1906). B. E. defines a "sleeveless story" as "a Tale of a Tub, or of a Cock and a Bull."

16. Cf. alternate form "Chaps" (pp. 153, 189).

17. In *A Proposal for Correcting, Improving and Ascertaining the English Tongue*, Swift argues that English is "overstocked with Monosyllables" (*A Proposal for Correcting the English Tongue, Polite Conversation, etc.*, ed. Herbert Davis and Louis Landa [Oxford, 1964], p. 11); and he praises the harmonies of Spanish, French, and Italian, while objecting to English, with its "Roughness and Frequency of Consonants" (p. 13).

18. *Irish Tracts and Sermons*, p. 68.

19. Cf. Hugh Sykes Davies, "Irony and the English Tongue," in *The World of Jonathan Swift*, ed. Brian Vickers (Oxford, 1968), p. 114: "Flatness of language, commonplaces, can itself serve as a key of the decoding of ironic messages, especially

when it is brought into vivid contrast with the opposing qualities of violence and outrageousness of expression."

20. See Glossary under "Deprecatory."

21. *A Letter*, p. 65. See Nowottny, chap. 2, for a fine discussion of lexical context.

22. Even the compilers of the *OED* were fooled, for they cite Swift's use of the verb "herd" as the first use in the sense "of things: to come together, to assemble"; rather, this is Swift's figurative use of the word in its older sense of the coming together of animals, here used derogatorily in reference to ideas. F. R. Leavis speaks of "that oddly concrete 'herd'" in "The Irony of Swift," rpt. in *Swift: A Collection of Critical Essays*, ed. Ernest Tuveson (Englewood Cliffs, N.J., 1964), p. 23.

23. See *A Letter*, pp. 65–68, and *A Proposal*, pp. 8–10. In *A Letter*, p. 68, Swift says: "And truly, as they say, a Man is known by his Company; so it should seem, that a Man's Company may be known by his Manner of expressing himself, either in publick Assemblies, or private Conversation."

24. Cf. Swift's note to p. 187, which reads, in part: "The curious were very Inquisitive whether those Barbarous Words, *Basima Eacabasa, &c.* are really in Irenaeus, and upon enquiry 'twas found they were a sort of Cant or Jargon of certain Hereticks, and therefore very properly prefix'd to a Book as this of our Author."

25. Barbara Strang, "Swift and the English Language: A Study in Principles and Practice," in *To Honor Roman Jakobson: Essays on the Occasion of His Seventieth Birthday* (The Hague, 1967), p. 1957, cites several such occasions where, she says, "the gap between use and approval is clearly marked out for us."

26. John Locke, *An Essay Concerning Human Understanding*, ed. John W. Yolton (New York, 1964), 3. 9. 7. In the *Tatler*, no. 230, in *Bickerstaff Papers and Pamphlets on the Church*, ed. Herbert Davis (Oxford, 1940), p. 177, Swift mentions "Sham" and "Banter" as examples of "modern Terms of Art." Cf. Glossary under "Bantring."

27. *The Correspondence of Jonathan Swift*, ed. Harold Williams (Oxford, 1963), 3:103.

28. *Gulliver's Travels*, ed. Herbert Davis (Oxford, 1965), p. 248. Cf. Locke, *An Essay Concerning Human Understanding*, 3. 10. 10.

29. *Gulliver's Travels*, p. 250.

30. Swift was by this time surely acquainted with Sir Edward Coke's *Commentary on Littleton* (he mentions Coke in *The Drapier's Letters*), and he may have drawn something from Coke's fragmented allusiveness, footnotes and marginalia, incessant etymologies, or even his references to "our author" (cf. *Tale*, pp. 115, 187).

31. 29°Car.II.c.4. *The Statutes of the Realm* (London, 1963), 5:844.

32. For this suggestion I am grateful to Professor Roger Manning, Department of History, Cleveland State University, Cleveland, Ohio. See Glossary under "Innuendo," "Nuncupatory," and "separate Maintenance."

33. *A Letter*, p. 61.

34. The *OED* suggests that even the words "Capacity" and "Conjecture" were not rare in religious contexts.

35. In "Oracles" Swift would appear to be punning on "orifices." The words sound something alike, and both may be traced to the same Latin or even Indo-European root; see the prefix "ōr-" in Julius Pokorny, *Indogermanisches Etymologisches Wörterbuch* (Bern, 1959). Cf. the *OED* definition of "oracle": "In Greek and Roman Antiquity: The instrumentality, agency, or medium, by which a God was supposed to speak or make known his will; the mouthpiece of the deity."

36. William Wotton, *A Defense of the Reflections Upon Ancient and Modern Learning*, p. 326.

37. Richard Bentley, Sermon 7, *Sermons Preached at Boyle's Lecture*, in *The Works of Richard Bentley*, ed. Alexander Dyce (1697; London, 1838), 3:163.

38. Swift's physical puns on "Corporeal" (p. 173) and "Motion" (p. 164) show what he is capable of doing with two of Bentley's words.

39. Both passages reflect the seventeenth-century fascination with air and space, and thus have at least a general connection with Boyle's *New Experiments Physico-Mechanical, Touching the Spring of Air and Its Effects* (1661).

40. Thomas Willis, *Of the Soul of Brutes*, in *Practice of Physick, Being the Whole Works of that Renowned and Famous Physician*, trans. S. Pordage (London, 1684), p. 182. In order to avoid confusion with the passage from Swift in which I have altered the original italics, I have deleted them here. Further proof of Swift's parody of medical writings is to be found in Thomas Sydenham, "Anatomie," in *Dr. Thomas Sydenham, His Life and Writings* (Berkeley, 1966); the unpublished draft of this work was written in 1668 and, except for the first sentence, was copied out in the hand of Sydenham's friend John Locke. Whereas Willis was a great advocate of anatomy, Sydenham thought it useless: "So I thinke it is cleare that after all our porings and manglings the parts of animals we know nothing but the grosse parts, see not the tools and contrivances by which nature works, and are as far off from the discovery we aim at as ever" (p. 87); "For poreing and gazing on the parts which we dissect without perceiving the very precise way of their working is but still a superficial knowledg, and though we cut into there inside, we see but the outside of things and make but a new superficies for ourselves to stare at" (p. 88). A remarkable number of words in these passages from Willis and Sydenham appear also in the central paragraph from "A Digression on Madness": "Tools," "cutting," "mangling," "Nature," "Outside," "In[side]," "Carcass," and "Superficies."

41. Cf. this recent account of an autopsy: "After that operation the patient's renal disease was aggravated, and he died about six weeks later. At the post-mortem examination we found huge lymph nodes throughout the mediastinum. Microscopically, they resembled the biopsy specimen, with a little more hyalinization. The gross examination of the lungs revealed many areas of fibrous scarring, an indication of healed sarcoidosis. In addition, granulomas, some with Schaumann bodies, were seen, evidence that there was still some activity of the process within the lungs. In the spleen we also observed a few granulomas, some of which were hyalinized" ("Case Records of the Massachusetts General Hospital," *New England Journal of Medicine* 290 [28 February, 1974]:509).

42. This is a subtle yet powerful satiric tool of Swift's. Cf. Glossary under "close in with."

43. The *OED* shows that although the contemptuous implications of the word date back to the sixteenth century, it continued to be used in its neutral sense until about 1750. Cf. "Carcass" (pp. 46, 80, 123, 186). Cf. "dead carcase" in the passage from Willis and Swift's sermon *On the Trinity*, in *Irish Tracts and Sermons*, p. 166.

44. John Boyle, Earl of Orrery, *Remarks on the Life and Writings of Jonathan Swift* (1752; facsimile ed., New York, 1974), p. 34.

45. *A Letter*, p. 66. Cf. Locke, *An Essay Concerning Human Understanding*, 3. 11. 10.

46. Cited in Harold Williams, ed., *The Poems of Jonathan Swift* (London, 1937), 1:xxxiv.

chapter four

Syntax and Rhythm

First expostulate the Case, then plead the Necessity of the Rod, from great Provocations, and conclude every Period with a Lash.

"With his extraordinary sensitivity to the effect of the tone of voice in writing," says Kathleen Williams of Swift, "style is frequently the embodiment of a particular way of thinking which is being set before us for our contemplation."[1] Thinking is in part caught in the syntax of Swift's sentences. It could be argued, of course, that to follow any writer's syntax is to follow his thoughts; but in Swift, where the actual thinking process is on many occasions more important than the thought itself, we must pay particularly close attention to the order of the words.[2] "Much of the Augustan dance of syntax," says one critic, "is based on the stately counter-change of antithesis";[3] yet although in *A Tale of a Tub* it is often possible to make out a bold antithesis, such symmetry is simultaneously obscured by cumulative organization, unfinished antitheses, and unrelenting qualification. Many of the sentences in the text are little dramas between right and wrong ways of thinking.

To me it is often more appropriate, however, to speak not of syntax (the static structure of a completed thought) but of rhythm (the movement of a thought through the mind). Writers in the seventeenth and eighteenth centuries were well aware of prose rhythm,[4] and Swift seems especially attentive to the subtle effects of sound. In the *Tale* he frequently manipulates syntax, along with stress pattern, alliteration, and even meaning, in order to set up a quasi-oratorical cadence, which he then breaks in order to suggest a more down-to-earth position. This struggle between one syntax or rhythm and another is an important aspect of Swift's irony.

Sometimes in the *Tale* the formality or informality implied in the syntax or rhythm clashes with the subject, diction, or tone; sometimes there is a sudden drop from a periodic, Ciceronian syntax to a loose, Senecan syntax; sometimes a certain prose rhythm is played off against a certain syntax, the rhythm suggesting one attitude toward the subject, the syntax another; and sometimes there is a shift from a formal, rounded rhythm to a shattered, more heavily stressed rhythm. Incongruity is at the root of all these devices. The *Tale* is poised precariously between what we might see as the Modern's rhetoric, which attempts all the techniques of balance, antithesis, and logic, and Swift's own loose, asymmetrical style of actual speech. And as with his juxtaposition of lexical field, Swift's juxtaposition of one syntax or rhythm and another implies a clash of two approaches to the world: the aloof and artificial, and the immediate and conversational.

As Morris Croll pointed out fifty years ago, the typical Ciceronian sentence represents the triumph of grammar and logic, whereas the typical Senecan sentence depicts the rhetoric of the mind: one style depicts a finished thought, the other a mind thinking.[5] To somewhat overstate it, the difference is between the balanced, periodic, symmetrical prose of Bacon, Milton, and to some extent Temple, and the looser, more cumulative, asymmetrical prose of Burton, Browne, and Marvell. "They knew," says Croll of the Senecans, "that an idea separated from the act of experiencing it is not the idea that was experienced. The ardor of its conception in the mind is a necessary part of its truth; and unless it can be conveyed to another mind in something of the form of its occurrence, either it has changed into some other idea or it has ceased to be an idea, to have any existence whatever except a verbal one."[6] Swift would agree wholeheartedly. Yet although he would seem to object more to the extremes of Ciceronianism than the extremes of Senecanism, he knew both styles well, and in *A Tale of a Tub* he exploits both in his subtle intermingling of symmetrical and asymmetrical syntax. The Modern's unsustained Ciceronian syntax represents his attempt at arranging his material in neat packages of ancient and modern, right and wrong, reasonable and unreasonable; but Swift makes his persona slip continually from balance and periodicity into a loose, absurdly cumulative rhythm that we ought to understand as his way of registering doubt concerning the Modern's proud categorizations.

A sentence or paragraph in the *Tale* often begins with a logical comparison or contrast but soon gets tangled in its own examples, parentheses, and qualifications and either dwindles away into an absurdity or attempts toward the end to reestablish some order or point, which is in most cases perversely ironic: "The Conclusion of a Treatise, resembles the Conclusion of Human Life, which hath sometimes been compared to the End of a Feast; where few are satisfied to depart, *ut plenus vitae conviva*: For Men will sit down after the fullest Meal, tho' it be only to *doze*, or to *sleep* out the rest of the Day" (p. 208). This sentence attempts to say something about the conclusion of a literary work, gets sidetracked by a trite analogy to a human lifetime, and is then led from there into another analogy to large dinners and their soporific effects. The incongruous Latin phrase merely underscores the Modern's pretentious attempts at meaning. And the end of the sentence is shaped into a homey aphorism that seems anticlimactic at best, and in this context ridiculously pat. The form of the Modern's aphorism suggests an authoritativeness that does not fit the ordinariness of his subject; this discrepancy is stressed by the shift in the final clauses to monosyllables, by the similar rhythm of the last two phrases, and by the sequence of vowels in "tho'," "only," and "doze," which rhymes with "Repose" in the next sentence. Here and elsewhere we could criticize the Modern for the same reason Swift criticizes Tindall: "He affecteth to form a few Words into the Shape and Size of a Maxim, then trieth it by his Ear, and according as he likes the Sound or Cadence, pronounceth it true."[7] Thus what begins as the Modern's self-assured, seemingly definitive statement on literary conclusions has by the end of the sentence been reduced to a lamely definitive statement on the behavior of men after big meals. Swift implies that some literary works may put their readers to sleep and, in fact, that such works may be deadly. Although there are far more complex examples of this type of syntax, the regression in this short sentence —from the sublime to the trivial—is a sort of microcosm of the whole book.[8]

The syntax of the *Tale* may be profitably set against the typical symmetries of seventeenth-century Ciceronianism. Take as an example the following sentence from Milton's *Areopagitica*, which I have laid out spatially so as to make its structure more clear. My method is a modified version of Francis Christensen's "generative rhetoric," where the main clauses or phrases are lined up along the left margin, and where each step to the right indicates an increasing degree of specificity.[9] "For," writes Milton,

as in a body,
when the blood is fresh,
the spirits pure and vigorous
not only to vital
but to rational faculties
and those in the acutest and pertest operations
of wit and subtlety
it argues
in what good plight and constitution the body is;
so [in a nation]
when the cheerfulness of the people is sprightly up,
as that it has
not only wherewith to guard well
its own freedom and safety,
but to spare, and to bestow
upon the solidest and sublimest points
of controversy and new invention
it betokens us
not degenerated nor drooping to a fatal decay,
but casting off the old and wrinkled skin of corruption
to outlive these pangs
and wax young again,
entering the glorious ways
of truth and prosperous virtue,
destined to become great and honorable
in these latter ages.[10]

Like other seventeenth-century prose writers, Milton has a keen sense of the weight and length of rhetorical members.[11] The sentence is periodic. It moves forward steadily and carefully, each of its two main divisions perfectly balanced: "as in a body . . . it argues," "so [in a nation] . . . it betokens us." This parallelism is based on the familiar analogy between the human body and the body politic, and indeed this is only the largest parallelism in the sentence, which is based at every level on balance or opposition. The syntax here is the picture of a complete thought, orderly, logical, and building climactically to an eloquent appeal to the English people (all its urgency captured in that final phrase). The sentence is architecturally perfect, its elements balanced down to the smallest detail, even alliteration (e.g., "solidest and sublimest") fixing the items in pairs. Milton speaks here from a position of sincere assuredness, and the neat parallelisms that dominate the sentence, plus its overall periodic movement, are the form of that assuredness.

The following sentence from the *Tale* shows how Swift has effectively reproduced much of the symmetry of Milton's Ciceronianism, while he is at the same time demonstrating the instability of such construction.

> Thus furnisht, and set out
>   with Gods,
>   as well as Devils,
> was the renowned Sect of Aeolists;
>   which makes at this Day
>   so illustrious a Figure in the World,
>   and whereof, that Polite Nation of Laplanders,
>   are beyond all doubt,
>   a most Authentic Branch;
>   Of whom, I therefore cannot,
>   without Injustice,
>   here omit to make honourable Mention;
>   since they appear to be
>   so closely allied
>   in Point of Interest,
>   as well as Inclinations,
>   with their Brother Aeolists among Us,
>   as not only to buy their Winds
>   by wholesale
>   from the same Merchants,
>   but also to retail them
>   after the same Rate and Method,
>   and to Customers much alike.
>
> (P. 160)

Swift reveals the ruins of Ciceronian symmetry: the opening clause sounds deceptively complete in itself, the leadoff "Thus" making it appear to be a summary; there are numerous pairs of terms here, although they are not as neatly laid out as in Milton; paradoxically, although the sentence would seem to pivot on logical-sounding conjunctions such as "and whereof," "since," and "as not only," the linkages are in fact quite loose and belie its logic and syntax;[12] and though most of the sentence is based, like Milton's, on a comparison, it is in this case difficult to tell exactly what is being compared. At first the Modern seems to want to discuss the Aeolists, but he then makes "honourable Mention" of the Laplanders, who are said to be "a most Authentick Branch" of the Aeolists; in mid sentence, however, he introduces a comparison between the Laplanders and "their Brother Aeolists among us," and he ends with a list of their similar practices in the buying and selling of winds. Swift means to make fun of the Aeolists as well as of the Modern himself (who is one of them), and this attempted classification is irrelevant to *his* argument. One thing seems clear: whereas Milton composes by large blocks of argument, Swift composes by clauses and phrases. The effect is to give the sentence from the *Tale* a rough, broken quality, a look of shattered unity.

Notice how Swift's sentence branches, to use Christensen's term, much more to the right than Milton's, each clause or phrase refining what was said immediately above. Whereas Milton keeps returning to, and indeed never gets too far away from, the main line of his argument, Swift permits himself to drift farther and farther to the right, and he never returns to his point of departure. Over and over Swift seems about to move back toward the left margin; after "so illustrious a Figure in the World," after "a most Authentic Branch," and again after "make honourable Mention," he would seem to be *required* by the conventions of syntax to touch base with his primary subject. But no. Here, as elsewhere, the reader of the *Tale* is frustrated. "A work has form," says Kenneth Burke, "in so far as one part of it leads a reader to anticipate another part, to be gratified by the sequence."[13] Certainly much the same may be said of the structure of a sentence. In the sentence from the *Tale*, however, the logic, comparison, and classification attempted by the Modern will not hold, because his assuredness ("beyond all doubt") is only as deep as his phraseology. His mind works in an essentially paratactic fashion and fails to impose form on thought.

Christensen makes the point that human thought is by nature cumulative and that the paratactic style is thus closest to the literal operation of the mind.[14] But the weakened force of logic and periodicity in the Senecan style makes it less appropriate for certain subjects. "The extremely loose sentence," advises Virginia Tufte, "has given up enough of its controlled patterning to be troublesome when its function is to contain a complex, logical thought."[15] Surely we could criticize the above sentence from the *Tale* on this ground. How can a complex, logical thought be conveyed adequately by means of a cumulative, one-plus-one syntax? I might make two observations here about Swift's style: it is less apt for projecting a fixed thought than it is for projecting a mind thinking (be it his own or his persona's); and, more importantly, it is precisely the failure of Swift's syntax to contain complex, logical thoughts that is one of his key devices for undermining the Modern's ideas.[16] Swift's meaning depends upon our picking up this collapse of logic and order. In a sense that collapse *is* his meaning.

Yet Swift's sentences can branch even more radically (and comically) to the right. In the following example, each subsequent clause or phrase is a modification of the item I have italicized in the clause or phrase immediately preceding.

> I ought in *Method,*
> to have *informed* the Reader
> about fifty Pages ago,
> of a *Fancy*
> Lord Peter took, and *infused*
> into his Brothers,
> *to wear* on their Coats
> *whatever Trimmings* came up in Fashion;
> never *pulling off* any,
> as they went out of the Mode,
> but keeping on *all together*;
> which amounted in time to a *Medley,*
> the *most Antick*
> you can possibly conceive;
> and this to a *Degree,*
> that upon the *Time*
> of their falling out
> there was hardly a *Thread*
> of the Original Coat to be seen,
> but an infinite Quantity of Lace, and Ribbands, and Fringe, and Embroidery, and *Points*;
> (I mean, *only those* tagg'd with Silver,
> for the rest fell off.)
>
> (P. 135)

Characteristically, the Modern begins here with one single thought, but this leads him to another thought, and another, and another; at each syntactic crossroad the new direction to be taken is determined by some signpost near the end of the previous clause or phrase. The Modern ends up wandering some *nine* modifications to the right of his starting point. So far has he strayed from periodicity that he concludes the sentence with a parenthesis, a tiny postscript, an insignificant addendum to what would seem an already insignificant detail. Although some of the Modern's phraseology suggests a sensitive, responsible author ("I ought in Method," for example), this is misleading, for there is little method to the Modern's madness, and his syntax proves it. This sentence is a good example of what Tufte calls "syntactical symbolism," the order of words suggesting a nonverbal analogue for meaning.[17] In this particular sentence we have a sort of symbol—"demonstration" would be better—of the Modern's failure of method; it is likewise a syntactic imitation of the absurd accretion ("keeping on all togther") that characterizes the brothers' coats. Swift seems to be interested not so much in what the Modern says as in how he says it, or, rather, in the incongruity between the two. Although in such works as Temple's *Essay upon Ancient and Modern Learning* or Swift's *Conduct of the Allies* syntax is the backbone of meaning, in *A Tale of a Tub* and Swift's other satires it is often ironically at odds with the persona's meaning and in keeping with Swift's.

Where did Swift find the model for his mock-Ciceronian syntax? Irvin Ehrenpreis argues credibly that for Swift Temple's style served as a kind of epitome.[18] Certainly one of the chief influences was the syntax and rhythm of his mentor's prose, which for the most part exhibits the typical symmetries of Ciceronianism, although it occasionally drops into a loose, more colloquial style that Swift would have found more to his liking. Swift seems to have taken from Temple his pervasive syntactic symmetry, then intentionally shattered that balanced structure, or played that structure off against his own ironic meaning. Compare the two following paragraphs from *An Essay upon Ancient and Modern Learning* and *A Tale of a Tub*:

> Besides, few men or none excel in all faculties of mind. A great memory may fail of invention; both may want judgment to digest or apply what they remember or invent. Great courage may want caution; great prudence may want vigour; yet are all necessary to make a great commander. But how can a man hope to excel in all qualities, when some are produced by the heat, others by the coldness of brain and temper? The abilities of man must fall short on one side or other, like too scanty a blanket when you are a bed, if you pull it upon your shoulders, you leave your feet bare; if you thrust it down upon your feet, your shoulders are uncovered.[19]

> This will stand as an uncontestable Argument, that our *Modern* Wits are not to reckon upon the Infinity of Matter, for a constant Supply. What remains therefore, but that our last Recourse must be had to large *Indexes*, and little *Compendiums; Quotations* must be plentifully gathered, and bookt in Alphabet; To this End, tho' Authors need be little consulted, yet *Criticks*, and *Commentators*, and *Lexicons* carefully must. But above all, those judicious Collectors of *bright Parts*, and *Flowers*, and *Observanda's*, are to be nicely dwelt on; by some called the *Sieves* and *Boulters* of Learning; tho' it is left undetermined, whether they dealt in

> *Pearls* or *Meal*; and consequently, whether we are more to value that which *passed thro'*, or what *staid behind*. (Pp. 147–48)

Temple and Swift develop their paragraphs in similar ways. Each begins with a general assertion, which is then supported by a series of parallel clauses and tied up with a balanced, aphoristic, quite homey metaphor. Temple's parallelism is neater and more pervasive; speaking for the moment only of structure, however, the paragraphs have a comparable shape, and these shapes are typical. But what about the differences? For all his symmetry, Temple manages a fairly straightforward, natural-sounding appeal to his readers. On the other hand, with the exception of the first proud sentence, Swift breaks up the Modern's thoughts with numerous caesuras (twenty-three, compared to Temple's fifteen), so much so that the rhythm of the paragraph is not balanced at all, but uneven, halting.[20] Swift's clausal and phrasal composition gives the paragraph an uncertain movement, and thus the Modern's symmetrical syntax is crossed by an opposing, broken sort of rhythm that discredits him. By the time we reach "and consequently," Swift's rhythm has destroyed the Modern's syntax altogether.

Contrast the conclusions of the paragraphs. Whereas Temple's analogy serves as a charming, human summary of his argument, Swift's rings false. The rhythm of Temple's paragraph gradually builds to the analogy; the rhythm of Swift's breaks up, splinters, and at last arouses our interest more in the analogy than in the thought it is supposed to illustrate. The Modern cites both sieves and boulters (fishing lines with several hooks) as metaphors for learning, drops the latter, alludes to sieves used in straining seawater for pearls, then to sieves used in straining meal, and finally tantalizes us (see the italics) into speculating on the relative value of "that which *passed thro'*, or what *staid behind*." Paradoxically, though Swift, who in the *Tale* defends Temple, models his own syntax on his mentor's, he uses it for diametrically opposed purposes. Temple's syntax is the basis of a calm, orderly, carefully reasoned argument. Swift's syntax in the end functions ironically as a faint reminder of order, and thus as a way of highlighting the unreason of his persona.

Temple's prose rises at times to a high, formal pitch, and at other times settles into an easy style approximating real speech; but in either vein his writing is powerfully and consciously rhythmical. As early as 1698 John Hughes contrasted Temple with L'Estrange this way: "There is the same Difference in the Styles of the two, as in those of *Cicero* and *Terence* in the Latin; in the first you find more of the *Orator*, and in the latter more of the *Englishman*."[21] "Sir William Temple," remarked Johnson to Boswell, "was the first writer who gave cadence to English prose. Before his time they were careless of arrangement, and did not mind whether a sentence ended with an important word or an insignificant word, or with what part of speech it was concluded."[22] The question of what Swift culled from the rhythm of Temple's prose is a difficult one, but it would seem that he learned from it the effects of rhythmical clauses at the ends of paragraphs, the role of parallelism and alliteration in establishing a rhythm, and the possibilities inherent in shifting stress patterns. Of course, as he did with every other element of Temple's style, Swift gave his mentor's cadences an ironic turn: whereas in Temple rhythm always echoes sense, in *A Tale of a Tub* they often contradict one another ironically.

Temple's style is almost as symmetrical as Milton's.[23] Although he is perfectly willing to break out of his formal syntax, and although in spite of the frequent symmetry he never achieves the neat profile of the more formal Ciceronians, it is clear that Temple's mind skips forward, typically, from one to another set of paired terms. Consider the following sentence, which I have set out spatially, so as to draw attention to its balances.[24]

> Such,
>   I am sure,
> Lucretius esteems
>   and describes
>   Epicurus to have been,
>   and to have risen,
>   like a prodigy of invention
>   and knowledge,
>   such as had not been before,
>   nor was like to be again;
> and I know not why others of the ancients may not be allowed
>   to have been as great in their kinds,
>   and to have built as high,
>   though upon different schemes
>   or foundations.[25]

The sentence is structured around a parallel between Epicurus, who is esteemed as a prodigy, and other ancients, whom Temple believes to be prodigies of different sorts. Every part of the sentence dwells on a pair of terms; every major noun, verb, or preposition calls forth a second term parallel to it. Interestingly, not one of these terms is in opposition to its sister term, which suggests that Temple is in his pairs amplifying ideas, not qualifying them. Three of the pairs move from an initial literal statement to a subsequent figurative one; "to have risen," "to have built as high," and "foundations" develop a single metaphor that serves to unify this architecturally structured sentence around an unobtrusive architectural image. The heavy use of parallelism gives the sentence a click-clack, click-clack rhythm, which is emphasized by like stress ("béen befóre"/"bé agaín") and slant rhyme ("been"/"risen," "kinds"/"high"). As with Milton, the overriding impression of order is the form of an apparent assuredness, and this is implied in Temple's "I am sure" and "I know not why others."

Swift's sentences are in his satires never as balanced as this one of Temple's. Yet it is often possible to discern a leaning toward balance and antithesis that is subtly knocked askew by the presence of certain asymmetrical elements—what Croll calls the "baroque"—in the same sentence.

I hold myself obliged
  to give as much Light as is possible,
    into the Beauties
    and Excellencies   of what I am writing,
because it is become the Fashion
                    and Humor
  most applauded among the first Authors
    of this Polite
    and Learned   Age,
  when they would
    correct the ill Nature of Critical,
or inform the Ignorance of Courteous   Readers.

(P. 130)

Like Temple, Swift would seem to display a predilection for balance and antithesis. But we must not forget that this is the Modern speaking. His coupled terms are just as redundant as Temple's ("Beauties"/"Excellencies"), just as rhythmical and alliterative ("Critical"/"Courteous"), and perhaps more trite and expected. The most notable difference between Temple's and Swift's sentences is that whereas in the former balance and antithesis form the rhetorical pattern on which the sentence is built, in the latter these devices are in effect mere rhetorical flourishes. In fact, Swift works just as hard to topple his balance and antithesis as he does to set it up. This is clearest in the neat parallelism that ends the sentence. Superficially, the last two phrases almost fall into the form of a couplet; Swift emphasizes his syntactic parallelism by means of rhythm, alliteration, and capital letters. On the other hand, notice how the parallelism does not here reinforce the Modern's meaning so much as it underscores the pride of the Modern and his put-down of the reader. The concluding syntax works ironically: although the sentence ends with a seemingly minor point, a mere dependent clause, this point is expressed in a neat parallelism that gives unwarranted emphasis to the idea. As it turns out, the Modern is not so much interested in his "obligation" or "the fashion" as he is in belittling the ill-natured or ignorant reader of *A Tale of a Tub*. Swift's sensitive readers, on the other hand, hate the Modern for his pride, resent his put-down, and generally see through his pat assertion at the end of the sentence. As in one of Pope's neat couplets, order is formally affirmed, only to be denied by some rhetorical incongruity.

In Swift's satire the complexity of relationship between form and meaning is connected to his characteristic complexity of point of view. We may read the above sentence as if a persona were speaking: though we are perhaps seduced by the sound of what the Modern says, we end up admiring the beauties and excellencies not of his rhetoric but of Swift's, which successfully undermines his persona's pretentiousness. Or we may read the sentence as if Swift himself were speaking: while agreeing with his ridicule of ill-natured or ignorant readers, we must at the same time remember that he did not write *A Tale of a Tub* for them anyway, but for attentive readers like ourselves.

Swift's ear was throughout his life attuned to the sound and rhythm of language. He is in all of his works attentive to alliteration, to the pattern of stressed syllables in a sentence, and, more generally, to the relationship between such sound devices and his intended meaning.[26] Swift's little language in the *Journal to Stella* is based on the sound of words: "Do you know that every syllable I write I hold my lips for all the world as if I were talking in our own little language to MD."[27] In *The Publick Spirit of the Whigs* Swift says of Steele: "He hath a confused Remembrance of Words since he left the University, but hath lost half their Meaning, and puts them together with no Regard, except to their Cadence."[28] Similarly, in

The Mechanical Operation of the Spirit he complains that "in Spiritual Harangues, the Disposition of the Words according to the Art of Grammar, hath not the least Use, but the Skill and Influence wholly lye in the Choice and Cadence of the Syllables."[29] And in *A Proposal for Correcting, Improving and Ascertaining the English Tongue* Swift speaks of "that Roughness of our Language," which he traces to its numerous monosyllables, the modern tendency toward contractions, and the absence of feminine softness from the professional, political, and business affairs of men.[30] And finally, perhaps most telling, is Faulkner's account that in 1735 Swift required that "the Editor should attend him every Morning, or when most convenient, to read to him, that the Sounds might strike the Ear, as well as the Sense the Understanding."[31] As we can see from these comments, Swift objected to the empty cadence, the cadence dissociated from meaning, and found the frequent harshness of the language disturbing. Yet it is not surprising that the Modern, like Steele, frequently slides into a cadence devoid of meaning, nor that Swift uses the abruptness of his native language as a way of interrupting the rounded tones of the Modern. As in most other matters, what Swift mocks in one place is what in another becomes for him a powerful satiric technique.

Swift's fascination with sound as an echo of sense is felt throughout *A Tale of a Tub*.[32] Of Fame, the Modern says that "her Trumpet sounds best and farthest, when she stands on a *Tomb*, by the Advantage of a rising Ground, and the Echo of a hollow Vault" (p. 186), and the balanced phrases and assonance at the end of the sentence set up an echo of their own. Swift's keen sensitivity to rhythm is clear from this wonderful instance: "Or, whether Fancy, flying up to the Imagination of what is Highest and Best, becomes over-shot, and spent, and weary, and suddenly falls like a dead Bird of Paradise, to the Ground" (p. 158). Swift here manipulates rhythm, as well as the sound of words, so as to match them to his meaning. Beginning hesitantly, the sentence speeds up after the word "Fancy" and runs on for a number of words without a caesura, then itself becomes overshot, wavers, and drops down with a series of heavy stresses, coming to rest on the word "Ground."

A further example of Swift's careful handling of sound occurs in the passage on Restoration theaters: "The whining Passions, and little starved Conceits, are gently wafted up by their own extreme Levity, to the middle Region, and there fix and are frozen by the frigid Understandings of the Inhabitants. Bombastry[33] and Buffoonry, by Nature lofty and light, soar highest of all, and would be lost in the Roof, if the prudent Architect had not with much Foresight contrived for them a fourth Place, called *the Twelve-Peny Gallery*, and there planted a suitable Colony, who greedily intercept them in their Passage" (p. 61). First, note in a general way how in these two sentences heavy "b" sounds are made to mingle with liquid "l" sounds, and how, more specifically, the paradox of "Bombastry and Buffoonry, by Nature lofty and light" is a phonetic demonstration of Swift's ironic meaning. Second, note how the alliteration of "fix" (active verb), "frozen" (passive verb), and "frigid" (adjective) suggests the freezing action itself. And third, note how the second sentence seems to escape the demanding caesuras for one longish clause, but is slowed down again, and intercepted at last by the insistent near-rhyme of "Gallery," "Colony," and "greedily." In the *Tale* Swift's imitative rhythms and sounds are fully as effective as Pope's in *Windsor Forest* and *The Rape of the Lock*.

A final, rather specialized but nonetheless very important phonetic device used by Swift in *A Tale of a Tub* is his intentional creation of and subsequent destruction of the cadences of classical and biblical oratory. It would be impossible here to summarize the difficult theory of cadence, its influence on seventeenth-century writers such as Browne and Milton, and the method of scansion used by Saintsbury, Tempest, Croll, and others.[34] Suffice it to say that the theory evolved from the practice of orators like Cicero, who, for emphasis, followed a certain few rhythmical patterns at the end of a large percentage of their clauses or phrases. It has been shown that the general effect of the cursus forms was closely adhered to in the Book of Common Prayer and the Authorized Version, although English cadences are somewhat less rigid than Latin.[35] The three major cadences, counting stressed syllables from the *end* of the clause or phrase, are as follows:

Planus:	5-2	("hélp ańd défénd uś")
	6-2	("supplications of thy people")
Tardus:	6-3	("governed and sanctified")
	7-3	("acknowledging our wretchedness")
Velox:	7-4-2	("punished for our offences")
	8-4-2	("defended by thy mighty power")[36]

Not coincidentally, Swift in *A Proposal for Correcting, Improving and Ascertaining the English Tongue* cites the Prayer Book and Bible as paragons of simple native eloquence, which, "being perpetually read in Churches, have proved a Kind of Standard for Language, especially to the common People."[37] Although Temple at times displays an awareness of the cursus, Swift's sensitivity to the oratorical cadences must have come to him more directly, through the rhythms of the two books he read every day and read aloud every Sunday morning. Cadencing in Swift's work is found where we would expect it—in passages of his sermons, in his three prayers for Stella, and in parts of *The Conduct of the Allies*. I have discovered little cadencing in *Gulliver's Travels*.[38] But Swift's sensitivity to rhythm and sound led him to see the potential effects of following the cursus forms in especially formal, pseudoserious passages of *A Tale of a Tub*; such cadencing is never sustained, but does for the moment prop up the Modern's swelling oratory, setting him up for a fall.

In a paragraph of the "Epistle Dedicatory" to the *Tale*, Saintsbury finds "a sort of grave oratorical rhythm—or a quiet caricature thereof."[39] I hope to show, as Saintsbury does not, just *how* Swift manages to create such a caricature. I give here only the first part of a paragraph, which I have set out clause by clause or phrase by phrase,[40] marking with an asterisk each sentence member that contains a cursus and italicizing the phrases where Swift has jammed two or more emphatic stresses up against one another.

*I profess to your Highness, (5-2)
in the Integrity of my Heart, (6-1)
that what I am going to say (4-1)
*is literally *true this Minute* I am writing: (6-2)
*What Revolutions may happen (5-2)
*before it shall be ready for your Perusal, (7-4-2)
I can by *no means warrant*: (4-3-2)
*However I beg You, (5-2)
to accept it as a Specimen of our Learning, (7-3-2)
our Politeness and our Wit. (5-1)
I do therefore affirm (4-1)
upon the Word of a *sincere Man*, (6-2-1)
*that there is now actually in being, (6-2)
a certain Poet *called John Dryden*, (4-3-2)
*whose Translation of Virgil (5-2)
was lately printed in a *large Folio*, (4-3)
well bound, (2-1)

and if diligent *search were made,* (3-2-1)
for *ought I know,* (3-2-1)
is yet to *be seen.* (4-2-1)

(P. 36)

Swift plays here with the Latin cadences. He opens the paragraph with a seeming commitment to the cursus (five out of the first eight endings); but he soon shows a preference for the stronger endings (4-1, 5-1, 6-1) that Norton Tempest calls "native cadences";[41] and he turns increasingly toward compounded stresses like "nó méans wárrant," "cálled Jóhn Drýden," and "óught Í knów." This shift in rhythm very subtly supports the intended effect of the passage, dropping it rather suddenly from the Modern's high-blown rhetoric down to Swift's commonsense meaning. "I profess to Your Highness," the Modern begins, in a phrase reminiscent of "Most merciful Father," which starts one of his prayers for Stella. But this supplicating cadence, though never completely abandoned, becomes more and more clogged with proper names,[42] initials, parentheses, caesuras, and a large number of compounded stresses. Although near the end of the paragraph there is a return to cadencing in the phrases "I vow to Your Highness" (5-2), "Friend of Your Governor" (6-3), and "utmost Politeness and Civility" (7-3)—it comes far too late to recover much of the Modern's previous formality. Swift's intentional undermining of his persona's oratorical cadences by means of his own arhythmical elements[43] proves the Modern's supplicating tones to be only the polite conventions of a very proud man. Like the subtle shifts in lexical field discussed in another chapter (note "Rheams" and "Squable" in this very proper paragraph), the subtle intermingling of knee-bent, trochaic cadences and self-assured, demanding spondees is an important element in the stylistic incongruity of *A Tale of a Tub.*

With the exception of the "Epistle Dedicatory" and perhaps the "Dedication to Lord Somers," however, Swift depends upon the cursus in the *Tale* for purely local effects. Thus in section 4, where the subject is Peter's proud politeness, Swift mixes the formal rhythms of the Latin cursus with the abrupt rhythms of English monosyllables in order to expose the pretentiousness of Peter as well as of the Modern.

In which Guise, (2-1)
whoever went to take him by the Hand (5-1)
*in the way of Salutation, (6-2)

Peter *with much Grace*, (3-2-1)
*like a well educated Spaniel, (6-2)
would present them with his Foot, (5-1)
*and if they refused his Civility, (6-3)
then he would raise it as high as their Chops, (4-1)
and give them a *damn'd Kick* on the Mouth, (4-1)
which hath ever since been call'd a Salute. (4-1)
Whoever walkt by, (4-2-1)
*without paying him their Compliments, (7-3)
having a wonderful *strong Breath*, (5-2-1)
he would *blow their Hats off* into the Dirt. (5-1)

(P. 115)

It is no accident that the cadences here all occur in phrases that refer to Peter's civility; though Swift employs the cursus sparingly in this passage, he uses it where it will have the most satirical force. What we hear are really two rhythms, each struggling for dominance: on the one hand, the polite cadences of "in the way of Salutation," and "paying him their Compliments"; on the other, the more heavily stressed, monosyllabic "damn'd Kick on the Mouth," and "would blow their Hats off into the Dirt." Swift is again juggling lexical fields (e.g., "Salutation" is equated with "Kick on the Mouth"), but the ironic juxtaposition of vocabularies is strengthened by the similarly ironic juxtaposition of prose rhythms. Simultaneously, Swift devotes his rhetorical energies to creating, if only for this moment, two styles, credible down to their quite different pacings and stress patterns. In documenting Peter's—and the Modern's—extreme civility, he employs a higher percentage of polysyllables, uses less emphatic endings, and depends upon a fairly slow, rounded sort of clausal and phrasal rhythm; in pointing up the superficiality of Peter's—and the Modern's—civility, he favors monosyllables, uses more emphatic endings, and lets the more frequent stresses break the longer rhythmic patterns. Swift's spondaic rhythms—what Albert Clark calls "hammer-stroke rhythm"[44]—throw the cadenced politeness into question. Shifting from one rhythm to another effectively jars our expectations (one of Swift's favorite games), sets up an ironic tension, and makes us catch the full impact of the deflating monosyllables.

Although in the above passage the emphatic rhythms of real speech win out, typically, over the stilted cadences of social graces, both have been felt by the reader. The compression Swift achieves here and elsewhere is remarkable: two rhythms, cleverly intermingled so as to suggest not just two ways of talking, but two approaches to life—the aloof, pseudopolite and the physical, impolite. Swift's ironic meaning is neither of these, and his peculiar sense of the absurd is what results from the incongruous mixing of these two styles as well as these two value systems, as in the simile "like a well educated Spaniel." The simile refers to Peter, but is just as apt for Swift himself, who under the "Guise" (the word is his) of civility presents us with his foot.

Let me end with a more general point. Don Cameron Allen suggests a direct connection between an author's rejection of periodicity and his philosophical uncertainty.[45] Not that I mean to use Swift's loose style as evidence of his skepticism. In his case the fragmentation of syntax and crisscrossing of rhythms are not signs of a personal lack of confidence but rather techniques for creating a voice separate from his own. Whereas a formal, balanced, periodic style—such as Milton's or to some extent Temple's—reminds us contantly of the author's aesthetic triumph over real life,[46] Swift's style tells us that the putative author has been unable either to sort out his experience or to control his literary form. The proud, authoritative tone of most Swiftian narrators is belied by their casual, drastically loose style; Swift's seemingly cavalier attitude toward form is his way of calling into question his assumed roles. Thus the giddy, incongruous rhythms of *A Tale of a Tub* contradict the Modern's attempts at logical and syntactic order, his know-it-all tone, and his staunch belief in the absolute efficacy of his masterpiece. The uncertainty implied in the style of the *Tale* is one of Swift's best devices for exposing the pretentiousness of his persona. But we can go further. What for the Modern is unclear thinking is for Swift a means of exploring complex ideas from several points of view. By contradicting the Modern's formal, pseudological style with the abrupt, broken style of real speech, Swift is able to look at the same idea, simultaneously, from at least two points of view. The Modern's uncertainty is Swift's complexity.

1. Kathleen Williams, *Jonathan Swift and the Age of Compromise* (Lawrence, Kans., 1958), p. 17.

2. Cf. Winifred Nowottny, *The Language Poets Use* (London, 1962), p. 9: "Of all the elements necessary to make an utterance meaningful, the most powerful is syntax, controlling as it does the order in which impressions are received and conveying the mental relations 'behind' the sequences of words."

3. Allan Rodway, "By Algebra to Augustanism," in *Essays on Style and Language: Lingusitic and Critical Approaches to Literary Style*, ed. Roger Fowler (London, 1966), p. 61. Rodway points up numerous antitheses in a passage from *Gulliver's Travels*.

4. The writers I am thinking of are Browne, Milton, Temple, Addison, and Johnson. In the eighteenth century John Mason published *An Essay on the Power and Harmony of Number* (1749), Joshua Steele published *Prosodia Rationalis* (1775), and Hugh Blair said a good deal about prose rhythm in his *Lectures on Rhetoric and Belles Lettres* (1783).

5. Morris Croll, "The Baroque Style in Prose," first published in 1929 and conveniently reprinted in *Style, Rhetoric, and Rhythm: Essays by Morris W. Croll*, ed. J. Max Patrick and Robert O. Evans (Princeton, 1966), pp. 207–33. Cf. George Williamson's revisions of Croll's theory in *The Senecan Amble: Prose from Bacon to Collier* (Chicago, 1951). In the margin of his copy of Clarendon's *History of the Rebellion*, Swift criticizes the author for "A long confounding Period"; in the margin of his copy of Burnet's *History of His Own Times*, he criticizes the author for his "Pretty jumping periods." See *Miscellaneous and Autobiogaphical Pieces, Fragments, and Marginalia*, ed. Herbert Davis (Oxford, 1969), pp. 304, 274.

6. Croll, "The Baroque Style in Prose," p. 210.

7. "Remarks upon a Book, intitled *The Rights of the Christian Church Asserted, &c.*," in *Bickerstaff Papers and Pamphlets on the Church*, ed. Herbert Davis (Oxford, 1966), p. 75. Cf. Sheridan Baker, "Fielding and the Irony of Form," *Eighteenth-Century Studies* 2 (December 1968):140: "Pope's most serious thoughts often seem flippant as the structural neatness of the couplet, so deftly balanced and contrasted, minimizes their depth, threatening irony or mirth."

8. I have borrowed Phyllis Joyce Guskin's term from her Ph.D. dissertation, entitled "The Microcosm of the Sentence: Syntax and Tone in Swift's Prose" (Vanderbilt University, 1968).

9. See Francis Christensen, "A Generative Rhetoric of the Sentence" and "A Generative Rhetoric of the Paragraph," both originally published in *College Composition and Communication* and rpt. in *The Sentence and the Paragraph: Articles on Rhetorical Analysis from "College Composition and Communication" and "College English"* (Urbana, Ill., 1966), pp. 1–7, 20–32. Cf. Brian Vickers's application of Christensen's method in "Syntactical Symmetry," chap. 4 of *Francis Bacon and Renaissance Prose* (Cambridge, Mass., 1968).

10. *John Milton: Complete Poems and Major Prose*, ed. Merritt Hughes (New York, 1957), p. 745.

11. I echo Morris W. Croll, "The Cadence of English Oratorical Prose," first published in 1919 and rpt. in *Style, Rhetoric, and Rhythm*, p. 332.

12. Louis T. Milic, in chap. 5 of *A Quantitative Approach to the Style of Jonathan Swift* (The Hague, 1967), pp. 122–36, cites numerous examples of Swift's pleonastic connectives and his use of them in a neutral sense, without their usual significance. But Milic's deduction (p. 136), that these connectives are nonetheless clear and persuasive, scarcely applies to *A Tale of a Tub*.

13. Kenneth Burke, "Lexicon Rhetoricae," *Counter-statement*, 2d ed. (Los Angeles, 1953), p. 124.

14. "A Generative Rhetoric of the Sentence," p. 2.

15. Virginia Tufte, *Grammar as Style* (New York, 1971), p. 157.

16. I have discussed this aspect of Swift's style in my article entitled "Swift's Correspondence: The 'Dramatic' Style and the Assumption of Roles," *Studies in*

English Literature 16 (Summer 1974): 357–71. Cf. Edward P. J. Corbett, "A Method of Analyzing Prose Style, with a Demonstration Analysis of Swift's *A Modest Proposal*," from *Reflections on High School English: NDEA Institute Lectures 1965*, ed. Gary Tate (Tulsa, Okla., 1966), rpt. in *Contemporary Essays on Style: Rhetoric, Linguistics, and Criticism*, ed. Glen A. Love and Michael Payne (Glenview, Ill., 1969), p. 89: "This tendency to ramify, qualify, or refine statements is evident too in the proposer's habit of compounding elements. I am referring not so much to the common eighteenth-century practice of using doublets and triplets, of which there are a conspicuous number in *A Modest Proposal*, as to the proposer's habit of stringing out words and phrases beyond the common triad, so that we get the effect almost of an exhaustive cataloguing of details or qualifiers."

17. Tufte, pp. 233–54.

18. Irvin Ehrenpreis, *Swift: The Man, His Works, and the Age*, vol. 1: *Mr. Swift and His Contemporaries* (Cambridge, Mass., 1962), p. 176.

19. *The Works of Sir William Temple*, ed. Jonathan Swift (1702; rpt. London, 1770), 3:459.

20. Note how here, as elsewhere in the *Tale*, Swift's italics contribute to such fragmentation by focusing our attention on individual words.

21. See John Hughes, "Of Style," in *Critical Essays of the Eighteenth Century, 1700–1725*, ed. Willard Higley Durham (New Haven, 1915), p. 84.

22. James Boswell, *The Life of Johnson*, ed. George Birkbeck Hill and rev. L. F. Powell (London, 1934–50), 3:257.

23. Cf. Croll, "The Baroque Style in Prose," p. 222, who mentions Temple as a late example of anti-Ciceronianism.

24. Again I have used a modified version of Christensen's "generative rhetoric," here taking care to group each of the paired terms together.

25. *The Works of Sir William Temple*, 3:447–48.

26. Very little has been written on this subject. But see Hugh Sykes Davies, "Irony and the English Tongue," in *The World of Jonathan Swift*, ed. Brian Vickers (Oxford, 1968), p. 153: "It seems to me very probable that Swift wished to indicate special intonations and stresses to the 'inner voice' of his readers by means of italic." And see A. Sanford Limouze, "A Note on Vergil and *The Battle of the Books*," *Philological Quarterly* 27 (January 1948), who points to several passages of what he describes as "limping blank verse" in *The Battle*. Finally, although (as will be seen) I disagree with her in part, I must quote Barbara Strang, "Swift and the English Language," in *To Honor Roman Jakobson: Essays on the Occasion of His Seventieth Birthday* (The Hague, 1967), p. 1950: "Euphony, especially in a rhythmical sense, is the only area in which he sees phonology as relevant to his concern; and although he was strikingly ignorant of phonology, synchronic or historical, he has, in rhythm, hit upon the most durable element in the organization of English sounds."

27. 4 May 1711. *Journal to Stella*, ed. Harold Williams (Oxford, 1948), 1:261. Cf. Paul Odell Clark, *A "Gulliver" Dictionary* (Chapel Hill, N.C., 1953), p. 3, who suggests that the code behind the invented words of *Gulliver's Travels* is likewise a phonetic one.

28. *Political Tracts 1713–1719*, ed. Herbert Davis and Irvin Ehrenpreis (Oxford, 1964), p. 36.

29. Guthkelch and Smith, p. 278.

30. *A Proposal for Correcting the English Tongue, Polite Conversation, etc.*, ed. Herbert Davis and Louis Landa (Oxford, 1964), pp. 11–14.

31. George Faulkner, "To the Reader," in *The Works of Jonathan Swift* (Dublin, 1762), vol. 1.

32. In *An Essay on Criticism* (1711), Pope argues that "The *Sound* must seem an *Eccho* to the *Sense*," and gives a series of classic examples: e.g., "That like a wounded Snake, drags its slow length along," "*Soft* is the Strain when *Zephyr* gently blows," and "The *hoarse, rough Verse* shou'd like the *Torrent* roar."

33. I have restored the reading of the fifth edition. See Glossary under "Bombastry."

34. George Saintsbury, *A History of English Prose Rhythm* (1912; rpt. Bloomington, Ind., 1967); Norton R. Tempest, *The Rhythm of English Prose: A Manual for Students* (Cambridge, 1930); Morris W. Croll, "The Cadence of English Oratorical Prose," in *Style, Rhetoric, and Rhythm*.

35. One of Croll's major contributions to the study of cadence is his demonstration of the English liberalization of the classical cursus patterns.

36. My examples are all from Croll, who has taken them from the Book of Common Prayer.

37. In *A Proposal*, p. 15. Interestingly enough, Swift in *The Mechanical Operation of the Spirit* (Guthkelch and Smith, p. 279) seems to draw a distinction between the music of classical and modern prose, the former based on syntax and rhythm, the latter on the sound of words or letters: "Now, the Art of *Canting* consists in skilfully adapting the Voice, to whatever Words the Spirit delivers, that each may strike the Ears of the Audience, with its most significant Cadence. The Force, or Energy of this Eloquence, is not to be found, as among antient Orators, in the disposition of words to a Sentence, or the turning of long Periods; but agreeable to the Modern Refinements in Musick, is taken up wholly in dwelling, and dilating upon Syllables and Letters. Thus it is frequent for a single *Vowel* to draw Sighs from a Multitude; and for a whole Assembly of Saints to sob at the Musick of one solitary *Liquid*."

38. Croll asserts that 40 percent of the endings in the Collects of the Book of Common Prayer fall into one of the three cursus forms. For what it is worth, my own rough count reveals the following percentages of cursus endings: five communion prayers in the Book of Common Prayer, 42 percent; Isaiah, chap. 40, in the Authorized Version, 22 percent; the first three paragraphs of chap. 5 of Browne's *Urn-Burial*, 32 percent; the first four paragraphs of Temple's *Essay upon Ancient and Modern Learning*, 28 percent; the first two Prayers for Stella, 42 percent; the entire sermon *On the Trinity*, 27 percent; the first four paragraphs of *The Conduct of the Allies*, 26 percent; book 4, chap. 4 of *Gulliver's Travels*, 18 percent; the first four paragraphs of the "Apology" to *A Tale of a Tub*, 36 percent; the "Epistle Dedicatory" to the *Tale*, 36 percent; and the "Conclusion" to the *Tale*, 23 percent. Although not too much weight should be put on these brief samplings, there are a couple of surprises. One is the high percentage of cursus endings in the "Apology"; the serious tone here must have led Swift into a serious use of the same cadences he elsewhere uses ironically.

39. Saintsbury, p. 243.

40. I follow Croll's acceptance of the cursus in what he calls "unitary phrases" in nonfinal positions. See "The Cadence of English Oratorical Prose," pp. 335–42.

41. Tempest, pp. 83–86. Swift is peculiarly sensitive to the final word of a clause; no better example can be found than his paragraph on reading books index first, where subsequent clauses conclude with "Tail," "Gate," "Back-Door," "Rear," "Behind," "Tails," "End," "Backwards," "Stockings," and "Foot" (p. 145).

42. It is perhaps not coincidental that the only italicization in the sentence is "*Your Highness*," "*John Dryden*," and "*Virgil*."

43. Paull Franklin Baum, in "Rhythm and A-Rhythm," chap. 7 of *The Other Harmony of Prose: An Essay in English Prose Rhythm* (Durham, N.C., 1952), gives an account of this phenomenon.

44. Albert C. Clark, *Prose-Rhythm in English* (Oxford, 1913), p. 13.

45. Don Cameron Allen, "Style and Certitude," *ELH* 11 (September 1948): 167–75.

46. I echo Sheridan Baker, "Fielding and the Irony of Form," p. 140: "In the eighteenth century, indeed, form tends to be comically ironic, at least potentially so, as when the couplet constantly reminds us of the artist's triumph over matters actual and conceptual." Cf. Ian Watt, "The Ironic Voice," *The Augustan Age* (New York, 1968), p. 108: "In both the heroic couplet and the periodic sentence, broadly speaking, the effort is for the speaker or writer to constrain or stabilize order, in some way to impose pattern, on the miscellaneous multifariousness of experience and individual attitudes."

chapter five

Language and Madness

It is usually conceived, that the Elder Brutus *only personated the* Fool *and* Madman, *for the good of the Publick.*

While reading, in another context, some contemporary studies of the language patterns and thinking processes of schizophrenic patients, I was struck by the fact that the major symptoms exhibited by those patients would serve well as a description of the major characteristics of the style of *A Tale of a Tub*. Transcriptions of schizophrenic language often sound like passages of the *Tale*. Although from this recognition I have been led back to studies of madness in the seventeenth century,[1] as well as to speculations on Swift's possible acquaintance with the language of madness, my approach remains essentially the one with which I began: the results of twentieth-century investigations of schizophrenic language and thinking can be used as a tool for describing and better understanding the style (and the thinking processes it depicts) of Swift's confusing satire.[2]

Swift is not, as some earlier readers believed, himself a madman; but neither is he, as our persona-critics would have it, clearly distinct from his Modern Author.[3] Although the Modern is often the butt of the joke, he is sometimes Swift himself, or at least he represents a point of view Swift could agree with. After all, Swift is —quite literally—a modern author,[4] and he has, in writing the *Tale*, explored his likeness to his persona as well as his difference from him, and also the ancient associations between madness and wisdom, pathology and creativity.[5] I share absolutely John Traugott's distaste for critics who argue away "the human condition that the living man risked his very sanity to think on."[6] Swift's choice of persona is all-important: in opting to deliver himself through the mind of a madman, and thus to tie himself to that persona's digressiveness, illogicality, and layered metaphors, Swift has, paradoxically, liberated his own mind. The madness of the Modern Author enables Swift to get at meanings he could not have otherwise. Focusing on the schizophrenic style of *A Tale of a Tub* can provide us with an awareness of the ambivalent relationship between Swift and his persona.

Swift and madness are often linked. There is, of course, the old legend that he was himself insane.[7] This view was in part spawned by Swift's fascination with the subject in his satires. "Madness," says Michael DePorte, "is their obsessive theme; they expose and isolate one source of insanity after another, and taken together they contain an alarming gallery of lunatics."[8] It is a fact that Swift was elected a governor of Bethlehem Hospital on 26 February 1714. And in later years he became concerned that Dublin had no public asylum like London's and resolved to use his modest fortune at his death to endow such a hospital.[9] But more interesting is Swift's knowledge of madness, along with its causes, effects, and cures, as displayed as early as *A Tale of a Tub*. Much of this knowledge reflects current seventeenth-century views of insanity and is specific enough to suggest that Swift's reading extended beyond Hobbes and Locke and into medical treatises such as Thomas Willis's *Practice of Physick* (translated in 1684), which included his historic *Anatomy of the Brain*.[10]

But Swift must also have gotten a good deal of his descriptive detail from firsthand observation at Bedlam, which had become by his day a popular Sunday tourist attraction. Note this entry in the *Journal to Stella*:

> *At Night*. Lady Kerry, Mrs. Pratt, Mrs. Cadogan, and I, in one coach; Lady Kerry's son and his governor, and two gentlemen in another; maids and misses, and little master (lord Shelburn's children) in a third, all hackney's, set out at ten o'clock this morning from Lord Shelburn's house in Picadilly to the Tower, and saw all the sights, lions, &c. then to Bedlam, then dined at the Chophouse behind the Exchange; then to Gresham College (but the keeper was not at home) and concluded the night at the Puppet-Shew, whence we came home safe at eight, and I left them.[11]

Distasteful as we may find the idea of Swift's visit to the King's menagerie, Bedlam, and a puppet show in a single day, it was in no way uncommon.[12] The sheer casualness of his account to Stella suggests both that this trip to Bedlam was not unique and that he was confident Stella would not be shocked by it; so too we may infer that Swift's appointment to a governorship was due to an interest in the hospital that was well known. At any rate, specific details in the *Tale* such as the "woodden Window" (p. 177) of one of Bedlam's cells argues for Swift's close attention during visits there. Although the Modern's cell-by-cell tour of the hospital has literary antecedents such as that in Ned Ward's *London-Spy* (1700), it may well be a thin fiction based on Swift's actual experience.

In Swift's era madness was commonly defined as an extreme subjectivity, as imagination beyond control of reason. One of its symptoms—and perhaps its cause—was seen to be pride.[13] DePorte suggests that the Augustans' association of madness and subjectivity was owing to their preoccupation with epistemology. "They were disturbed," says DePorte, "by the arguments of Descartes, Hobbes, and Locke that the secondary qualities of objects—their colors, smells, and tastes—were not inherent. The question of how much of what we perceive in things is inherent and how much a construct of the mind unsettled them. If normal experience involved such mental constructs must one not be on guard against further impositions? Might it not, in fact, be the mind's inclination to impose?"[14]

Swift in particular seems to have recognized the intimate connection between an understanding of madness and the theory of knowledge; no one work illustrates these concerns of the late seventeenth and early eighteenth centuries better than *A Tale of a Tub*, which combines so closely the problem of madness with the problem of epistemology. "For whatsoever in this state," argues the humanitarian Thomas Tryon in 1695, "is represented unto the Soul by the uncontrolable and unbounded Imagination, is essential unto them, whether it be good or evil."[15] Similarly, the psychiatrist Silvano Arieti has said recently that "what for us are truth and error share for the patient equal right to existence, inasmuch as they are both acts of consciousness."[16] Ignoring both sense data and moral dicta, madness was in the Augustan age usefully exploited as an example of our tendency toward mental distortion, or at least as a metaphor for such distortion. Swift uses it as both. "How fade and insipid do all Objects accost us that are not convey'd in the Vehicle of Delusion?" (p. 172), exclaims the Modern, and his rhetorical question betrays his madness as well as the unempirical basis of his epistemology; in fact, the former becomes a metaphor for the latter. To speak more generally, madness is for Swift the *cause* of the

Modern's ridiculous modernism as much as it is the *effect* of that modernism, and also a convenient *symbol* for the pervasive errors of his time.

"The central issue for Swift is cognition," says Martin Price.[17] "Swift's typical mode, therefore, is the ironic dramatization of the mind that chooses not to see. Such a mind may, and in fact usually does, have great energy. It is prompted by strong passions which capture the imagination, freeing it from the control of reason and its adherence to truth. (The relationship of imagination to truth may be oblique, but its existence remains, for the Augustans, a test of all serious art.) Once the imagination is given rein, its fertility is enormous and its energy untiring."[18] In *A Tale of a Tub* Swift interweaves the style of madness with the style of reason and discovers that there is often truth in the former and error in the latter. The sheer energy of the *Tale*'s style results from the dramatic interplay between the rational, commonsensical Swift and the irrational, jumble-headed Modern Author. Yet both are Jonathan Swift. No wonder we find the meaning of the *Tale* to be so elusive: what we have is the inconsistent style of a madman, or rather, the electric current that jumps incessantly, unpredictably, between Swift's style and point of view and the Modern's.[19] The result seems to fit one of Jerome S. Bruner's "conditions of creativity": "I would like to suggest that it is in the working out of conflict and coalition within the set of identities composing the person that one finds the source of many of the richest and most surprising combinations."[20] The Modern's insanity becomes for Swift a means to a brilliant creativity. In writing the *Tale* Swift confronted the madness not only in the world but also in himself, and discovered there a source of great inspiration.[21]

The warp and woof of the *Tale* are a logical, step-by-step, "vertical" way of thinking and an analogical, associative, "horizontal" way of thinking. The difference between these two modes of thinking is the difference between what Freud calls "primary" and "secondary" processes.[22] Primary process thinking is pleasure-oriented thinking characteristic of the child and is dominated by the untroubled coexistence of opposites, thinking by allusion or metaphor, and the absence of any apparent intellectual goal. Secondary process thinking, on the other hand, is thinking characteristic of the mature adult and is dominated by the rules of Aristotelian logic, conventional syntactic patterns, and a sense of working toward some goal. Primary thinking is inborn, private, and unconscious; secondary thinking is learned, socialized, and altogether conscious.

Of course, as Freud pointed out, primary process thinking is not restricted to the yet-to-be-socialized child but is dominant also in dreams, jokes, slips of the tongue, and certain forms of mental illness.[23] The artist likewise taps into this more primitive kind of thinking. Thus Brendan A. Maher sees in schizophrenic writing examples of "the literary imagination gone mad": "It would seem, therefore, that the mental substrata in which certain kinds of poetry are born probably are associative in a more or less schizophrenic way. . . . The intelligence that shapes, cuts, edits, revises and erases is fed by many unconscious sources, most of them cultural; but the wellsprings seem to be, as poets have been telling us for centuries, sort of divine and sort of mad."[24] In "A Digression on Madness" Swift deliberately explores this connection between the artist and the madman. The Modern Author admits that he was formerly an inmate of Bedlam: "that honourable Society, whereof I had some Time the Happiness to be an unworthy Member" (p. 176).[25] His writing is a kind of therapy: "My Friends will never trust me alone, without a solemn Promise, to vent my Speculations in this, or the like manner, for the universal Benefit of Human kind" (p. 180).

In *A Tale of a Tub* Swift simultaneously exhibits two styles and two sorts of thinking, the secondary or logical and the primary or analogical. Swift *in principle* mocks both the Modern's logic and his redundant, farfetched metaphors; however, though he *in effect* demonstrates the absurdity of formal logic, he utilizes the Modern's crazy metaphors for his own purposes. Swift undermines both the socialized style of secondary thinking and the eccentric style of primary thinking. But many of the satiric meanings of the *Tale* are found in the Modern's associative, metaphorical madness, which we can understand only if we ourselves respond on a primary level.[26]

A general awareness of the distinction between primary and secondary thinking existed in Swift's day and is found especially in seventeenth-century discussions of the differences between madness and dreams on the one hand and sane, waking life on the other. To Hobbes and Locke the distinction is between a runaway "Trayne of Thoughts" (Hobbes) or "Association of Ideas" (Locke) and those kept in check by judgment.[27] "Without Steddinesse, and Direction to some End," argues Hobbes, "a great Fancy is one kind of Madnesse;

such as they have, entring into any discourse, are snatched from their purpose, by every thing that comes in their thought, into so many, and so long digressions, and Parentheses, that they utterly lose themselves."[28] Locke traces madness to the uncontrolled connection of ideas in the mind: "I shall be pardoned for calling it by so harsh a name as *madness*, when it is considered that opposition to reason deserves that name and is really madness; and there is scarce a man so free from it but that, if he should on all occasions argue or do as in some cases he constantly does, would not be thought fitter for Bedlam than civil conversation."[29] Locke's view of madness as a mere exaggeration of perfectly normal thought patterns is a bold departure from earlier accounts of mental illness and one that may have influenced Swift. But for the moment we ought to notice the distinction in both Hobbes and Locke between rational and irrational thought, between disproportionate ideas and unconventional connections on the one side and orderly, proportionate, conventional thinking on the other.

Imagination must be restrained always by reason, as in the Modern Author it is not: "I my self, the Author of these momentous Truths, am a Person, whose Imaginations are hard-mouth'd, and exceedingly disposed to run away with his *Reason*, which I have observed from long Experience to be a very light Rider, and easily shook off" (p. 180).[30] Swift in part may be talking here about himself; after all, it is *his* galloping imaginations we meet in *A Tale of a Tub, Gulliver's Travels,* and his other works. As G. S. Rousseau says of Addison, Swift, and Pope, "the role of imagination in literature was perhaps the most vexing aesthetic problem of their time."[31] By exploring the nature of madness in the *Tale*, and by making his mad persona also a writer, Swift faces this problem head-on. As an artist Swift knew, as did Freud, that primary process thinking is not the sole property of children, dreamers, and madmen.

As we have seen, Hobbes and Locke suggest that the difference between a sane man and an insane man is often a difference in speech patterns. This distinction is made even more explicitly by Thomas Tryon, that independent-minded merchant and sometime student in physic who wrote in his *Treatise of Dreams and Visions*: "The one speaks and forms every thought into words: having not the Bridle of sense nor Reason to restrain him; the other often times cuts off such and such thoughts and Imaginations in the Budd, or at least shuts the grand Gate, the *Mouth*, and keeps those Stragglers in, not suffering the Organs and Properties of Nature to form them into Articular Expressions."[32] Swift makes a very similar distinction in *Some Thoughts on Free-Thinking*:

> Discoursing one day with a prelate of the kingdom of Ireland, who is a person of excellent wit and learning, he offered a notion applicable to the subject, we were then upon, which I took to be altogether new and right. He said, that the difference betwixt a mad-man and one in his wits, in what related to speech, consisted in this: That the former spoke out whatever came into his mind, and just in the confused manner as his imagination presented the ideas. The latter only expressed such thoughts, as his judgment directed him to chuse, leaving the rest to die away in his memory. And that if the wisest man would at any time utter his thoughts, in the crude indigested manner, as they come into his head, he would be looked upon as raving mad.[33]

Again I am reminded of Freud's primary and secondary process thinking. The madman, and to some degree the artist, speaks as his imagination prompts him; the mature,"normal," properly socialized man speaks only those ideas his judgment chooses from among the many presented by the imagination. In *A Tale of a Tub* Swift shows over and over the collapse of the Modern's judgment and demonstrates thereby the positive and negative effects of alogical, unconventional, and digressive speech and thinking.

Swift's fascination with the language of schizophrenia is apparent in his emphasis on speech throughout "A Digression on Madness." The Modern refers to philosophers as "Persons Crazed, or out of their Wits, having generally proceeded in the common Course of their Words and Actions, by a Method very different from the vulgar Dictates of *unrefined* Reason" (p. 166)—and the italicization only heightens Swift's irony.[34] Philosophers, enthusiasts, and critics in this digression all deliver their doctrines in unconventional language. And in the Modern's tour of Bedlam, each inamte is marked by a peculiar style of speech: one is "eternally talking, sputtering, gaping, bawling, in a Sound without Period or Article" (p. 176); another is "in much and deep Conversation with himself" (p. 177); another "has forgot the common *Meaning* of Words, but an admirable Retainer of the *Sound*" (p. 178); and yet another is "very sparing in his Words, but somewhat over-liberal of his Breath" (p. 178). Swift must have paid close attention to the speech patterns of the madmen he encountered inside—as well as outside!—Bedlam, and he seems to have modeled his style in *A Tale of a Tub* as much on what he heard there as on the style of the *Anatomy of Melancholy* or *The Rehearsal Transpros'd*. It is not hard to see that the speech habits of the Bedlamites in "A Digression on Madness" are characteristic also of the style of the Modern Author himself.

I introduce here two recent examples of what John D. Benjamin terms "schizophrenic pseudo profundity."[35] Their relevance to a study of the mad style of the *Tale* is readily apparent:

> The players and boundaries have been of different colors in terms of black and white and I do not intend that the futuramas of supersonic fixtures will ever be in my life again because I believe that all known factors that would have its effect on me even the chemical reaction of ameno acids as they are in the process of combustronability are known to me.[36]

> The subterfuge and the mistaken planned substitutions for that demanded American action can produce nothing but the general results of negative contention and the impractical results of careless applications, the natural results of misplacement, of mistaken purpose and unrighteous position, the impractical serviceabilities of unnecessary contradictions. For answers to this dilemma, consult Webster.[37]

As psychiatrist Maria Lorenz says of the language of one of her patients: "The words swell with an implication of meaningful thought. But the full fruition of *a* thought, *a* meaning, does not occur."[38] There is in both passages a veritable rush of ideas, too many ideas for too few sentences. "In my head," explained one patient after recovery, "there ran like an endless clockwork of a compulsive, torturing, uninterrupted chain of ideas. Naturally, they were not too sharply defined or clearly developed. There were joined idea upon idea in the most remarkable and bizarre associations although there was always a certain definite or inherent connection from link to link."[39] This rush of ideas is behind the associational quality of most schizophrenic language and is the source of the chaining effect such as that in the latter half of the second passage above.

Another major characteristic of these passages is that described by Eugen Bleuler (who in 1911 first introduced the term "schizophrenia") in his groundbreaking *Dementia Praecox or the Group of Schizophrenias*: "The wording is preferably bombastic; indeed it is not so merely in the passages which are intended to convey emphasis or feeling. The patients utter trivialities using highly affected expressions as if they were of the greatest interest to humanity."[40] As schizophrenics often are, the authors of these two passages are proud in their belief that they are communicating something of immense importance: the signs of that self-satisfaction are the pseudo-scientific polysyllables ("futuramas," "supersonic," "subterfuge") and vague Latinisms ("reaction," "contention," "applications"), plus the phrase "all known factors . . . are known to me" in the first paragraph and the cocky reference to Webster in the second. Although the effect here is of the presence of great meaning, or at least potential meaning, none emerges because the patients feel the pressure of too many ideas, or ideas of overblown significance, and are unable to edit some of them out, judge their relative importance, or bring them together into a unified whole.[41] "The schizophrenic," says Norman Cameron, "is shooting at the target with a verbal shotgun where he should be sighting along a rifle."[42] That everything I have said here concerning these two examples of schizophrenic writing would apply as well to the Modern's style in *A Tale of a Tub* is, I suggest, no mere coincidence: Swift put his keen ear for speech to good use on his visits to Bethlehem Hospital.

But there are other similarities between the language of madness and the style of the *Tale*. Schizophrenics often give undue emphasis to the mere verbalization of words,[43] as in the second of the above passages, where there is a toying with prefixes (e.g., "*sub*terfuge" and "*sub*stitution," "*mis*taken" and "*mis*placement"), and where the reference to Webster shows that the lexicographical nature of the passage even hits the patient himself. And there is in each paragraph a neologism, typical in schizophrenic language:[44] "combustronability," a noun where an adjective is required, seems to mean "combustible" but looks like an inaccurate fusion of "combustion" and "ability"; "serviceabilities," an adjective converted to a noun, seems in fact to mean simply "service," and like "combustronability" it demonstrates the schizophrenic's unconventional play with words and parts of words. Moreover, the reason in each case for the patient's heightened concern for expression is helpful in understanding the Modern's similar concern. In *The Divided Self* R. D. Laing points out that the schizophrenic is desperately afraid of being exposed and thus spends most of his energy maintaining a "false-self system" for keeping others at a distance; one aspect of the patient's cultivated persona or personas (he frequently adopts more than one) is his kaleidoscopic, fragmented, intentionally misleading talk, what Laing calls "red-herring speech."[45] When one of the patients quoted above says, "I do not intend that the futuramas of supersonic fixtures will ever be in my life again," he is for a split second revealing his terrible fear and also attempting to hide that fear behind a string of big words. Analogously, in the *Tale* the insane Modern Author distances his readers by means of his continual verbal flamboyance;[46] yet we are meant to discover behind his deflecting style Swift's very sane meanings. The Modern—like many schizophrenics—has little more than a verbal existence. In this powerfully paradoxical work, Swift pretends to be psychotic, and the Modern is a sort of grotesque caricature of himself,[47] just as the style of the *Tale,* though essentially Swift's own, is in fact a caricature of that style.

As a basis for discussing these characteristics of the style of *A Tale of a Tub* in greater detail, here is a paragraph from "A Digression in the Modern Kind":

> To this End, I have some Time since, with a World of Pains and Art, dissected the Carcass of *Humane Nature,* and read many useful Lectures upon the several Parts, both *Containing* and *Contained*; till at last it *smelt* so strong, I could preserve it no longer. Upon which, I have been at a great Expence to fit up all the Bones with exact Contexture, and in due Symmetry; so that I am ready to shew a very compleat Anatomy thereof to all curious *Gentlemen and others.* But not to Digress farther in the midst of a Digression, as I have known some Authors inclose Digressions in one another, like a Nest of Boxes; I do affirm, that having carefully cut up *Humane Nature,* I have found a very strange, new, and important Discovery; That the Publick Good of Mankind is performed by two Ways, *Instruction,* and *Diversion.* And I have farther proved in my said several Readings, (which, perhaps, the World may one day see, if I can prevail on any Friend to steal a Copy, or on certain Gentlemen of my Admirers, to be very Importunate) that, as Mankind is now disposed, he receives much greater Advantage by being *Diverted* than *Instructed*; His Epidemical Diseases being *Fastidiosity, Amorphy,* and *Oscitation*; whereas in the present univeral Empire of Wit and Learning, there seems but little Matter left for *Instruction.* However, in Compliance with a Lesson of Great Age and Authority, I have attempted carrying the Point in all its Heights; and accordingly throughout this Divine Treatise, have skilfully kneaded up both together with a *Layer of Utile* and a *Layer of Dulce.* (Pp. 123–24)

In this paragraph the seemingly knowledgeable Modern speaks first of his dissection of human nature (which has died?) and how he reassembled the bones "with exact Contexture, and in due Symmetry." For all his talk of symmetry, however, he soon catches himself digressing, apologizes for it, then wanders off into further digressions. "Their Phantasies or Imaginations," says Willis of madmen, "are perpetually busied with a storm of impetuous thoughts."[48] The Modern is plagued with so many thoughts—the dissection, the symmetry of bones, the problem with digressions, his other writings, his friends, his admirers, and so forth—that he cannot work them into a coherent whole. Like the symmetry of human nature, the symmetry of this paragraph breaks down and its meaning becomes confused. Although the Modern speaks in the aloof, bombastic language of the intellect, and although he has an overweaning pride in the efficacy of his book ("this Divine Treatise"), his arguments have little direction, and he proceeds from one association to another with very little logic. The *Tale* is fractured at every level—chapters, paragraphs, and sentences—because Swift intends to give the impression of a fractured authorial consciousness. The Modern lacks integrity in part because his creator does not mean for him to be a full-bodied, consistent character like Gulliver; but Swift must also have realized that a madman lacks integrity and is apt to flip from one false self to another.

Swift in addition recognized that an overemphasis on verbalization is a characteristic feature of a madman's speech. Notice how the Modern's ideas cease to have much beyond a purely lexical significance: a dissected corpse becomes the italicized "*Humane Nature*"; there is a play on the words "Containing" and "Contained," from Wotton;[49] the Modern takes times out for a consideration of literary digressions; he draws attention to his *writings* on the subjects (as if they were new!) of instruction and diversion; the words "Fastidiosity" and "Amorphy" are the Modern's neologisms;[50] and the concluding aphorism is a lexical absurdity cooked up from a classical writer. In schizophrenia even the autonomy of words may be disrupted, as when the three brothers (two of whom are mad) break up the word "knot" into its constituent letters so as to manipulate its meaning the way they want (pp. 82–84). "A word," says Lorenz, "is denatured and neutralized by converting it into an alphabetical object,"[51] just as, in a more general way, troubling reality is denied by converting it into a purely verbal phenomenon. As Freud tells us, for the schizophrenic "word-presentation" replaces "object-presentation."[52] Nothing truer could be said of Swift's Modern Author.

But so far I have not commented on one of the chief features of this and other passages of the *Tale*: the Modern's loose handling of categories and his inability to distinguish between the literal and the figurative, the particular and the general. "Such qualities as being fictitious, metaphorical, potential, assumed, and presumed," says Arieti, "are not always possible for schizophrenic ideation."[53] There is an unnerving imprecision to the Modern's thinking processes. For example, though he alludes to what would seem to be a real autopsy of a real corpse, this corpse is called "Humane Nature" and would thus seem to be an abstraction, and the dissection a metaphor for a rigorous study of mankind. But the Modern subsequently admits that "at last it *smelt* so strong, I could preserve it no longer," thereby reasserting the real existence of a certain overripe corpse. "Having carefully cut up *Humane Nature*," a phrase that follows the Modern's short digression on digressions, jams the literal and figurative up against one another, the verb suggesting the one, the noun the other. By the time we get to the Modern's discovery itself—"that the Publick Good of Mankind is performed by two Ways"—we are unsure what to think, although the second half of the paragraph would suggest that "Humane Nature" is indeed to be understood in its generic sense; even here, however, the term "Epidemical Diseases" implies a literal corpse. And more generally, when at the end of the paragraph the Modern refers to his "Compliance with a Lesson of Great Age and Authority" (note the Milnesque use of capitals), we can only wonder why he has been making so much of his inductive method, when he has in fact been working deductively from some ancient principle.

As psychiatrists frequently have pointed out, schizophrenics lack the capacity to make generalizations and tend to jump quickly from the hypothetical to the real. Maurice J. Quinlan has shown that the literalization of metaphor is one of Swift's favorite rhetorical devices;[54] but it is in the *Tale* that he first discovered the satirical virtues of this trick, and it may be that his attempt to duplicate the language of madness inspired him to it.[55] Like most schizophrenics, the Modern exhibits a concrete attitude toward his ideas and seems incapable of making an unreal assumption or of accepting a fictitious situation.[56] One of the most pervasive and disturbing features of the style of the *Tale* is this slippage of meaning between the general and the particular, the metaphorical and the literal. The tiniest instances of such slippage are the schizophrenic's characteristic punning,[57] such as the Modern's word "Layer" at the end of the above passage; together with the verb "kneaded up" (here meaning "molded" or "shaped"), "Layer" (used frequently at this time with reference to cookery) suggests a sort of Horatian layer cake.

This ambiguity between the literal and the figurative infuses the *Tale* at every level, even affecting its structure: Arieti says that in an advanced stage of schizophrenia a patient may think of some people who once came to visit him, and as he does so he quite literally sees those people before his eyes;[58] similarly, as the Modern, who was once an inmate of Bedlam, begins to speak of the hospital, he suddenly seems to be there and slides into an account of his tour through the building—in the present tense—as if he were walking through it at that very moment. "At once confounding things past with things present, or to come," says Willis of madmen.[59] As in the Modern's case, a patient may confuse the present place—"the very Garret I am now writing in" (p. 169)—with somewhere else, or the present time—"what I am going to say is literally true this Minute I am writing" (p. 36)—with some future or past occurrence. Thus while writing in his garret the Modern (should we say Swift?) may imagine he is touring Bethlehem Hospital, his presence there neither past nor future, but *right now*; like one of the schizophrenics Laing describes whose life is totally contemporaneous,[60] for him a thing is modern or it is nothing. Confusing fact with fiction at every level, the speech of the schizophrenic Modern is Swift's epitome of modern man's epistemological daydreaming, which is a kind of madness.

Another passage will shed more light on the relation between fact and fiction—and how each relates to Swift's satiric "truth"—in *A Tale of a Tub*. This amazing sentence takes up an entire paragraph of section 11 and is nevertheless only the second half of the Modern's extended comparison of riding and writing. Swift puns on "rides."

> On the other side, when a Traveller and his *Horse* are in Heart and Plight, when his Purse is full, and the Day before him; he takes the Road only where it is clean or convenient; entertains his Company there as agreeably as he can; but upon the first Occasion, carries them along with him to every delightful Scene in View, whether of Art, of Nature, or of both; and if they chance to refuse out of Stupidity or Weariness; let them jog on by themselves, and be d--n'd; He'll overtake them at the next Town; at which arriving, he Rides furiously thro', the Men, Women, and

> Children run out to gaze, a hundred *noisy Curs* run *barking* after him, of which, if he honors the boldest with a *Lash of his Whip*, it is rather out of Sport than Revenge: But should some *sourer Mungrel* dare too near an Approach, he receives a *Salute* on the Chaps by an accidental Stroak from the Courser's Heels, (nor is any Ground lost by the Blow) which sends him yelping and limping home. (Pp. 188–89)

At the start the sentence would seem to be following a certain logical form: "*when* a Traveller"; "*when* his Purse"; "[*then*] he takes the Road." It is only with the phrase "*but* upon the first Occasion" that we get the first alteration of direction of the Modern's thinking; by the time we reach the clause "and if they chance to refuse," however, we have relinquished logic altogether. This disturbance of the logical function is one of the most frequently mentioned symptoms of schizophrenic thinking; recent studies indicate that such disturbances are the result of lapses in the person's attentional abilities.[61] Maher explains the proliferation of associational linkages in this way: "The schizophrenic in his use of language may therefore be seen as suffering from a process whereby irrelevant associations reach a strength equal to those of relevant associations, leading to a breakdown in the discriminations necessary to the precise use of words."[62] Notice how the Modern's logic shatters precisely at the moment his tone changes from polite ("every delightful Scene in View") to antagonistic ("out of Stupidity or Weariness"); when he thinks of a possible objection to a rider's—or writer's—meanderings, the Modern gets angry, and logic is replaced by concrete narrative.

Having once left rational argument behind, the mere mention of the next town leads the Modern to describe his traveler's reception; his reference to men, women, and children compels him to think also of barking dogs; and barkings dogs prompts him to consider how such beasts should be dealt with. By the conclusion of the sentence the Modern has been foolishly derailed by his own thoughts into an account of a single rider's dealings with a single dog.[63] What begins as a quite general argument concerning a typical, hypothetical traveler has by the middle of the paragraph slipped into a pseudoautobiographical adventure story, which, finally, dwindles into a parenthetical phrase and a dependent clause.[64] The Modern has difficulty dealing with the hypothetical and tends to concretize his arguments. Yet it is important to recognize that it is the Modern alone who loses his rational grip;

Swift temporarily gives over his style to his persona but himself uses the Modern's lapse into concrete narrative as a way of laying bare his own satiric truth. Since writing is like riding, the movement of the sentence demonstrates both the dangers and the possibilities of a spontaneous approach to traveling and, likewise, to the digressive approach to writing. The image of the dogs barking at the egocentric rider-writer has a double function: it is Swift's hint as to how we should respond to the Modern and his runaway imagination; it is also his prognostic nose-thumbing at anyone who dares criticize his way of writing. To say this, however, is not to turn Swift into a great compromiser, but rather to suggest that he suspects logic and relies instead on concrete situations chock full of implications to get across his meanings.[65] Above all we should not overlook the fact that it is the Modern's craziness that *allows* Swift to make his points, and brilliantly.

Swift makes fun of formal logic. The Modern says, seemingly satisfied with the Aeolists' reasoning: "First, it is generally affirmed, or confess'd that Learning *puffeth Men up*: And Secondly, they proved it by the following Syllogism; *Words are but Wind; and Learning is nothing but Words*; Ergo, *Learning is nothing but Wind*" (p. 153).[66] Swift here shows how one can prove anything at all by logic. Although the structure of the syllogism—it follows the form Barbara—is impeccable, its major premise is absurd, and thus what results is a formally valid conclusion that is nevertheless in its content quite unacceptable.

Swift may have lifted a page here from Aristotle. In the *Tale* he alludes disparagingly to Aristotle's *Dialectica*, "and especially that wonderful Piece *De interpretatione*, which has the Faculty of teaching its Readers to find out a Meaning in every Thing but it self" (p. 85). The reference to the *Dialectica*, however, is apparently to any compendium of Airstotle's logical treatises, including *De sophisticis elenchis*, which contains a collection of logical fallacies like the following:

> There must be sight of what one sees.
> One sees the pillar.
> Therefore, the pillar has sight.[67]

As Aristotle explains it, the problem here arises from a verbal ambiguity or "amphiboly," for the word "sight" in this syllogism may refer either to that which sees or that which is seen. It is interesting that many of the Modern's supposedly logical arguments are betrayed by the double meaning of words, as above "wind" means both "breath" and "hot air." In such instances the reader must catch the pun in order to catch Swift's irony. "It is a general rule in dealing with arguments that depend on language," says Aristotle, "that the solution always follows the opposite of the point on which the argument turns."[68] This is sound advice for the unraveler of Swift's fallacious logic in the *Tale*.

But beyond this, though Swift seems to have despised every minute of his enforced two years of logic at Trinity College, he seems also to have remembered many of its forms and phrases.[69] As with so much in the *Tale*, we are led back ultimately to Swift's simultaneous dislike of and fascination with the same rhetorical device. Imagine Swift's frustrated endeavors at Trinity to make sense of such labyrinthine scholasticism as this from *De interpretatione*:

> Yet from the proposition "it may be" it follows that it is not impossible, and from that it follows that it is not necessary; it comes about therefore that the thing which must necessarily be need not be; which is absurd. But again, the proposition "it is necessary that it should be" does not follow from the proposition "it may be," nor does the proposition "it is necessary that it should not be." For the proposition "it may be" implies a twofold possibility, while, if either of the two former propositions is true, the twofold possibility vanishes.[70]

On the other hand, what earlier had been a student's frustration was transformed in the *Tale* into a budding writer's pseudoacademic parody of the subject he hated most. Swift gets the last laugh. Yet the Modern's stubborn attempts to reason through literally everything by means of Aristotelian logic—or a semblance of it—is in truth not Swift's parody of Aristotle but of the discipline of logic, which he saw as so much hot air. Whether he is recalling Aristotle directly or the manual of logic written by his teacher Narcissus Marsh, Swift surely was aware of the absurdity of a speculative science that busied itself with logical and linguistic paradox rather than confronting the world's very real contradictions.

Swift would have found equally absurd Antoine Arnauld's popular *La logique ou l'art de penser* (Paris, 1662),[71] a so-called Cartesian logic that departed from scholastic logics in its emphasis not on the memorization of forms but on the usefulness of logic in the real world. "Had we written," says Arnauld, "an arid logic employing the ordinary examples of animal and horse, however, precise and methodical our book, it would have served only to increase the world's already overabundant supply of such texts—none of them read."[72] Instead Arnauld aims to furnish examples "which allow a student to see both the principle and the practice of logic at one and the same time." He offers a practical as opposed to a speculative science, a logic that might be applied to *everyday experience*.[73] Since a great deal of the satire of *A Tale of a Tub* is directed at attempts to apply logic to real circumstances, this may represent Swift's parody of *L'art de penser*. Recall, for example, the Modern's several rationalizations of a reeking human carcass, Peter's "thundring Proof" that a crust of bread is a leg of mutton, and Jack's spontaneous logicalizations upon knocking his head against a post.

But Swift goes well beyond parody of formal logic. Again and again he shows the Modern drawing on the grammar of logic without being able to maintain its logical force.

> The *True Criticks* are known by their Talent of swarming about the noblest Writers, to which they are carried meerly by Instinct, as a Rat to the best Cheese, or a Wasp to the fairest Fruit. So, when the *King* is a Horse-back, he is sure to be the *dirtiest* Person of the Company, and they that make their Court best, are such as *bespatter* him most. (P. 103)

> The following Maxim was of much Weight; That since *Wind* had the Master-Share, as well as Operation in every Compound, by Consequence, those Beings must be of chief Excellence, wherein that *Primordium* appears most prominently to abound; and therefore, *Man* is in highest Perfection of all created Things. (P. 151)

> And therefore, I the Author of this miraculous Treatise, having hitherto, beyond Expectation, maintained by the aforesaid *Handle*, a firm Hold upon my gentle Readers; It is with great Reluctance, that I am at length compelled to remit my Grasp; leaving them in the Perusal of what remains, to that natural *Oscitancy* inherent in the Tribe. (P. 203)

Although in each case the Modern's pseudosyllogistic thinking works ploddingly but correctly from a questionable premise toward some conclusion, which, if arrived at at all, is scarcely worth the trouble, he at the same time slips repeatedly into an analogical way of thinking that is the source of many of his misconceptions. In the above passages the Modern gets sidetracked by analogies that obviously strike him as more compelling than his logic. His analogies are for him quite literal: court flatterers *are* critics; wind *is* human breath; and readers *are* held by handles. In I. A. Richards's terms, the Modern is repeatedly seduced by his own rhetoric into mistaking "vehicles" for "tenors." Secondary process thinking in the *Tale* keeps regressing to that primary process thinking characteristic of madmen and artists.

We are now in a position to consider in greater detail the nature of logical dysfunction in the *Tale*. As a point of departure, I introduce a transcription of an interview with a schizophrenic patient who seems to have some of the same difficulties with language as the Modern Author:

> In the, the halls of the Justice Department there is an understanding of a bona fide agreement between any people scheduled to meet within government circles, within government triangles, within government rectangles or any place else. It is hard to speak with a language which has an idiom of opposition. I mean insofar as there are so many bulwarks in historical content representative of a, the revolutionary victory won over an English prosidium. It's made this country great in its self-containment. It might be of interest but it's hard to understand what I mean through a nonutilization of English grammar books. A small faction usually arises to call themselves leaders, forever after apologizes for it, who oppose learning. I don't know whether that's wholly correct or not, but Jimmy Cagney in one of his movies specified the fact that people who come up from the depths usually have a right to authority. The depths of the Anglo-Saxon language has no use for anything that is nonutilized, that is nonutility. What I mean is that progress is foolish when you consider the fact that through language and leadership you can augment the process of future generations being of foreign parentage.[74]

Irvin Ehrenpreis speaks of the Modern's "gestures of logic," a phrase reminiscent of Julius Laffal's reference to the schizophrenic's "show of logic."[75] Although in the above passage there is a hint of logical argument—or perhaps of more than one—that argument never comes off. The characteristic markers of rational discourse are here ("I mean insofar as," "It might be of interest," "when you consider the fact that," for example), as are a proliferation of intellectual-sounding, quite separable phrases that seem as if they *ought* to mean something ("understanding of a bona fide agreement," "bulwarks in historical content," "the depths of the Anglo-Saxon language"). But the connectives only give the illusion of connection, and the fine phrases jangle in their contexts. Although we can discern two major themes—language and government—in the passage, we cannot make out their relationship, nor exactly what the speaker is attempting to say about each of them. These two subjects come together at several points in the paragraph, most notably in the alliterating "language and leadership" and the neologism "prosidium," which could be a pun on "presidium" and "prose idiom."[76] Is the speaker saying that politics has so corrupted our language that it is difficult to make meaning out of it? Or is he perhaps praising the American conquest of the English language? Although his words tantalize us with potential meaning, the patient would appear to be totally illogical and this passage a good example of what is commonly termed schizophrenic "word salad."

But to describe this passage and others like it as illogical is too easy. What we have here is not *il*logical so much as it is *a*logical or *para*logical—a way of thinking quite apart from the rules of Aristotelian logic.[77] In primary process thinking there is no such thing as a logical contradiction, and a proposition may both be and not be at the same time.[78] Thus in this paragraph the patient seems simultaneously to be praising the American system while condemning it, applauding revolution while lamenting it, and attempting to bring his two subjects together while keeping them safely apart. Much of the difficulty here stems from the patient's failures to maintain accepted grammatical connectives and his dependence instead on purely associative, often emotional linkages that have meaning only within the private world of the schizophrenic himself; for example, the allusion to Jimmy Cagney in the midst of such a serious argument seems quite out of place and entirely personal to the speaker. Other associations are equally idiosyncratic: there is a playful repetition of words ("nonutilization," "nonutilized," and "nonutility"); a linkage due only to the application of a word within different contexts ("people who come up from the *depths*," "*depths* of the Anglo-Saxon language"); and an absurd instance of what David Rapaport calls "phrase completion" ("within government circles, within government triangles, within government rectangles").[79] The schizophrenic typically gets trapped in word, phrase, or sound associations that he cannot repress and that completely override any logic he may be pretending to. Schizophrenic thinking is primary process thinking, and if we manage to identify in a patient's speech some fragments of society's logic, his thinking is nevertheless at its core decidely eccentric and egocentric. In this passage it is not even clear that government and language are both real topics for the patient, for it is possible that one may exist in his mind as a metaphor for the other. Yet through the verbal smoke screen we can make out a desperate concern for communication: "It is hard to speak with a language that," "it's hard to understand what I mean," and "I don't know whether that's wholly correct or not." There is in this passage a tension between a terrible desire to be understood and a terrible fear of being understood.

Willis says that the madman's speech contains "contrary or opposite things" and that "some evilly joined or wonderfully divided, are confounded with others, the imagination suggests manifold *Phantasms*, and all of them only incongruous."[80] In the following passage from "A Digression on Madness" we find some of the same incongruities we discovered in the speech of the schizophrenic discussed above:

> For, if we take a Survey of the greatest Actions that have been performed in the World, under the Influence of Single Men; which are, *The Establishment of New Empires by Conquest: The Advance and Progress of New Schemes in Philosophy; and the contriving, as well as the propagating of New Religions*: We shall find the Authors of them all, to have been Persons, whose natural Reason hath admitted great Revolutions from their Dyet, their Education, the Prevalency of some certain Temper, together with the particular Influence of Air and Climate. Besides, there is something Individual in human Minds, that easily kindles at the accidental Approach and Collision of certain Circumstances, which tho' of paltry and mean Appearance, do often flame out into the greatest Emergencies of Life. For great Turns are not always given by strong Hands, but by lucky Adaption, and at proper Seasons; and it is of no import, where the Fire was kindled, if the Vapor has once got up into the Brain. For the *upper Region* of Man, is furnished like the *middle Region* of the Air; The Materials are formed from Causes of the widest Difference, yet produce at last the same Substance and Effect. Mists arise from the Earth, Steams from Dunghils, Exhalations from the Sea, and Smoak from Fire; yet all Clouds are the same in Composition, as well as Consequences: and the Fumes issuing from a Jakes, will furnish as comely and useful a Vapor, as Incense from an Altar. Thus far, I suppose will easily be granted me; and then it will follow, that as the Face of Nature never produces Rain, but when it is overcast and disturbed, so Human Understanding, seated in the Brain, must be troubled and overspread by Vapours, ascending from the lower Faculties, to water the Invention, and render it fruitful. Now, altho' these Vapours (as it hath been already said) are of as various Original, as those of the Skies, yet the Crop they produce, differs both in Kind and Degree, meerly according to the Soil. I will produce two Instances to prove and Explain what I am now advancing. (Pp. 162–63)

The Modern gives the superficial impression of being rational; like Swift he has learned his logical figures well. Indeed, the whole argument is laid out in a formally acceptable fashion: the Modern suggests first a survey of new systems, says the authors of these systems were all mad, traces the origin of such madness to his theory of vapors,[81] and draws a series of analogies for their effect on the brain.[82] "Thus far," he interjects, "I suppose will easily be granted me," apparently convinced that the mere appearance of logic will pass as honest thought. But Swift's irony is that though formally we may accept the Modern's argument, we ought to be dubious about his conclusion—"then it will follow"—that vapors, like rain, water the invention and bring it to positive fruition. Madmen, says Locke, "do not seem to have lost the faculty of reasoning, but having joined together some ideas very wrongly, they mistake them for truths, and they err as men do that argue right from wrong principles."[83] In this passage from the *Tale* it is not the form of the Modern's argument that we question, but rather his assumptions concerning the value of new systems, the validity of such a meteorological analogy, and perhaps the existence of bodily vapors in the first place. When at the end of the paragraph the Modern says, "I will produce two Instances to prove and Explain what I am now advancing," we realize that such proofs and explanations will be no more valid than the Modern's premises. It takes a madman to argue so forcefully from a purely surface similarity between weather conditions and the human understanding.

Ernst von Domarus has said that the difference between logical and paralogical thinking is that whereas in the former there is argument from identical subjects, in the latter there is argument from identical predicates.[84] It is the difference between this logic:

> All men are mortal.
> Socrates is a man.
> Therefore, Socrates is mortal.

and this:

> Butterflies are beautiful.
> Helen is beautiful.
> Therefore, Helen is a butterfly.

In the first syllogism the identical concept is the subject "man"; in the second the identification is made on the basis of the predicable "beautiful" as it is shared by two subjects. "The paralogical thinker," says von Domarus, "finds identity of subjects whenever and wherever he finds identity of predicables."[85] Of course, the second "syllogism" is not really a syllogism at all, but an example of argument by analogy. Thus the schizophrenic discussed above would seem to confuse language and government simply because he discovers that they have "opposition," "revolution," or "nonutilization" in common, just as, coincidentally, the words "language" and "leadership" have a sound in common, or "circles" have something in common with other geometric figures.

But for our purposes what is important is this: that whereas the true syllogism yields no new knowledge (since the concept "man" belongs by implication to Socrates, and he thus by definition shares man's common mortality),[86] the paralogical "syllogism" yields an absurdity that is in its way quite new, creative, and incisive (since it brings together, within a single context, two things not ordinarily thought of together). It is interesting that Freud cited wit as an example of the working of primary thinking and showed how its success often depends upon a short-circuiting of logic.[87] To say that language is like government—or *is* government—is perhaps illogical, but it is at the same time fresh, jarring, and full of possibilities. Analogies can sometimes grasp things that syllogisms cannot: Helen is a butterfly.

I find von Domarus's account of this feature of schizophrenic thinking to be especially useful in discussing the faulty reasoning in the *Tale*. The Modern Author's mind works in a dangerously predicative way. "The Hack is quite literally a crazy man with a metaphor," says Ronald Paulson.[88] Thinking of vapors rising from some source, he connects mists rising from dung hills, exhalation from the sea, smoke from a fire, fumes from a jakes, and incense from an altar. What matters to the Modern is neither the *differences* between "mists," "exhalations," "smoke," "fumes," and "incense" nor those between "dung hills," "sea," "fire," "jakes," and "altar"; because he senses a similarity in the outward effects—the predicables —of vapor rising in each case, he *identifies* the quite different types of vapors and also the quite different sources of vapors.[89] Moreover, a larger confusion is the Modern's mixing of meteorology with the workings of the human understanding, which is again based on a few predicative parallels between the two. Having mentioned near the beginning of the passage that one's reasoning abilities are determined by "the particular Influence of Air and Climate," the Modern cannot let this idea go; he introduces more and more references to the weather—"at proper Seasons," "Clouds are the same in Composition," and so forth—as he proceeds, until at last the idea overtakes him, and he concludes with an explicit, fully developed, and quite absurd analogy between the weather and the human understanding. What begins as a minor point becomes for the Modern a subject equal to his real subject. Notice how he uses weather metaphors for describing human beings ("to water the Invention, and render it fruitful") as freely as he uses personification in describing the weather ("as the Face of Nature never produces Rain"). In all of these instances the error is one of treating mere predication as if it were identification, of confusing what is predicated of a subject with the subject itself. As we can see here the madness of the Modern is not so much his failure with logic as it is his inability to see differences between things.[90]

Thus in the *Tale* there is an interweaving of the logical, syllogistic approach to knowledge and the paralogical, analogical approach. However, though each seems to be satirized, and though it is clear that we are meant to see the fallacies inherent in each, we must recognize that it is not logical but analogical thinking that makes possible many of the powerful meanings of Swift's satire. His view of logic is comparable to Locke's: "I am apt to think that he who shall employ all the force of his reason only in brandishing of *syllogisms* will discover very little of that mass of knowledge which lies yet concealed in the secret recesses of nature, and which, I am apt to think, native rustic reason (as it formerly has done) is likelier to open a way to and add to the common stock of mankind rather than any scholastic proceeding by the strict rules of mode and figure."[91]

Swift uses the Modern's ridiculous analogies as a way of getting at some of these meanings beyond logic. As Paulson says, Swift "exploits resemblance for all it is worth, but makes us see the difference; his metaphors reveal rather than overcome difference."[92] For example, he wants us to see the *resemblance* between fumes from a jakes and incense from an altar (for that metaphor contains a swipe at Catholicism), but he likewise intends for us to see the *difference* between the two and thereby to separate him trom his crude persona: the odor of incense is indeed pungent, and its value as a spiritual cleanser suspect; but Swift wants us to identify neither fumes with incense nor a jakes with a Catholic altar. The analogy is true in one sense and certainly untrue in another. Thus we can see how the effect of this passage depends not upon the force of its specious logical argument, but upon a whole array of imaginative associations and counterassociations: aside from the analogies themselves, we are meant to see that Swift is continuing the "air" theme of the previous section, that the mere use of the words "Dunghils" and "Jakes" in connection with the human understanding ironically degrades reason's confidence in its own powers, and that the Modern's mental leapfrogging demonstrates that his own brain has become vaporized. Swift typically makes the Modern's difficulty in fixing reality our difficulty as well. Confusions between fact and fiction are simultaneously mad and poignant.

Metaphors compress judgments into simple and instantaneous perceptions of things.[93] Swift uses them boldly in the *Tale*, forcing on us perception after perception, a mass of tiny judgments, each one containing a great deal of the Modern's fiction, but more than a little of Swift's satiric truth. As readers we must be willing to go some distance with the *Tale*'s primal metaphors without rejecting them out of hand as mere symptoms of the Modern's madness. I think we can say of Swift's persona what Arieti says of other paralogical thinkers: "In a certain way the universe of the schizophrenic, of the primitive, and of the child is closer to the immediate perception, to the phenomenological world, at the same time it is farther from the truth than ours because of its extreme subjectivity."[94] Paradoxically, the solidest reality in the *Tale* is to be found in its metaphors. Fumes, jakes, razors, cheese, maggots, hemp, ladders, horses, barking dogs, wasps, asses, stockings, and corpses: these things are in effect not metaphorical at all, but pinprick realities employed by Swift to deflate his persona's high-flying argumentation.

In the madness of his Modern, Swift discovered a freedom from propriety, conventionality, and single-mindedness. Tryon sees in madmen something of the innocence of children, for "they no longer remain under a Mask or Disguise, but appear even as they are, which is very rare to be known in any that retain their Senses and Reason."[95] And in *The London-Spy* one of Ned Ward's Bedlamites tells him:

> Prithee come and Live here, and you may talk what you will, and no Body will call you in Question for it: *Truth* is persecuted every where Abroad, and flies hither for Sanctuary, where she sits as safe as a *Knave* in

> a *Church*, or a *Whore* in a *Nunnery*. I can use her as I please, and that's more than you dare do. I can tell Great Men such bold Truths as they don't love to hear, without the danger of a Whipping-Post, and that you can't do: For if ever you see a Madman Hang'd for speaking the Truth, or a Lawyer Whip'd for Lying, I'll be bound to prove my *Cap* a *Wheel-Barrow*.[96]

The Modern's unwitting contradictions, perfectly acceptable in a madman, permit Swift to explore his subjects from several points of view at the same time; like Picasso in his cubist period, he can argue simultaneously *for* something and *against* it, make fun of the Modern and speak through him. So too his persona's insane running together of the specific and the general, the literal and the metaphorical, and the accidental and the substantial allows Swift to raise the questions: What is real? What is fiction? Why is it so important to distinguish between them? Furthermore, the liberation of opinion in the madman is precisely the position the satirist requires: when the Modern speaks of "the Art of exposing weak Sides, and publishing Infirmities" (p. 172), he is talking about the art of satire, which is, perhaps, nothing but the art of impersonating the madman. But of course that impersonation can never be complete. "In listening to a schizophrenic," says Laing, "it is very difficult to know 'who' is talking";[97] this is precisely the difficulty we have in reading *A Tale of a Tub*. DePorte suggests that Swift utilized the seventeenth-century notion of the madman's "lucid intervals" as a model for the style of the *Tale*.[98] The importance of this symptom for Swift is that is allows him to speak out in his own voice without destroying the credibility of his persona. Yet Bedlam gave him something more: I suggest that Swift's tours of the asylum demonstrated to him the peculiar flux of mad talk, and that he intentionally reproduced this effect in creating one of the most brilliant, difficult styles in English.

Swift does not advocate—as does the Modern Author—the release of all inmates of Bedlam; but neither does he share the paranoia of many of his contemporaries concerning the insane. As Michel Foucault has shown, the so-called Age of Reason feared unreason more than anything else.[99] The sane locked up the insane in asylums like Bedlam and kept them out of sight except on tour days, when they could be viewed through a grate or watched as if they performed before an audience or jury of "normal" people. Even Willis was able to write that in hospitals for the insane we "may behold, not without wonderful spectacle, as it were a new and monstrous nation of men, contrary to rational people, as it were our Antipodes."[100] Swift's view was closer to Locke's and Tryon's. Locke saw that sanity and insanity were not antipodes but were on a spectrum, and Tryon asked: "Are not all those Intemperances, Violence, Opression, Murder, and savage Evil, and Superfluities deservedly to be accounted the worst Effects of Madness? As also Lying, Swearing, vain Imaginations, and living in and under the power of Evil Spirits, more to be dreaded than the condition of those that want the use of Senses and Reason; and therefore are esteemed Mad?"[101]

The Modern argues that Epicurus, Lucretius, Descartes, and others, "if they were now in the World, tied fast, and separate from their Followers, would in this our undistinguishing Age, incur manifest Danger of *Phlebotomy*, and *Whips*, and *Chains*, and *dark Chambers*, and *Straw*" (p. 166). Of course, at least part of Swift would have thought that these thinkers, in the cause of good sense, should be used this way. But I take "this our undistinguishing Age" to be Swift talking, for the failure to distinguish, as we have seen, is the Modern's chief error.[102] The boldest technique of *A Tale of a Tub*—Swift's partial identification of himself with his mad persona—by itself proves that he did not care to write about modern insanity from the safe position of modern sanity. The responsibility for distinguishing between sanity and insanity, truth and error, is in the *Tale* turned over to us; the Modern, himself insane, cannot do it, and Swift does it only indirectly, through irony. Swift agreed with Dryden that "Great wits are sure to madness near allied": he chose a madman as his persona and used the style and perceptions of that persona in order to score his own points—or, rather, in order to force us to experience an alternate, quite mad approach to a quite mad world.

1. In particular, Michel Foucault, *Madness and Civilization: A History of Insanity in the Age of Reason*, trans. Richard Howard (New York, 1965); and Michael V. DePorte, *Nightmares and Hobbyhorses: Swift, Sterne, and Augustan Ideas of Madness* (San Marino, Calif., 1974). Here at the start I acknowledge my special debt to DePorte. Against the background of abnormal psychology in seventeenth-century England, he defines Swift's attitude toward the imagination, and then goes on to show how the Modern Author's madness affects the structure and style of *A Tale of a Tub*. I have pursued DePorte's connection between madness and style and have found, contrary to him, that Swift is not patly critical of the Modern's runaway imagination, but uses it for his own purposes.

2. It is interesting that one psychiatrist has urged the opposite, that literary

criticism might be used as a tool for understanding schizophrenia. See Maria Lorenz, "Criticism as Approach to Schizophrenic Language," *Archives of General Psychiatry* 9 (September 1963): 235–45. See also two recent books: Marshall Edelson, in *Language and Interpretation in Psychoanalysis* (New Haven, Conn., 1975), and Richard Bindler and John Grinder, in *The Structure of Magic*, vol. 1 (Palo Alto, Calif., 1975), recommend using transformational grammar as a tool for understanding patients in therapy. Edelson's discussion of linguistic "deviance" in literature and psychoanalysis is particularly relevant to the present study.

3. We ought to listen to R. D. Laing's warning in *The Divided Self: An Existential Study in Sanity and Madness* (1960) and *The Politics of Experience* (1967) that we have been too quick to clamp the term "schizophrenic" on certain unconventional people. We have also been too quick to call Swift's persona "mad."

4. In Swift's day the word "modern" could mean one thing in reference to the ancients-and-moderns controversy and another in reference to a contemporary author. Thus in *The Battle of the Books* Swift says: "This Temple having been educated and long conversed among the *Ancients*, was, of all the *Moderns*, their greatest Favorite, and became their greatest Champion" (p. 228).

5. "Great wits are sure to madness near allied," says Dryden in *Absalom and Achitophel* (lines 163–64); but the idea is found in Aristotle, Seneca, Shakespeare, Burton, and elsewhere.

6. John Traugott, "*A Tale of a Tub*," in *Focus: Swift*, ed. C. J. Rawson (London, 1971), p. 78.

7. For a discussion see Irvin Ehrenpreis, "Madness," chap. 6 of *The Personality of Jonathan Swift* (Cambridge, Mass., 1958).

8. DePorte, p. 58.

9. E. G. O'Donoghue, *Story of Bethlehem Hospital from Its Foundation in 1247* (London, 1914), pp. 249–51.

10. Thomas Willis, *Practice of Physick, Being the Whole Works of that Renowned and Famous Physician*, trans. S. Pordage (London, 1684).

11. 13 December 1710. *Journal to Stella*, ed. Harold Williams (Oxford, 1948), 1:121–23.

12. In the *Tatler*, no. 30 (18 June 1709), Steele speaks of taking three boys (ages 12, 14, and 16) "a-rambling, in a hackney-coach, to show them the town, as the lions, the tombs, Bedlam, and the other places which are entertainment to raw minds, because they strike forcibly on the fancy" (*The Tatler*, ed. George A. Aitken [London, 1898], 1:247).

13. Willis, p. 205. Cf. Thomas Tryon, *A Treatise of Dreams and Visions . . . to which is added, a Discourse of the Causes, Natures and Cure of Phrensie, Madness or Distraction* (London, 1695), p. 256.

14. DePorte, p. 32.

15. Tryon, p. 252.

16. Silvano Arieti, "Schizophrenic Cognition," in *Psychopathology of Schizophrenia*, ed. Paul H. Hoch and Joseph Zubin (New York, 1966), p. 43.

17. Martin Price, *Swift's Rhetorical Art: A Study in Structure and Meaning* (1953; rpt. London, 1963), p. 87.

18. Martin Price, *To the Palace of Wisdom: Studies in Order and Energy from Dryden to Blake* (Garden City, N.Y., 1964), p. 190.

19. John C. Nemiah, *Foundations of Psychopathology* (New York, 1961), p. 204, cites a patient who said to him: "I know what I was saying, but it doesn't seem as though I'm saying it to you; it seems as if I'm saying it to myself."

20. Jerome S. Bruner, "The Conditions of Creativity," in *Contemporary Approaches to Creative Thinking*, ed. Howard E. Gruber et al. (New York, 1962), p. 17.

21. This is not, of course, the same as *equating* the madman and the artist. See Arieti, "Schizophrenic Cognition," p. 41; and J. S. Kasanin, *Language and Thought in Schizophrenia* (Berkeley, 1944), p. 102.

22. Freud outlined the main differences in a brief essay entitled "Formulations on the Two Principles of Mental Functioning" (1911); but the theory lies also behind *The Interpretation of Dreams* (1900), *Jokes and Their Relation to the Unconscious* (1905), and *The Relation of the Poet to Day-Dreaming* (1908). Cf. Henry B. Veatch's distinction in *Two Logics: The Conflict between Classical and Neo-Analytic Philosophy* (Evanston, Ill., 1969). It is interesting that Veatch begins his book with a lengthy discussion of Swift's *Battle of the Books*, and carries throughout an opposition between what he calls "spider-logic" and "bee-logic."

23. For a good discussion of Freud's two types of thinking, see Charles Brenner, *An Elementary Textbook of Psychoanalysis* (New York, 1955), pp. 155–62.

24. Brendan A. Maher, "The Shattered Language of Schizophrenia," *Psychology Today* 2 (1968): 60. Maher's major scholarly study is *Principles of Psychopathology: An Experimental Approach* (New York, 1966).

25. And "happiness," we ought to recall, has been defined above as "a perpetual Possession of being well Deceived" (p. 171).

26. Cf. Brenner, p. 159: "From this point of view we may say that an activity like wit involves for *both* author and audience the partial and temporary reinstatement of the primary process as the dominant mode of thought."

27. Thomas Hobbes, *Leviathan*, ed. A. D. Lindsay (New York, 1950), 1. 1; and Locke, *An Essay Concerning Human Understanding*, ed. John W. Yolton, 2 vols. (New York, 1961), 2. 33. 5. Locke added his discussion of the association of ideas to the fourth edition (1700) of his *Essay*.

28. Hobbes, 1. 8.

29. Locke, 2. 33. 4.

30. Swift has literalized the common metaphor of the "unbridled" imagination as it is used, for example, by Willis (p. 201). Paradoxically, horseback riding was at this time recommended by some doctors as a treatment for madness.

31. G. S. Rousseau, "Science and the Discovery of the Imagination in Enlightened England," *Eighteenth-Century Studies* 3 (Fall 1969): 116.

32. Tryon, pp. 278–79. Cf. this other riding metaphor in Tryon, pp. 255–56: "The heart akes, the inward Body seems to swell, and becomes too little for the Soul . . . and flings up the Reins of Government, and lets *Reason*, like a wilde Horse that hath cast off Bit and Bridle, and thrown his Rider, ramble confusedly whithersoever the Imagination shall hurry it." It is interesting that both Tryon and Swift use riding metaphors to describe the relationship between reason and imagination; but in Tryon reason is either the bridle or the horse, whereas in Swift reason is the overthrown rider.

33. In *A Proposal for Correcting the English Tongue, Polite Conversation, etc.*, ed. Herbert Davis and Louis Landa (Oxford, 1964), p. 49.

34. Cf. Willis, p. 202: The animal spirits, "whilst they flow, they produce unaccustomed notions, and very absurd, whence there is a necessity, that the distempered do speak, and imagine for the most part incongruous and discomposed things."

35. J. D. Benjamin, "A Method for Distinguishing and Evaluating Formal

Thinking Disorders in Schizophrenia," in Kasanin, *Language and Thought in Schizophrenia*, p. 83.

36. Quoted in Maher, *Principles of Psychopathology*, p. 395.

37. Ibid., p. 402.

38. Lorenz, p. 239.

39. Quoted in Eugen Bleuler, *Dementia Praecox or the Group of Schizophrenias* (1911), trans. Joseph Zinkin (New York, 1950), p. 33.

40. Ibid., p. 157. Cf. Norman Cameron, "Experimental Analysis of Schizophrenic Thinking," in Kasanin, *Language and Thought in Schizophrenia*, p. 55; and Kasanin, "The Disturbance of Conceptual Thought in Schizophrenia," ibid., p. 46.

41. See Bleuler, *Dementia Praecox*, pp. 374–76; and Kasanin, "Conclusion," in *Language and Thought in Schizophrenia*, p. 131.

42. Cameron, pp. 53–54.

43. Arieti, *Interpretation of Schizophrenia* (New York, 1955), pp. 209–19. Cf. Rudolph Arnheim, who in *Art and Visual Perception: A Psychology of the Creative Eye* (Berkeley, 1954), p. 104, points out that formalism is characteristic of the pictures produced by schizophrenics: "The secluded intellect weaves fantastic cosmologies, systems of ideas, visions, and grandiose missionary projects. Since the sensory sources of natural form and meaning are clogged and the vital passions dried up, formal organization remains, as it were, unmodulated. The tendency to simple shape operates unhampered in the void. The result is order as such, with little left to be ordered. Remnants of thoughts and experiences are organized, not according to their meaningful interaction in the world of reality, but by purely formal similarities and symmetries."

44. Bleuler, *Dementia Praecox*, pp. 150–52.

45. R. D. Laing, *The Divided Self* (1960; rpt. London, 1965), p. 164. Cf. Kasanin, "Conclusion," pp. 127–28: "When his security with others is impaired the language is not used for communication and something else takes place. The language becomes individualistic, eccentric, and contains elements of magic. Things happen in the world of thought which do not happen in the world of reality. Because a schizophrenic has given up hope of communication with others, he uses language to counteract his sense of insecurity."

46. Cf. Lorenz, p. 243: "Language thus ceases to *in*form, although it continues to *per*form."

47. Cf. case studies described by Laing in *The Divided Self*, pp. 104, 164.

48. Willis, p. 201.

49. See Guthkelch and Smith, p. 123 n. 2.

50. See Glossary under both words.

51. Lorenz, p. 242.

52. See Freud's essay *The Unconscious* (1915), esp. chap. 6 and app. C.

53. Arieti, "Schizophrenic Cognition," p. 42.

54. Maurice J. Quinlan, "Swift's Literalization of Metaphor as a Rhetorical Device," *PMLA* 82 (December 1967): 516–21.

55. Ned Ward's *London-Spy, Compleat* (1700; rpt. London, 1924) offers a couple of examples of madmen's confusion of the real with the hypothetical: literalizing a common metaphor, one Bedlamite is seen stomping on the floor and explains, "I am trampling down *Conscience* under my Feet" (p. 65); another inmate, when asked why he does not petition the Man in the Moon for some much-wanted claret, replies,

"I sent to him for a Dozen Bottles t'other day, and he swore by his Bush, his Cellar had been dry this six Months" (p. 63).

56. Cf. Kurt Goldstein, "Methodological Approach to the Study of Schizophrenic Thought Disorder," in Kasanin, *Language and Thought in Schizophrenia*, p. 24.

57. Cf. Bleuler's term "clang associations," in *Dementia Praecox*, pp. 24–26. On the cause of such sound derailment, see Maher, "The Shattered Language of Schizophrenia," pp. 30ff. See also chap. 2 above for further examples and a discussion of puns in the *Tale*.

58. Arieti, "Schizophrenic Cognition," p. 42.

59. Willis, p. 202. Cf. Arieti, *Interpretation of Schizophrenia*, p. 240; Brenner, p. 60; and Bleuler, "Autistic Thinking," in *Organization and Pathology of Thought: Selected Sources*, trans., with commentary, by David Rapaport (New York, 1951), p. 410.

60. Laing, *The Divided Self*, p. 197.

61. See Maher, "The Shattered Language of Schizophrenia," pp. 30ff. See also Donald Pavy, "Verbal Behavior in Schizophrenia: A Review of Recent Studies," *Psychological Bulletin* 70, no. 3 (1968): 171.

62. Maher, *Principles of Psychopathology*, p. 413.

63. Cf. Arieti, *Interpretation of Schizophrenia*, p. 243: "The more paleologically a person thinks, the more deprived he becomes of concepts or of Plato's universals. His ideas become more and more related to specific instances."

64. Swift's change in punctuation from the fuller stop of the semicolon to the lesser stop of the comma is indicative of the movement of this runaway sentence.

65. See my article "Dramatic Elements in Swift's *Journal to Stella*, " *Eighteenth-Century Studies* 1 (Summer 1968): 332–52. Cf. Ricardo Quintana, "Situational Satire: A Commentary on the Method of Swift," *University of Toronto Quarterly* 17 (1948): 130–36.

66. For further examples of Swift's syllogistic parodies, see Helen O'Brien Molitor's Ph.D. dissertation entitled "Traditional Logic and Rhetoric in Jonathan Swift's *A Tale of a Tub* and Later Works" (University of Minnesota, 1967), pp. 162–69.

67. Aristotle, *De sophisticis elenchis*, trans. W. A. Pickard-Cambridge, in *The Works of Aristotle*, ed. W. D. Ross (Oxford, 1928), 1:166a.

68. Ibid., p. 179a.

69. On Swift's study of logic, see Irvin Ehrenpreis, *Mr. Swift and His Contemporaries*, vol. 1 of *Swift: The Man, His Works, and the Age* (Cambridge, Mass., 1962), pp. 47–50, 58–63.

70. *De interpretatione*, trans. E. M. Edghill, in Ross, *The Works of Aristotle*, 1:22b.

71. In England the work came to be known as *The Port-Royal Logic*. According to Wilbur S. Howell, *Logic and Rhetoric in England, 1500–1700* (New York, 1961), p. 351, there were eight London editions between 1664 and 1700, including three English translations (1685, 1693, and 1696).

72. I quote from the most recent translation by James Dickoff and Patricia James, *The Art of Thinking* (New York, 1964), p. 21. Arnauld alludes in this passage to the commonplaces of the scholastic logics: "homo est animal rationale," "nullus equus est rationale," and so forth. See Ehrenpreis, pp. 49–50.

73. Arnauld, pp. 21–22. See Howell, "Descartes and the Port-Royalists," *Logic and Rhetoric in England*, pp. 342–63.

74. Quoted in Julius Laffal, *Pathological and Normal Language* (New York, 1965), pp. 131–32.

75. Ehrenpreis, p. 200; and Laffal, p. 29.

76. Laffal, p. 132 n. 1.

77. On this feature of schizophrenic thinking see Bleuler, *Dementia Praecox*, p. 23; and Arieti, *Interpretation of Schizophrenia*, p. 256.

78. See Bleuler, "Autistic Thinking," p. 409; and Nemiah, p. 214.

79. Rapaport, *Organization and Pathology of Thought*, p. 602 n. 2.

80. Willis, pp. 202, 182.

81. Willis's discussions of the role of animal spirits in causing madness may have influenced Swift, and he may even be parodying Willis's water and fire metaphors. Cf. Willis: "the Animal Spirits, together with the juice watering the Brain" (p. 203); and "being agitated by the former, and as it were inkindled, cause as it were a flamy, though most thin contexture" (p. 103).

82. Cf. Rapaport's "phrase completion" cited above. The *Tale* is full of examples of this phenomenon, although none more humorous than the following: "The other Instance is, what I have read somewhere, in a very antient Author, of a mighty King, who for the space of above thirty years, amused himself to take and lose Towns; beat Armies, and be beaten; drive Princes out of their Dominions; fright Children from their Bread and Butter; burn, lay waste, plunder, dragoon, massacre Subject and Stranger, Friend and Foe, Male and Female" (p. 165).

83. Locke, 2. 11. 13.

84. Ernst von Domarus, "The Specific Laws of Logic in Schizophrenia," in Kasanin, *Language and Thought in Schizophrenia*, pp. 104–14. Cf. Aristotle's fallacy of argument based on mere accidents of things in *De sophisticis elenchis*, 1:168b.

85. Von Domarus, p. 112.

86. Ibid., pp. 109–10.

87. Sigmund Freud, *Jokes and Their Relation to the Unconscious*, vol. 8 of *The Complete Psychological Works of Sigmund Freud*, ed. James Strachey (London, 1960), pp. 60, 63, 126, and others.

88. Ronald Paulson, "What is Modern in Eighteenth-Century Literature?", in *Studies in Eighteenth-Century Culture*, vol. 1: *The Modernity of the Eighteenth Century*, ed. Louis T. Milic (Cleveland, 1971), p. 82.

89. Cf. John Wilkins, *An Essay Towards a Real Character, and a Philosophical Language* (1668; facsimile ed., Menston, England, 1968), p. 58. Classified under "Air" see "Vapor," "Exhalation," "Fume," "Smoke," and "Steam." Under "Water" see "Cloud," "Mist," and "Rain." Swift has created a sort of ironic version of Wilkins's thesaurus of words and things.

90. Cf. Aristotle, *De sophisticis elenchis*, 1:176b: "One solves merely apparent arguments by drawing distinctions."

91. Locke, 4. 17. 6.

92. Paulson, p. 82.

93. See Walter J. Ong, "Metaphor and the Twinned Vision," *Sewanee Review* 62 (Spring 1955): 193–201.

94. Arieti, *Interpretation of Schizophrenia*, p. 213.

95. Tryon, p. 261.

96. Ward, *The London-Spy*, p. 65.

97. Laing, *The Divided Self*, p. 195.

98. DePorte, p. 77. Cf. p. 119, where Swift refers to Peter's "lucid Intervals," and p. 209, where the Modern excuses the "short fits or Intervals of Dullness" he encountered in writing the *Tale*. Cf. Swift's *Discourse of the Contests and Dissentions Between the Nobles and the Commons in Athens and Rome* (1701): "This encourages me to hope, that during the present lucid Interval, the Members retired to their Homes, may suspend a while their *acquired Complexions*; and, taught by the Calmness of the Scene, and the Season, re-assume the native Sedateness of their Temper."

99. Foucault, *Madness and Civilization*, for example, p. 76: "More effectively than any other kind of rationalism, better in any case than our positivism, classical rationalism could watch out and guard against the subterranean danger of unreason, that threatening space of an absolute freedom."

100. Willis, p. 208.

101. Locke, 2. 33. 4; and Tryon, p. 267.

102. Swift's concern for distinguishing is suggested by the following phrases from sections 9, 10, and 11 of the *Tale*: "a Point of the nicest Conduct to distinguish" (p. 168); "It will be a very delicate Point, to cut the Feather, and divide the several Reasons" (pp. 169-70); "the sole Point of Individuation" (p. 170); "Upon so nice a Distinction we are taught" (p. 175); "between whom and the former, the Distinction is extreamly nice" (p. 185); and "it was a Point of great Difficulty to distinguish" (p. 195).

chapter six

Reality and the Limits of Mind

With Relation to the Mind or Understanding; 'tis manifest, what mighty Advantages Fiction has over Truth.

Critics in our century show a naive reluctance to acknowledge the crucial place of *A Tale of a Tub*—or *Gulliver's Travels,* for that matter—in the history of the English novel. Our tendency to treat satire and novel as separate genres has divided Swift from Defoe, Richardson, and even Fielding. But Swift's first satire offers us the unique opportunity of watching a major English writer wrestling in the 1690s with some of the literary-philosophical issues implied in the form of the novel itself. For Swift the very act of creating a work of art raised the question of the correspondence between that work and external reality—what Ian Watt calls "essentially an epistemological problem."[1]

The *Tale* is an odd combination of satiric fiction and philosophical tract. Some twenty years before *Robinson Crusoe,* Swift turned out what is in effect an antinovel not unlike Sterne's *Tristram Shandy,* Beckett's *Watt,* or Barth's *Lost in the Funhouse.*[2] In the *Tale,* as in these works, the frustrated endeavor to tell a story, to make order and sense out of the raw materials of fiction, is inseparable from the endeavor to comprehend the world, to make order and sense out of physical and intellectual experience. Working through the madness of the Modern Author, Swift pushes himself (and us with him) to the outer reaches of thinking, into that strange territory where art and life, meaning and absurdity, rationality and irrationality border on one another, mixing freely. In that rarified atmosphere narrative order fails; but in the failure of his narrative Swift manages to question the effects of literary form, the relationship between form and reality, and beyond—the very limits of human knowledge.

All of Swift's satire rests on a suspicion of speculative philosophy. "The Philosopher's Way in all Ages," he says in *A Tale of a Tub*, "has been by erecting certain *Edifices in the Air*" (p. 56). The Modern Author twice refers to himself as a philosopher (pp. 57, 71) and is in a sense a caricature of the philosophical rationalist who builds such unfounded systems. Surely the point is Swift's when the Modern asks rhetorically: "For, what Man in the natural State, or Course of Thinking, did ever conceive it in his Power, to reduce the Notions of all Mankind, exactly to the same Length, and Breadth, and Height of his own? Yet this is the first humble and civil Design of all Innovators in the Empire of Reason" (pp. 166–67).[3] In the *Tale* the plot concerning the three brothers is minimal and trite, and Swift's Modern philosopher becomes—like Descartes in the *Meditations on First Philosophy*—essentially a disembodied mind grinding away impassively at all that is nonmind. But to see the world in terms of a personal intellectual system is to ignore the separable "facts" of experience, or at least to distort these facts in order to make them fit preexisting pigeonholes.

A Tale of a Tub turns in general on the opposition between the Cartesian rationalism of the Modern and the Lockean empiricism of Swift himself.[4] Swift's quasi novel focuses on the problematic trustworthiness of the medium of print, the danger of forcing history into literary form, the relation between mathematics and style, the paradox of the Modern's verbose nothingness, and the possibility of finding truth in a work of fiction. In all of these matters—each of which has for Swift its epistemological implications—the Modern Author presumes one answer while Swift suggests another. Proceeding like Descartes, Swift's persona builds a "*Romantick* System" (p. 167) of concepts and words and touches on real experience simply as a sort of analogy to his ideas. Swift, on the other hand, repeatedly undermines such Cartesianism and implies that the Modern stupidly ignores the "ocular Conviction" (p. 36) of concrete objects of perception.

Swift follows Locke in holding that the external world is real, that our senses give a true report of it, and that truth can be discovered by the individual through his senses. "Perception," says Locke in *An Essay Concerning Human Understanding*, "is the first operation of all our intellectual faculties, and the inlet of all knowledge in our minds."[5] Swift would agree. "In truth," says Locke elsewhere in the *Essay*, "the matter rightly considered, the immediate object of all our reasoning and knowledge is nothing but particulars."[6] Again Swift would agree. And Swift's philosophical position suggests the basis of his satiric technique: he continually undermines the Modern's categorizing, generalizing mind with images of particular things and everyday experiences described with sensory precision. As we have seen in preceding chapters, throughout the *Tale* things eventually overcome mere words, low style interrupts high style, and the rhythm of speech shatters the Modern's more formal cadences. Behind the Modern we sense always a larger consciousness: to reason with him, Swift seems to say, is to turn life into a purely intellectual construct, to create, literally, nothing out of something.

A Tale of a Tub is a satiric dramatization of the type of mind that denies everything outside the mind.[7] Neither the woman flayed nor the carcass of the beau per se troubles the Modern; these phenomena scarcely exist until interpreted. If the Modern can only transmute his two corpses into a neat generalization on *outsides* versus *insides*, he will be able to relax, conscience and sensation safely under control of intellect. The *Tale* is marked by strange denials of the facts of physical experience. Jack's encounter with a post is a good example:[8]

> He would shut his Eyes as he walked along the Streets, and if he happened to bounce his Head against a Post, or fall into the Kennel (as he seldom missed either to do one or both) he would tell the gibing Prentices, who looked on, that *he submitted with entire Resignation, as to a Trip, or a Blow of Fate, with whom he found, by long Experience, how vain it was either to wrestle or to cuff; and whoever durst undertake to do either, would be sure to come off with a swinging Fall, or a bloody Nose. It was ordained*, said he, *some few Days before the Creation, that my Nose and this very Post should have a Rencounter; and therefore, Nature thought fit to send us both into the World in the same Age, and to make us Country-men and Fellow-Citizens. Now, had my Eyes been open, it is very likely, the Business might have been a great deal worse; For, how many a confounded Slip is daily got by Man, with all his Foresight about him? Besides, the Eyes of the Understanding see best, when those of the Senses are out of the way; and therefore, blind Men are observed to tread their Steps with much more Caution, and Conduct, and Judgment, than those who rely with too much Confidence, upon the Virtue of the visual Nerve, which every little Accident shakes out of Order, and a Drop, or a Film, can wholly disconcert*. (Pp. 192–93)

We get a page and a half of Jack's mad philosophizing; and, tellingly, the Modern praises "the Force of his Reasoning upon such abstruse Matters" (p. 194). What, we might ask, is abstruse about a post?

Jack hardly notices what has occurred to him, nor learns anything from his experience. He pretty much ignores what happens to his body, so anxious is he to fit this particular, physical event into some sort of rational schema. He explains it away (1) by identifying this blow as simply one in a series of blows, and (2) by interpreting the whole series as evidence for the workings of "Fate" or "Nature."[9] Yet to rationalize the arbitrary is ridiculous; the boys who laugh at Jack have the right idea. Notice how Jack never gets around to asking "Why?" or evey "Why me?" What we have here is a sort of archetype of the absurd Sisyphus; for Swift he is a stoic clown-philosopher—like the Modern himself—who responds to physical stimulus as if it were rational meaning. And Jack's experience is not unique: it is relevant how often sheer *things* in the *Tale,* despite man's efforts to control them, knock him down, make him look foolish, and assume mastery over him; clothes, wills, nuts, barrels, a crust of bread, and of course paper and the printer's type all defeat man in one way or another.

Nor does Swift keep himself clear of the comedy. *A Tale of a Tub* belongs to that strange breed of introverted novel that assumes as one of its chief subjects the writing of the novel. Swift associates himself with his narrator simply by turning that narrator into a peculiarly self-conscious author.[10] At the same time, the equation of author and pseudoauthor is denied by the pseudoauthor's difficulty in composing his own story. Or does this difficulty in fact underline the equation? Typically, in Swift things are ambivalent, double-edged; thus in the *Tale* the ventriloquist is simultaneously incriminated by his dummy and excused because he is the manipulator of him. Kathleen Williams says: "Swift, with his restless energy, the inexhaustible inventiveness which produced the *Tale* itself and the fabulous voyages of Gulliver, knew only too well the seductiveness of undisciplined speculation, and his delight in it, as well as his disapproval of it, is made to contribute to satiric effect."[11] The author of the *Tale* has arranged things in such a way that he can satirize his speaker's mismanaged narration and at the same time recognize the irony of his own struggles. One of Swift's most winning traits is his ability to laugh at himself.

Swift repeatedly draws attention to the epistemological problems inherent in telling a story in a book. Although the Modern distinguishes between an idea "wholly neglected or despised in *Discourse*" and "its Preferment and Sanction in *Print*" (p. 210), Swift refutes this claim on every page of the *Tale*.[12] He denies the likelihood of fixing ideas into any kind of black-and-white assertiveness.

> The *Ladder* is an adequate Symbol of *Faction* and of *Poetry*, to both of which so noble a Number of Authors are indebted for their Fame. Of *Faction*, because * * * * * * * * *
> *Hiatus in* * * * * * * * * * *
> *MS.* * * * * * * * * * *
> * * * * * * * Of *Poetry*, because its orators do *perorare* with a Song; and because climbing up by slow Degrees, Fate is sure to turn them off before they can reach within many Steps of the Top: And because it is a Preferment attained by transferring of Propriety, and a confounding of *Meum* and *Tuum*. (Pp. 62–63)

It is possible that such blank spaces may be Swift's literalization of Locke's description of the beginning mind as "white paper void of all characters."[13] At any rate, it is no coincidence that at precisely the moment when the Modern is speaking of a "Symbol"—a literary device for fixing meaning—his manuscript itself gives way. One effect of such blank spaces in the text is to demonstrate that ideas committed to paper are guaranteed no certainty. A few of Swift's footnotes point up the same thing. For example, one tells us that the "O. Brazile" mentioned in the text is only a figment of the cartographer's imagination: "This is an imaginary Island, of Kin to that which is call'd the *Painters Wives Island*, placed in some unknown part of the Ocean, meerly at the Fancy of the Map-maker"(p. 125).[14] And another footnote undermines our faith in the informative nature of footnotes themselves: "I cannot conjecture what the Author means here, or how this Chasm could be fill'd, tho' it is capable of more than one Interpretation" (p. 179). Such footnotes caution us that at one level the *Tale* too is only a figment of the Modern's imagination, and that if he is saying anything, what he is saying is open to more than one interpretation. Swift sees that thoughts are for the most part too complicated, variable, and subjective to be fixed by mere ink and paper. It is interesting that the story of Peter, Jack, and Martin is itself about the fate of a manuscript; what fixity is there in writing if a document can be interpreted any way at all?

The persona's difficulties with the book as book draw attention to the tangential connection between history and truth. The Modern attempts to convince us of his accuracy: he refers three times to his keeping of a commonplace book (pp. 54, 148, 209); and his use of such phrases as "Here the Story says" (p. 74), "says my Author" (p. 115), and "By what I have gathered out of antient Records" (p. 151) imply that he is working from various earlier sources. But depending upon sources, no matter how meticulous one may be, opens up the possibility of several sorts of errors. Swift reminds us of this throughout the story of the three brothers, but nowhere more specifically then in his satire of Jack's reliance on his father's will: "Having consulted the Will upon this Emergency, he met with a Passage near the Bottom (whether foisted in by the Transcriber, is not known) which seemed to forbid it" (p. 191). Jack may depend entirely on his father's words, but if those words are written down, they are not to be trusted absolutely.[15]

The Modern's own manuscript was severely damaged before it reached the bookseller. In addition to the visible gaps in the text, we have this marginal note to tell us so: "The Title Page in the Original was so torn, that it was not possible to recover several Titles which the Author here speaks of" (p. 71). Thus the Modern's mangled, incomplete, tampered-with history of the three brothers is a perfect example of the impossibility of arriving at a true or factual account of some past occurrence. Swift's apparently half-serious talk in the "Apology" of how his corrected papers got out of his control (p. 12), how the bookseller published from a surreptitious copy (p. 17), and how his go-between took the liberty of expunging a few passages (p. 21) all suggest his very real mistrust of print as a vehicle of truth. We are throughout the *Tale* reminded that we are at several removes from what was, and that the truth may never be recovered by any means.

Despite the haphazard appearance of *A Tale of a Tub*, its effects are carefully calculated by its real author. The formlessness of the book is meant to reflect the trouble the Modern encounters in his attempts to make literary sense out of the mishmash of actual events and personal opinions. Whereas in *Robinson Crusoe* and most of its successors reality is accepted pretty much at face value, and literary form is worked out on the basis of this assumption,[16] the *Tale* has a raggedy profile precisely because its author has arrived at no such easy assumption on which to build. It is as if we have been carried back to some primitive stage in order to be shown how things are during the transformation into art. We are invited to watch the

Modern Author actually making numerous Ur-decisions—while Swift makes different ones—in which he opts not only for one way of telling the story of the brothers over another but for one view of reality over another. Thus the *Tale* is not fiction in the ordinary sense, but rather a book about the folly of assuming that one can freeze evanescent reality into fictional form. In *Madness and Civilization* Michel Foucault, mentioning Swift, speaks of that unique type of literature that exposes that "central incertitude where the work of art is born."[17] Swift in this respect prefigures Sterne, Beckett, and Barth, all of whom have given us disordered works of art and tentative explorations of knowledge.

In this context Swift's handling of the beginning, ending, and chapter divisions of his book takes on special importance. Thus the multiple embarcations ("Apology," "Dedication," "Bookseller to the Reader," and so on) are so many false starts; similarly, the book simply winds down, as the Modern (the reader too) simply gets tired, despairs of inserting anything more from his "laborious Collection of Seven Hundred Thirty Eight *Flowers*" (p. 209), and concedes that "there seems to be no Part of Knowledge in fewer Hands, than That of Discerning *when to have Done*" (p. 208). But the problems inherent in organizing a narrative are best shown in the following passage, where the Modern's typically poor memory has gotten him into difficulty: "The Necessity of this Digression, will easily excuse the Length; and I have chosen for it as proper a Place as I could readily find. If the judicious Reader can assign a fitter, I do here empower him to remove it into any other Corner he pleases. And so I return with great Alacrity to pursue a more important Concern" (p. 149). The Modern is so mixed up that he expresses a willingness to surrender authorship to his reader. Although a desire for propriety and symmetry is an understandable human trait, it cannot be fulfilled. As Swift's bad example, the Modern is intensely concerned about matters of organization, but his book is a record of his repeated organizational catastrophes. The mock-serious tone of this passage should not obscure a basic idea: it is ultimately impossible to squeeze contingent reality into neat beginnings, endings, and chapter divisions; by permitting contingency to enter between the covers of his book, Swift underscores not only the arbitrariness of literary form but also, by extension, the arbitrariness of judgments about the world.[18]

Narrative art has always been balanced uneasily between fact and fiction: a narrator desires to describe what happened at the same time that he feels pressure to shape, to improve, and to embellish his story.[19] Storytelling is in a sense the art of compromising between these two extremes. Before Swift this nervous and vibrant compromise was explored most self-consciously—and inconsistently—in *Don Quixote*. Although Swift's toying with point of view in *A Tale of a Tub* surely owes a good deal to Cervantes, his contribution was to spotlight in England at this particular time the problem of narrative strategy.[20]

In a joking but nevertheless quite serious way Swift mocks his narrator's insistence on playing both Lodge and Locke: "I have placed *Lord Peter* in a Noble House, given Him a Title to wear, and Money to spend. There I shall leave Him for some Time; returning where common Charity directs me, to the Assitance of his two Brothers, at their lowest Ebb. However, I shall by no means forget my Character of an Historian, to follow the Truth, step by step, whatever happens, or where-ever it may lead me" (p. 133). The Modern Author is suspended precariously between the roles of careful historian and God-like creator. Thus he can describe himself at one point as mere Secretary of the Universe (p. 123), while employing elsewhere the storyteller's formula, "Once upon a Time" (p. 73), and peppering his narrative with the editorializations "I cannot but bewail" (p. 125), "I record it with Tears" (p. 138), and the like. But Swift's irony should not deceive us. Just as philosophically the *Tale* depends from beginning to end on an opposition between the empirical and rationalistic views of life, so too Swift's novelistic concern with the opposition between narrator as historian and narrator as fabricator is crucial to his conception of the work.

Swift likewise questions the possibility of discovering meaning through the method of the philosophical rationalists. The Modern is typically sober and reasonable: he argues in a meticulous, point-by-point fashion, often separating an idea into its components for more intensive study; he supplies a plethora of information about every subject that comes up, taking time out to explain here and qualify there. Of course, this is not enough. The following discussions of the paradoxical notions of "empty" and "full"—from Descartes and Swift—are amazingly alike in method, not to mention subject matter, and demonstrate how effectively Swift has caught the mind that believes it can make significance out of anything at all. Descartes takes issue with the philosophical view of vacuum—"a space in which there is no substance"—because he cannot conceive that anything, even space, should not possess extension and thus be a substance. "When we take this word vacuum in its ordinary sense," argues Descartes, "we do not mean a place or space in which there is nothing, but only a place in which there are none of those things which we expected to find there."

> And if, in place of keeping in mind what we should comprehend by these words—vacuum and nothing—we afterwards suppose that in the space which is termed vacuum there is not only nothing sensible, but nothing at all, we shall fall into the same error as if, because a pitcher is usually termed empty since it contains nothing but air, we were therefore to judge that the air contained in it is not a substantive thing.[21]

Descartes stoutly defends the paradox that nothing is something, that emptiness is in fact fullness; Swift turns the paradox around to show how we mistake the dark of emptiness for the dark of fullness:

> I conceive therefore, as to the Business of being *Profound*, that it is with *Writers*, as with *Wells*; A Person with good Eyes may see to the Bottom of the deepest, provided any *Water* be there; and, that often, when there is nothing in the World at the Bottom, besides *Dryness* and *Dirt*, tho' it be but a Yard and half under Ground, it shall pass, however, for wondrous *Deep*, upon no wiser Reason than because it is wondrous *Dark*. (Pp. 207–8)[22]

The Modern sounds good. But there is a flabby virtuosity to both arguments, resulting partly from the twists and turns of mind, but also from the fact that both deal not with objects but with concepts —indeed, with words. In both instances the solid, physical world of real containers is brought in as mere analogy for the ideas of emptiness and fullness. But note the all-important difference: whereas Descartes assumes, by definition, that something is in the pitcher although there appears to be nothing, Swift argues that although we are sometimes tricked into thinking that a well wondrous dark is a well wondrous deep, this is not always the case. Swift, in other words, like Descartes, says that what appears to be so —even to a "Person with good Eyes"—may not be so; but whereas Descartes uses analogy to support his frail preconception concerning vacuums, Swift's analogy undercuts the Modern's equally frail argument, showing that some dark authors, like some dark wells, are truly deep and others are quite empty. Although Swift's method is close to Descartes's method, his analogy is in effect not secondary to his argument but the basis of it. Don't be fooled by the apparent depth of modern wells, Swift warns; they are not necessarily full, as Descartes would tell us, simply because philosophically we refuse to acknowledge the possibility of emptiness.

Notice in the above passage from the *Tale* how the effect of logical conjunction and careful qualification quickly breaks down; the Modern's "therefore," "however," and "because" fail to screen the basically cumulative nature of his argument.[23] Throughout the *Tale* he asserts that a thing means this, or this, or perhaps this, but the multiplicity of his interpretation suggests to us that whatever the thing means, its meaning is beyond the mind of the speaker. Kenner's comment on Beckett's *Watt* might be applied as aptly to *A Tale of a Tub*: "The detached, encyclopaedic style more and more evidently rehearses not facts but possibilites, not evidence but speculation."[24]

Swift is veritably obsessed with logical probability, a subject very much in the air in the latter half of the seventeenth century.[25] In the *Tale* sentence segments and words are commonly grouped in series of three, four, five, or more; beyond this, Swift seems fascinated by the notion of infinite series (the word "infinite" appears frequently). And the Modern concludes many of his lists with trailers such as : "forty other Qualifications of the like Stamp, too tedious to recount" (p. 75); "two and thirty Points, wherein it would be too tedious to be very particular" (p. 151); and "these Events, I say, and some Others too long to recite" (p. 183). In fact, open-endedness pervades the work at every level. Toying with the idea of infinite series, Swift sneaks "*Etcaetera* the Elder" and "*Etcaetera* the Younger" into his family tree of critics (p. 94). The Modern Author admits to Prince Posterity that he is nothing more than the most recent modern and can claim only that "what I am going to say is literally true this Minute I am writing" (p. 36). On a couple of occasions he even threatens us with other books. The series that crowd every page of Swift's satire are further indications of the failure of the Modern's categorical thinking; no matter how many items in a series, that series remains incomplete, at least theoretically open to one more item. In *De sophisticis elenchis* Aristotle suggests that in order "to exhaust all possible refutations we shall have to have scientific knowledge of everything"; in the *Discourse on Method* Descartes expresses a similar aim "to make enumerations so complete and reviews so general that I could be certain of having omitted nothing."[26] For Swift, to aim at exhausting all possible refutations or enumerating all factors involved in a situation is an unrealistic goal. *A Tale of a Tub* satirizes all such hopes for assembling *complete* evidence on any subject.

The Modern Author uses mathematics the same way he uses rational argument—as a tool for systematizing experience; and the greater abstraction of number promises that it will succeed in quieting reality where logic, print, and literary form have not. The Modern loves to quantify. He suggests that the Grub Streeters' worth might be calculated by hiring an arithmetician (if he had "*Capacity* enough") to count their books (p. 64). "It is intended that a large Academy be erected," he says elsewhere, "capable of containing nine thousand seven hundred forty and three Persons; which by modest Computation is reckoned to be pretty near the current Number of *Wits* in this Island" (p. 41). And he advocates meditation on the mystical numbers[27] seven, nine, and especially three: "Now among all the rest, the profound Number *THREE* is that which hath most employ'd my sublimest Speculations, nor ever without wonderful Delight. There is now in the Press, (and will be publish'd next Term) a Panegyrical Essay of mine upon this Number, wherein I have by most convincing Proofs, not only reduced the *Senses* and the *Elements* under its Banner, but brought over several Deserters from its two great Rivals *SEVEN* and *NINE*" (pp. 57–58). Reduced the senses! The Modern's overweening pride, his reference to a forthcoming publication, and his conflation of "Panegyrical Essay" and "convincing Proofs" are all Swift's means of divorcing himself from what his persona is saying. The trouble with mathematics is that it gives us the abstract outlines of things, or turns things into symbols, and thus makes sense only if we happen to be more interested in outlines or symbols than in things themselves.[28] The man in the *Tale* who stops in the street to take the dimensions of ordure is truly out of his mind (p. 93); to turn excrement into science is to deny reality.

The mathematics of *A Tale of a Tub* is related to one of its most important themes—that of nothingness.[29] As if his book has not demonstrated it well enough, in "The Conclusion" the Modern Author admits the failure of his imagination, even passes it off as a sort of modern virtue: "I am now trying an Experiment very frequent among Modern Authors; which is, to *write upon Nothing*; When the Subject is utterly exhausted, to let the Pen still move on; by some called, the Ghost of Wit, delighting to walk after the Death of its Body" (p. 208). By Swift's time there was a minor tradition of writings on the subject of nothing.[30] But what the Modern says here is perhaps related to the "method of exhaustion" developed by Archimedes, the so-called founder of infinitesimal analysis.[31] Elsewhere Swift's persona denies the infinity of matter (p. 147) and seems shocked to learn that all of the moderns' previous writings should have disappeared, the paper itself becoming "wholly annihilate" (p. 35). Swift was clearly fascinated by the intangible notions of infinity, vacuum, and annihilation. In *A Tritical Essay upon the Faculties of the Mind* (1704) he makes fun of those philosophers who dispute endlessly the existence of vacuums and those scientists who devote their lives to the search for perpetual motion.[32] Counting on his reader's general awareness of these standard topics of seventeenth-century mathematics, logic, and science, Swift utilizes them as analogies for the vacuity of his mad Modern Author. Swift's position is this: "There is no inventing Terms of Art beyond our Idea's; and when Idea's are exhausted, Terms of Art must be so too" (p. 50). With no ideas to start with, the Modern should never have picked up a pen—what he writes is so many words.

The *Tale* is an attempt at fictional meaning that must fail because it has at its core an unconquerable nonmeaning. Near the end of his book the Modern graciously interjects a few "Innuendo's"[33] to assist our interpretation of his ideas: "And First, I have couched a very profound Mystery in the Number of O's multiply'd by *Seven*, and divided by *Nine*. Also, if a devout Brother of the *Rosy Cross* will pray fervently for sixty three Mornings, with a lively Faith, and then transpose certain Letters and Syllables according to Prescription, in the second and fifth Section; they will certainly reveal into a full Receit of the *Opus Magnum*" (pp. 186–87). Surely Swift senses the irony of his equation:

$$\frac{X \times O \times 7}{9} = O$$

What is "couched" here is more than the Modern knows. Even the "O" of "Opus" echoes Swift's playful hint to the reader that the meaning of his persona's *Tale of a Tub* is zero, nothing.[34] The talkative Modern has nothing whatsoever to say: his blather about prayers, syllables, and vague prescriptions as much as proves it. The

Modern talks and talks and talks, sounding as if he is saying something but in fact saying nothing at all. Swift pushes the art of tedium about as far as it will go. Minus the continuous hints in the *Tale* that he himself knows full well what is going on, we would not read much more than a page.

In the *Tale* the theme of nothingness is paralleled by a couple of other ideas, like the notion of wind or breath. Aeolists of the past, we are told, while at sea stored wind in casks or barrels (p. 155); we are, of course, meant to see the connection with the tub itself. There are likewise in the *Tale* numerous references to silence, as when the Modern criticizes "the Silence of Authors" (p. 96) and insists on filling the quiet. At the same time noise is tied paradoxically to nothingness; arriving at the city, the three brothers "Rhymed, and Sung, and Said, and said Nothing" (p. 74).[35] Moreover, we ought to view the disintegration of the manuscript and the proliferation of word blanks in the *Tale* as physical demonstrations of (or glimpses into) the nothingness lurking behind the thousands of words that make up the text; these lacunas are, quite literally, holes in the Modern's thinking. Wind, silence, and white paper become in Swift's satire metaphors for nothingness, which is itself a metaphor for madness. Or perhaps it would be more accurate to say that madness becomes a metaphor for nothingness.

For all his rationalism the Modern is unmistakably irrational; and if irrationality is the absence of meaning, then he is nothing. Foucault points to the paradox of madness:

> Joining vision and blindness, image and judgment, hallucination and language, sleep and waking, day and night, madness is ultimately nothing, for it unites in them all that is negative. But the paradox of this *nothing* is to *manifest* itself, to explode in signs, in words, in gestures. Inextricable unity of order and disorder, or the reasonable being of things and this nothingness of madness! For madness, if it is nothing, can manifest itself only by departing from itself, by assuming an appearance in the order of reason and thus becoming the contrary of itself.[36]

I cannot imagine a better description of the fullness-emptiness paradox at the heart of *A Tale of a Tub*. The Modern explains his title: "Sea-men have a Custom when they meet a *Whale*, to fling him out an empty *Tub*, by way of Amusement, to divert him from laying violent Hands upon the Ship" (p. 40). Swift mocks here the Modern's *Tale of a Tub* (but not his own), which is empty, and also the mind that produced such a book. The *Tale* is chock-full of images, ideas, metaphors, numbers, allusions, jokes, quotations, and especially words; but its copiousness paradoxically betrays its absolute emptiness. Of course Swift subtly communicates something through his crazy persona. Madness masquerades as reason; then, ironically, madness becomes intelligible.

As a coalition of the various lacunas in Swift's satire, Bedlam is its climactic metaphor. It is more than a single image standing for the madness of the Modern, Jack, Wotton, and the others; it becomes a sort of ship of fools, an extremely open, suggestive symbol for all that is rotten in philosophy, religion, science, politics, criticism, and literature. And since madness is in the *Tale* a brimful nothingness, Bedlam becomes an epitome not only of the madness of the modern world, but also of its meaninglessness, and even, from Swift's point of view, its nothingness.

Michael V. DePorte speakes of "the great fascination throughout most of the eighteenth century with testing the limits and possibilities of reason."[37] *A Tale of a Tub* does just that. Swift's interest in the boundaries of the mind was perhaps fanned by a reading of Locke, who in book 4 of *An Essay Concerning Human Understanding* devotes an entire chapter to "The Degrees of Our Knowledge" and another to "The Extent of Human Knowledge." With Locke Swift questions the assumption that reason can locate verifiable, fixed, certain meanings about things; he depicts a mind repetitiously and ridiculously sifting experience through language, logic, and mathematics; finally, he shows the futility of expecting to make rational sense out of the facts of everyday experience, or, much more, the ultimate meaning of life.

"If Truth be not fled with Astrea," Swift says in *A Tritical Essay*, "she is certainly as hidden as the Source of the Nile, and can be found only in Utopia"; in the same work he makes the point that Socrates, "who said he knew nothing, was pronounced by the Oracle to be the wisest Man in the World."[38] Significantly, Swift's sermon *On the Trinity* argues that religious mysteries (like some earthly mysteries) are beyond human reason and must remain essentially mysterious, acceptable only on grounds of faith.[39] We have seen how the *Tale* has at its comic and epistemological core an obsession with awful, limitless everythings that prove to be, paradoxically, mere nothings. As Rosalie Colie says of such paradoxes: "At either end of the conceptual scale, 'nothing' and 'infinity' both bring man to the same impassable intellectual position, where he is himself by definition no longer the measure of all things, nor even the meásure of anything at all."[40] Swift dramatizes rational man's failure when he is confronted with the complex, the subtle, and the basically irrational.

In this paragraph the Modern discusses the limits of the mind and, ironically, exceeds those limits himself.[41]

> And, whereas the mind of Man, when he gives the Spur and Bridle to his Thoughts, doth never stop, but naturally sallies out into both extreams of High and Low, of Good and Evil; His first Flight of Fancy, commonly transports Him to Idea's of what is most Perfect, finished, and exalted; till having soared out of his own Reach and Sight, not well perceiving how near the Frontiers of Height and Depth, border upon each other; With the same Course and Wing, he falls down plum into the lowest Bottom of Things; like one who travels the *East* into the *West*; or like a strait Line drawn by its own Length into a Circle. Whether a Tincture of Malice in our Natures, makes us fond of furnishing every bright Idea with its Reverse; Or, whether Reason reflecting upon the Sum of Things, can, like the Sun, serve only to enlighten one half of the Globe, leaving the other half, by Necessity, under Shade and Darkness: Or, whether Fancy, flying up to the imagination of what is Highest and Best, becomes over-shot, and spent, and weary, and suddenly falls like a dead Bird of Paradise, to the Ground. Or, whether after all these *Metaphysical* Conjectures, I have not entirely missed the true Reason. (Pp. 157–58)

A brilliant paragraph. Careful reading makes the gist of Swift's (not the Modern's) argument quite clear. The mind of man "naturally" attempts too much, believes it can wrap up the world in neat packages of high and low, light and dark, good and evil, and fools itself into thinking it can achieve order and perfection. Boldly, Swift allows his mad narrator to score points for him: the Modern tells us what Swift would tell us, that man puts too much faith in his own reasoning, tries to reach understandings impossible for him, and overlooks the existence of paradox in the world. After all, is not east sometimes west? High sometimes low? Good sometimes evil? While speaking through the Modern, Swift simultaneously uses the Modern to demonstrate the ridiculous, dangerous pitfalls of thought. Notice how the pairing of terms suggests a nice balance of ideas at the same time that the fragmented, run-on style undermines such facile organization. In considering why we see mental alternatives, the Modern slides into an or-or-or syntax that is itself an example of exactly what he is talking about; and the last sentence explodes the series, the Modern admitting that this sequence of explanations is incomplete and perhaps infinite.

Swift's point is that the world is beyond easy schematization and is apt to be disturbingly paradoxical. The heavy, metaphorical quality of the passage finally gets the best of the Modern's high-flying argument and throughout keeps us aware of an opposing world of real objects and real experiences. The circle image (reinforced by the globe) suggests at once everything and nothing.[42] It is at the start an ironic metaphor for "what is most Perfect, finished, and exalted" but has become, by the time we reach the last sentence, a metaphor for the circular reasonings of modern man, which "doth never stop."[43] Perhaps we may take the circle as a metaphor for the circularity of *A Tale of a Tub* as a whole, for its copiousness, nothingness, and paradox.

In the *Tale* Swift disparages unempirical "Belief in Things invisible" (p. 169) and cautions us against those who "advance new Systems with such an eager Zeal, in things agreed on all hands impossible to be known" (p. 166). This is his persona's way. Throughout the *Tale* the Modern pigeonholes real experience into genus and category, transforms real things into aphorisms and maxims, and argues everything into abstract system, analogy, or personal theory. Swift's position is clear: rationalist philosophers, he would say, are like "Men in a Corner, who have the Unhappiness of conversing too little with *present Things*" (p. 97).

It is no coincidence that what strikes us most forcefully in *A Tale of a Tub* is not the mental configurations stamped by the Modern over the face of palpable reality but that reality itself. Although we come away from the *Tale* with little sense of the Modern Author as a real person, we retain a keen memory of a ladder, a post, a ragged coat, a rotten cheese, a barrel, a well, a crust of bread, a bellows, a cadaver, and a Bedlamite dabbling in his own urine. The Modern's rationalism is likewise undermined by Swift's moments from everyday life: a child whipped with a birch, a man splattered by the horse ahead of him, a fly feeding first on a honeypot and then on excrement, and many other things. The sheer accumulation of these various empirical fragments is itself an appeal to the reader's common sense; on every page they call into question the Modern's purely intellectual approach to the world. It is perhaps true, as Watt says, that in 1709 the *Tatler* was being ironic when it introduced Swift's "Description of the Morning" as a work where the author had "run into a way perfectly new, and described things as they happen."[44] But by the late 1690s Swift had already made a commitment to empiricism, a commitment that is at the roots of that formal realism characteristic of the novels of Defoe, a good deal of *Gulliver's Travels,* and the genre of the novel itself.[45]

But what does such a commitment mean to Swift? After all, the objects of sense perception themselves change, and two people may be able to agree on very little. At one point the Modern remarks on "the transitory State of all sublunary Things" (p. 66) and says in his "Epistle Dedicatory":

> If I should venture in a windy Day, to affirm to *Your Highness,* that there is a large Cloud near the *Horizon* in the Form of a *Bear,* another in the *Zenith* with the Head of an *Ass,* a third to the Westward with Claws like a *Dragon;* and *Your Highness* should in a few Minutes think fit to examine the Truth, 'tis certain, they would all be changed in Figure and Position, new ones would arise, and all we could agree upon would be, that Clouds there were, but that I was grossly mistaken in the *Zoography* and *Topography* of them. (P. 35)[46]

Swift is here making fun of man's attempt to label configurations of insubstantial air. For what "Truth" is there amidst the ever-changing objects of our sense perceptions? Yet such sensory data is all we have to go on. Although the empirical world sometimes plays tricks on our senses (recall the dark but shallow well), Swift would tell us that our eyes and other sense organs are nevertheless the source of what knowledge we have and the gatherers of that evidence we must base our judgments on, if we are to agree at all. Thus items of real experience become the lowest common denominators of *A Tale of a Tub* and Swift's other satires: empirical touchstones against which all else must be tested.

1. Ian Watt, *The Rise of the Novel: Studies in Defoe, Richardson, and Fielding* (1957; rpt. Berkeley, 1959), p. 11.

2. See my article entitled "The Epistemology of Fictional Failure: Swift's *Tale of a Tub* and Beckett's *Watt,*" *Texas Studies in Literature and Language* 15 (Winter 1974): 649-72.

3. Even Martin is willing to wrench the will in order to defeat "Contradiction" (p. 139).

4. I ought to say at the outset that my views as expressed here are generally in opposition to those of Walter J. Ong, "Swift and the Mind: The Myth of Asepsis,"

Modern Language Quarterly 15 (September 1954): 208–21. Ong unwittingly describes what is the Modern's—not Swift's—notion of mind.

5. John Locke, *An Essay Concerning Human Understanding*, ed. John W. Yolton, 2 vols. (New York, 1961), 2. 9. 15.

6. Ibid., 4. 17. 8.

7. In this sense Swift's satire anticipates Berkeley, who in *A Treatise Concerning the Principles of Human Knowledge* (1710) denied the existence of material substance independent of perception.

8. Cf. Locke, 2. 4. 11: "A studious blind man, who mightily beat his head about objects . . ."

9. "Nature" in 5th ed.; editions 1–4 read "Providence." See Guthkelch and Smith, p. 193 n. 2.

10. For a discussion of the depths as well as dangers of this kind of writing, see Richard Poirier, "The Politics of Self-Parody," chap. 2 of *The Performing Self: Compositions and Decompositions in the Languages of Contemporary Life* (New York, 1971).

11. Kathleen Williams, *Jonathan Swift and the Age of Compromise* (Lawrence, Kans., 1958), p. 17.

12. On this matter of the early eighteenth century distrust of print, see Marshall McLuhan, *The Gutenberg Galaxy: The Making of Typographic Man* (1962; rpt. New York, 1969), esp. pp. 301–13.

13. Locke, 2. 1. 2.

14. "O Brazile" actually does occur elsewhere; see Guthkelch and Smith, p. 125 n. 2. Cf. Robert South, *Sermons Preached Upon Several Occasions*, 6 vols. (1679; new ed., London, 1737), 3:250: "Some *O Brazile* in Divinity." South and Swift seem to be using the term to refer to unnecesary mystic arcana in subjects that should be treated plainly.

15. Nor may we be sure of ideas transmitted by word of mouth. "Brothers," says Peter, overly confident of oral tradition, "if you remember, we heard a Fellow say when we were Boys, that he heard my Father's Man say, that he heard my Father say, that he would advise his Sons to get *Gold Lace* on their Coats, as soon as ever they could procure Money to buy it" (p. 86).

16. Cf. Hugh Kenner, *The Counterfeiters: An Historical Comedy* (Bloomington, Ind., 1968), p. 81, who calls *Robinson Crusoe* "the first notable triumph of the new esthetics of fraud." Of course, to describe Defoe's book as a fraud is in one sense quite accurate; on the other hand, I would argue that though Defoe intentionally deceives us into believing that Crusoe's adventures are real, he does so precisely because he and his readers have such an implicit faith in the tangible world around them.

17. Michel Foucault, *Madness and Civilization: A History of Insanity in the Age of Reason*, trans. Richard Howard (New York, 1965), p. 229.

18. See Frank Kermode, "Literary Fiction and Reality," chap. 5 of *The Sense of an Ending: Studies in the Theory of Fiction* (Oxford, 1967), for an interesting discussion of the assumptions about reality implied in a novelist's handling of form.

19. For a history of these two tendencies, see Robert Scholes and Robert Kellogg, "Point of View in Narrative," chap. 12 of *The Nature of Narrative* (Oxford, 1966).

20. For a discussion of the peculiar philosophical and literary atmosphere, see Watt, "Realism and the Novel Form," chap. 1 of *The Rise of the Novel.*

21. *The Principles of Philosophy*, in *The Philosophical Works of Descartes*, trans. Elizabeth S. Haldane and G. R. T. Ross (Cambridge, 1967), 1:262–63.

22. I have already shown in chap. 1 how the italics in this passage highlight Swift's irony.

23. On Swift's use of conjunctions, see Louis T. Milic, "Words Without Meaning," chap. 5 of *A Quantitative Approach to the Style of Jonathan Swift* (The Hague, 1967).

24. Hugh Kenner, *Flaubert, Joyce, and Beckett: The Stoic Comedians* (Boston, 1962), p. 81.

25. In the seventeenth century the subject was treated most memorably by Antoine Arnauld in *La logique ou l'art de penser* (Paris, 1662), pt. 4. Cf. Locke's discussion of probability, 4. 3. 14 and, more generally, 4. 15–17.

26. Aristotle, *De sophisticis elenchis*, trans. W. A. Pickard-Cambridge (Oxford, 1928), in *The Works of Aristotle*, ed. W. D. Ross (Oxford, 1908–31), 1:170a; and Descartes, *Discourse on Method, The Philosophical Works of Descartes*, 1:192. In his discussion of probability, Arnauld quotes Descartes's precept; see *The Art of Thinking*, trans. James Dickoff and Patricia James (1662; rpt. New York, 1964), p. 309.

27. See *A Tale of a Tub*, p. 58 n. 1. And on Swift's satire of mysticism, cabalism, and alchemy, see Guthkelch and Smith's "Notes on Dark Authors," pp. 353–60.

28. Cf. the Laputans, who, if they "praise the Beauty of a Woman, or any other Animal, they describe it by Rhombs, Circles, Parallelograms, Ellipses, and other Geometrical Terms" (*Gulliver's Travels*, ed. Herbert Davis [Oxford, 1965], p. 163).

29. Cf. W. B. Carnochan's somewhat different emphasis in "Swift's *Tale*: On Satire, Negation, and the Uses of Irony," *Eighteenth-Century Studies* 5 (Fall 1971): 122–44. Kathleen Williams likewise mentions this theme in *Jonathan Swift and the Age of Compromise*, pp. 132–46.

30. The most prominent seventeenth-century examples of this genre are Sir William Cornwallis's essay "Prayse of Nothing" (1616) and the Earl of Rochester's poem "Upon Nothing" (1691). See Henry K. Miller, "The Paradoxical Encomium with Special Reference to its Vogue in England, 1660–1800," *Modern Philology* 53 (1956): 162–65. See also Rosalie L. Colie's fine discussions in chaps. 7 and 8 of *Paradoxia Epidemica: The Renaissance Tradition of Paradox* (Princeton, 1966).

31. See Tobias Dantzig, *Number: The Language of Science* (New York, 1954), pp. 128–29.

32. In *A Tale of a Tub and Other Early Works, 1696–1707*, ed. Herbert Davis (Oxford, 1965), pp. 249–50. In *Dr. Swift*, vol. 2 of *Swift: The Man, His Works and the Age* (Cambridge, Mass., 1967), p. 192, Irvin Ehrenpreis warns that although we should view *A Tritical Essay* as a parody of simplistic methods of argument, the ideas are Swift's own.

33. See Glossary.

34. See Dantzig, pp. 31–33, for a discussion of the importance of zero as a symbol for both "emptiness" and "nothing."

35. Cf. *Macbeth*, 5. 5. 26–8: "It is a tale/Told by an idiot, full of sound and fury,/ Signifying nothing."

36. Foucault, p. 93. Foucault goes on to say that madness violates the rule of either-or, discovering paradox where the rational mind sought unity and order.

37. Michael V. DePorte, *Nightmares and Hobbyhorses: Swift, Sterne, and Augustan Ideas of Madness* (San Marino, Calif., 1974), p. 32.

38. *A Tritical Essay*, pp. 248, 247. See n. 31 above. Cf. *The Works of Sir William Temple*, ed. Jonathan Swift (1702; rpt. London, 1770), 3:501.

39. In *Irish Tracts 1720–1723 and Sermons*, ed. Herbert Davis (Oxford, 1968), pp. 159–68.

40. Colie, p. 219.

41. Cf. *The Mechanical Operation of the Spirit*, in Guthkelch and Smith, p. 286: "I find there are certain Bounds set even to the Irregularities of Human Thought, and those a great deal narrower than is commonly apprehended."

42. This point about the circle is made by Colie, p. 228. As background, see Georges Poulet, *Metamorphoses of the Circle*, trans. Carley Dawson and Elliot Coleman (Baltimore, 1967), and Majorie Hope Nicolson, *The Breaking of the Circle: Studies in the Effect of the "New Science" on Seventeenth-Century Poetry*, rev. ed. (New York, 1960).

43. Walter R. Davis, "The Imagery of Bacon's Late Work," *Modern Language Quarterly* 27 (June 1966): 165–67, points out that Bacon uses the circle not to represent perfection and order but as a metaphor for giddy, perpetual, useless motion. Other circles appear in the *Tale*: the Modern observes that wit "is observ'd to run much in a Line, and ever in a Circle" (p. 61); and speaking of the Aeolists, he says that "At other times were to be seen several Hundreds link'd together in a circular Chain, with every Man a Pair of Bellows applied to his Neighbor's Breech" (p. 153).

44. Watt, *The Rise of the Novel*, p. 28.

45. John Henry Raleigh, in "Henry James: The Poetics of Empiricism," chap. 1 of *Time, Place, and Idea: Essays on the Novel* (Carbondale, Ill., 1968), suggests that Locke's philosophy in a general way influenced not only James but the novel as a genre.

46. Guthkelch and Smith note the parallel between this passage and *Antony and Cleopatra*, 4. 14. 1–11. Cf. *Hamlet*, 3. 2. 393–405.

Glossary for *A Tale of a Tub*

What follows is a select glossary of neologisms, archaisms, and odd usages to be found in the *Tale*. Although the list pretends to no completeness, it does include all of Swift's coinages that I have been able to discover, plus examples of his various other word games in this work. As a whole the Glossary amply documents Swift's Janus-like parody of, and participation in, the virtual lexical explosion of the previous half century.

I have of course relied heavily on the *The Oxford English Dictionary*, but I have also consulted: Henry Cockeram, *The English Dictionarie; or, An Interpreter of Hard English Words* (1623; 4th ed., London, 1632); Thomas Blount, *Glossographia; or, A Dictionary, Interpreting all such Hard Words . . . as are now used in our refined English Tongue* (London, 1656); Edward Phillips, *The New World of Words, Or a General English Dictionary* (1658; 4th ed., London, 1678); Thomas Blount, *Nomo-Lexicon: A Law Dictionary* (1670; facsimile ed., Los Angeles, 1970); Elisha Coles, *An English Dictionary* (1676; 10th ed., London, 1678); B. E., *A New Dictionary of the Terms Ancient and Modern of the Canting Crew* (1690; rpt. London, 1906); John Harris, *Lexicon Technicum; or An Universal English Dictionary of Arts and Sciences* (1704; facsimile ed., New York, 1966); John Kersey, *Dictionarium Anglo-Britannicum; or, A General English Dictionary* (London, 1708); Nathan Bailey, *An Universal Etymological Dictionary* (1721; 3rd ed., London, 1726); Samuel Johnson, *A Dictionary of the English Language* (1755; rpt. London, 1822); and Eric Partridge, *A Dictionary of Slang and Unconventional English*, 2 vols. (1937; 5th ed., London, 1970). Two other books have been especially useful: De Witt T. Starnes and Gertrude E. Noyes, *The English Dictionary from Cawdrey to Johnson, 1604–1755* (Chapel Hill, 1946); and W. K. Wimsatt, Jr., *Philosophic Words: A Study of Style and Meaning in the "Rambler" and "Dictionary" of Samuel Johnson* (New Haven, 1948). I have, of course, checked the words recorded here against the two volumes of the supplement to the *Oxford English Dictionary* published to date.

ABORTION (p. 206). The *OED* gives the first use in a figurative sense as 1710, meaning "a failure of aim or promise." This is Swift's meaning, although the sexual imagery of the previous section, plus the puns in this very sentence ("Going too short," "Labors of the Brain") keep us aware at the same time of the earlier medical meaning of the term.

ACADEMY (p. 166). One of Swift's frequent puns. He means both a university and a brothel, a low sense of the word found in B. E.'s *Dictionary of the Canting Crew*. Thus the "Academy of Modern Bedlam" becomes a very open symbol of corruption of all sorts—simultaneously a madhouse, a university, and a brothel. According to Partridge, "academy" as a colloquialism came to mean "lunatic asylum" ca. 1730–90.

ADAPT (p. 172). Swift's adjectival use is cited first in the *OED*, which suggests that the word was developed on the basis of an analogy with others like "content," "distract," and "erect," all of which are "in form identical with verbs, though really adaptations of Latin participles in *-tus*." Yet there is no Latin "*adaptus*"! Cf. "*Afflatus*" and "*Inflatus*" (p. 151).

AEOLIST (p. 150 and elsewhere). Swift's use is unique. The term is derived from "Aeolus," the Greek god of winds.

AMORPHY (p. 124). Swift's use of the word is cited in the *OED* as the first in English. It is derived from either the French "amorphie" or the Greek word for "shapelessness." Cf. "amorphous," the adjective, which apparently did not come into being until sometime in the 1720s or 1730s.

ANNEXT (p. 87). An example of the sort of contraction Swift objected to in the *Tatler*, no. 230, and *A Proposal for Correcting, Improving and Ascertaining the English Tongue*. On the same page the word is spelled "annexed"; perhaps, despite his theoretical objection to that foolish opinion "that we ought to spell exactly as we speak," Swift was himself less than consistent. Or was he satirizing the instability of spelling by using both forms on the same page? Cf. "shipwreckt" (p. 107), "fatning" (p. 169), and especially "bantring" (p. 19), which appears in the

"Apology," though in an ironic context. It is significant that in his *Reflections on Dr. Swift's Letter to Harley* (1712) John Oldmixon criticizes the intentionally absurd contractions of Swift's "Humble Petition of Frances Harris" (1701).

ANNIHILATE (pp. 35, 43). Although the verb "to annihilate" (p. 32) and the noun "annihilation" were common in the seventeenth century, the adjective seems to have been quite rare. In the eighteenth century "annihilate" was replaced by the past participle "annihilated." Note how Swift heightens the irony in each case by prefixing a humorously redundant intensifier: "wholly annihilate" and "utterly annihilate."

ASTRIDE (p. 171). The *OED* lists this as the first figurative use of an older word, and Swift's italics draw attention to it. The word appears in its literal sense in *Hudibras*: "Does not the Whore of Bab'lon ride / Upon her horned Beast astride?" Swift is fond of riding metaphors: cf. "Man, when he gives the Spur and Bridle to his Thoughts" (p. 157), and "a Person, whose Imaginations are hard-mouth'd" (p. 180).

BANTRING (p. 19). This instance is cited in the *OED* as the first use of this form of the word, and Swift's attitude toward it is clear: "Of this Bantring as they call it . . . " The mock—or is it?—etymology of "Banter" immediately above may well suggest that both words were common in speech long before they appeared with any frequency in print. Cf. "Banter" (pp. 13, 19, 207), a word Johnson described as "barbarous." In the *Tatler*, no. 230, Swift refers to "Banter" as a word "invented by some *Pretty Fellows*" that is "now struggling for the Vogue." According to Partridge, "banter" was slang in 1688 but during the eighteenth century came gradually to mean "harmless raillery." Cf. Glossary under "annext."

BATE (p. 148). This verb is defined in the *OED* as "to omit, leave out of count, except," and Swift's use is cited as the last in this particular sense. Cf. Glossary under "flesht."

BIGOTTED (p. 122). The *OED* defines this word as "blindly attached to some creed, opinion, or party" and gives its first use in the construction "bigotted to [something]" as 1704. In this 1710 footnote Swift is apparently employing a brand new phrase.

BOMBASTRY (p. 61). "Bombastry" did not come in until the fifth edition of 1710. True to the first four editions, Guthkelch and

Smith opt for "Bombast" and explain: "evidently a printer's coinage due to assimilation with 'Buffoonry.' No other instance of this form appears to be known." But Swift was clearly behind most of the changes in the fifth edition and probably liked the ironic rhythm of "Bombastry and Buffoonry"; cf. "Clergy, and Gentry, and Yeomantry" (p. 181). Later in the *Tale* Swift refers to Paracelsus as "Bumbastus" (p. 152), a humorous abbreviation of the alchemist's name, Philippus Aureolus Theophrastus Bombastus von Hohenheim; with "Bumbastus" Swift puns on "bum-baste," which Partridge defines as "to beat hard on the posteriors." Swift is speaking here of flatulation, and thus it is relevant that Partridge further notes that "bum" probably had an echoic origin and cites the Italian "bum," the sound of an explosion.

BONAE NOTAE (p. 68). Lois M. Scott-Thomas, "The Vocabulary of Jonathan Swift," *Dalhousie Review* 25 (1946): 445, points to this as one of the foreign terms that owes its introduction into English to Swift. Cf. Swift, "Introduction" to *Polite Conversation*: "I did therefore once intend, for the Ease of the Learner, to set down in all Parts of the following Dialogues, certain Marks, Asterisks, or Nota Bene's (in *English*, Mark-well's) after most Questions, and every Reply or Answer."

BOTTOM (p. 191). On the surface Swift means simply the "bottom" of the page, but the excremental context ("urgent Juncture," "Way to the Backside," "Make himself clean again") suggests that he is implying also the posteriors, although in the *OED* 1794 is the earliest citation in this sense. Cf. Glossary under "Occasion," which occurs in the same passage.

BOUTADE (p. 115). Although the first *OED* reference is to Bacon's *King James* (1614), Swift felt the need of an explanatory note: "This Word properly signifies a sudden Jerk, or a Lash of an Horse, when you do not expect it." Wotton's note on the word in his personal copy of the *Tale* likewise underscores its strangeness: "Any Body but Sr W. Temple would have said *Sally*" (Guthkelch and Smith, p. 314). And for Swift "Boutade" must have held some novelty even as late as 1734, when in a letter he explained to his friend Mrs. Pendarves: "It is, you know, a French word, and signifies a sudden jerk from a horses hinder feet which you did not expect, because you thought him for some months a sober animal."

BRIGUING (p. 65). The *OED* gives the substantive "brigue" two meanings: (1) "strife, quarrel, contention," which was adopted from the Italian "briga" in the fourteenth or fifteenth century; and (2) "intrigue, faction," which was adopted from the French "briguer" around 1700 and was much used in the first half of the eighteenth century. This second meaning is Swift's. Guthkelch and Smith note that the word is used by Rabelais and occurs frequently in Bernier's *Histoire du grand mogol* (1670), which appears in Swift's list of books read in the year 1697. Kersey marks the word as an archaism; neither "brigue" nor "briguing" are found in Johnson.

BULLY (pp. 19, 140, 165). In the *Tatler*, no. 230, Swift calls this one of "the modern Terms of Art." Etymologically complicated, this word had since the sixteenth century meant "sweetheart," had recently taken on the meaning "swash-buckler," and about this time began to refer to a hired protector of prostitutes. Cf. Swift's use: "The very same Principle that influences a Bully to break the Windows of a Whore, who has jilted him . . . " (p. 165).

CACKLING (p. 66). Another of Swift's obscene puns. He means both the chittering of a hen and farting, a low sense of the word found in B. E.'s *New Dictionary*. According to Partridge, "cackling fart" was at this time slang for an egg; Swift is clearly toying with this meaning without using it per se.

CHOCOLATE-HOUSES (p. 74). The first references in the *OED* are to 1694 and 1695, the latter to Congreve's *Love for Love*.

CLAIMANT (p. 21). A word that does not appear in any seventeenth-century dictionaries, although Phillips defines the root word "claim" in this way: "A Law term, is a challenge of interest in any thing that is out of ones possession, as Claim by Charter, or descent, &c." Johnson gives "claimant" a more general application: "He that demands any thing, as unjustly withheld from him." The first *OED* citation is 1741. Cf. Glossary under "Innuendo."

CLEANLILY (p. 192). The first *OED* reference is 1698. In the edition of 1711 this apparently rather rare form was altered to "cleanly." Cf. "cleanly" (p. 93).

CLINAMINA (p. 167). The *OED* cites this as the first use in English. Guthkelch and Smith observe that the word comes from Lucretius, who used it to mean "the bias or deviation from a straight line which was supposed to explain the concourse of atoms."

CLOSE IN WITH (p. 188). Meaning "to draw near to, or advance into contact with," this use is the first cited in the *OED*. But it is Swift's frequent practice to intensify ironic verbs by the addition of prepositions, as in "spy out" (p. 93), "kneaded up" (p. 124), "twirl over" (p. 131), "hymning out" (p. 156), "falls down plum into" (p. 158), and "fly off upon" (p. 174).

CONTRIVANCE (p. 61). Although the word is found in Browne's *Vulgar Errors*, John Woodward's *Natural History of the Earth* (1695) is the first place it appears in the sense of an "adaptation of means to an end"; Swift owned a copy of the *Natural History* in a 1714 Latin edition but may well have read it earlier. Woodward's phraseology seems to be echoed in the *Tale*: "Proofs of Contrivance in the Structure of the Globe," says Woodward; "there is something yet more refined in the Contrivance and Structure of our Modern Theatres," says Swift.

COTEMPORARY (p. 38). In his *Dissertation upon the Epistles of Phalaris* (1697) Bentley calls this form "a downright barbarism." Under "contemporary" the *OED* gives a discussion of the etymology of the two words and their relationship.

COURT-CUSTOMERS (p. 177). Apparently a coinage, this word represents Swift's parodic echo of the virtual flood of new combinations such as "court-favorite" (1647), "court-ladies" (1661), and "court-poet" (1697). Barbara Strang, "Swift's Agent-Noun Formations in *-Er*," in *Wortbildung, Syntax, und Morphologie: Festschrift Zum 60. Geburtstag von Hans Marchand*, ed. Herbert E. Brekle and Leonhard Lipka (The Hague, 1968), pp. 217–29, points out that although there is only a normal frequency of such formations in Swift, these instances attract attention precisely because they are dispensable, because they have quite obviously been chosen over the constructions "one who" or "those who." See "Answerer" (p. 11), "Opposer" (p. 12), "Arbiter" (p. 31), "Undertaker" (p. 41), "Peruser" (p. 44), "Deliverer" (p. 52), "Smatterers" (p. 130), "Hatcher" (p. 177), "Rectifier" (p. 183), and so forth. In all of these cases Swift creates an ironic class name in order to put someone he dislikes into it.

CRITICK (p. 209). First found as a verb in Dryden's *Virgil* (1697): "Those who can Critick his *Poetry*, can never find a blemish in his *Manners*."

DEFAULTS (p. 132). A noun meaning a defect, a blemish, or simply a fault. Both Temple and Swift are cited in the *OED*, although the word appears by the early eighteenth century to have been used rarely in this sense.

IN DEFERENCE TO (p. 61). Although "deference" first appeared some forty years earlier, Swift may have been the first writer to employ the phrase "in deference to," which the *OED* does not cite before the mid nineteenth century.

DELICATESSE (p. 80). A French word not entirely naturalized into English. The first use in an English text was in Vanbrugh's *Provoked Wife* (1698). Swift had a special dislike of John Vanbrugh and may be mocking him here: his poems "Vanbrug's House" (1703), "The History of Vanbrug's House" (1706), and "V———'s House" (1708–9) all deal with his shortcomings both as an architect and as a dramatist. As elsewhere, Swift seems to have been attracted to the sound of "abundance of Finesse and Delicatesse." Words of French origin heighten the impact of the story of the effete brothers; cf. Glossary under "Amorphy," "Boutade," and "Briguing."

DEPRECATORY (p. 92). The *OED* cites Swift's use as the first in the sense of "expressing a wish or hope that something feared may be averted." Typically, the rhythm of "Expostulatory, Supplicatory, or Deprecatory" must have appealed to Swift. Cf. "-tory" in the *OED*. And cf. Glossary under "Bombastry" and "Yeomantry."

DIRT-PELLETS (p. 10). Swift's use is the single citation in the *OED*. But various analogous combinations existed before; for example, "dirt-pie"—meaning "mud pie"— dates from 1641 and appears in Congreve's *Love for Love*. Cf. Swift's use of the verb "to dirt" in his *Thoughts on Various Subjects* (1706): "Ill Company is like a Dog, who dirts those most whom he loves best" (altered to "fouls" in *Works*, 1735).

DISPLODING (p. 155). Swift's use is cited, but the first reference in the *OED* is to Milton, *Paradise Lost*: "In posture to displode their second tire/Of thunder." Perhaps Swift was the first author to use the word in its "-ing" form.

DISPOSETH (p. 171). One of the intentionally archaic forms used by Swift in the *Tale* to heighten the formality of the Modern; cf. the proverb (originally from Thomas à Kempis) "Man proposeth but God disposeth." Henry C. K. Wyld, in *A History of Modern*

Colloquial English (New York, 1956), p. 334, says that by Swift's day the "-eth" ending had an archaic feel about it; see also Thomas Pyle, *The Origins and Development of the English Language* (1964; 2d ed., New York, 1971), pp. 216–17. In addition, Swift once uses the form "doth" (p. 157) and often uses "hath" (pp. 10, 19, 60, 66, 69, 77, and elsewhere). Barbara Strang, "Swift and the English Language: A Study in Principles and Practice," in *To Honor Roman Jakobson: Essays on the Occasion of His Seventieth Birthday* (The Hague, 1967), p. 1956, says that at least in Swift's correspondence "hath" becomes increasingly the mark of formality and coldness.

DOZEN (pp. 68, 210). John Oldmixon, in his *Reflections on Dr. Swift's Letter to Harley* (1712), objects to Swift's imprecise "Affection to the Word Dozen": "I have several good Reasons why, if I were to be of this Academy, I would banish the word Dozen out of our Dictionary, and the Doctor has no doubt his to be fond of it, and fixing it there forever."

DUPE (p. 171). The *OED* suggests that the use of this word in the substantive sense began with Temple and credits Swift with the first use of the verb, meaning "to make a dupe of; to deceive, delude, befool."

EXANTLATION (p. 67). One of Swift's frequent, quite self-conscious hard words in the *Tale*. In their "Introduction" Guthkelch and Smith say this word was apparently suggested by its use in Browne's *Vulgar Errors*. Phillips defines the term as "an overcoming with much labour and difficulty"; but according to the *OED* it was usually employed in the figurative sense of "the action of drawing out, as water from a well." Swift's phrase "to draw up by Exantlation" reminds his reader of the well metaphor.

EX CATHEDRA (p. 90). Another of the foreign terms that owes its introduction into English literature to Swift. It means literally "from the chair" and refers to the Pope's infallible pronouncements on matters of dogma—cf. "infallibly" (p. 110). Cf. Glossary under "*bonae notae*."

EXCHANGE-WOMEN (p. 140). The first *OED* reference is 1697, although "exchange-man" and "exchange-wench" go back further. This is a good illustration of Swift's delight in hyphenated nouns: "Chocolate-Houses," "Dirt-Pellets," "Meal-Tubs," "Shop-lifters," "Snap-Dragon," "State-Arcana," and such. These words force the reader to pay special attention to their etymologies.

EXPEDITION (p. 145). There are two major definitions in the *OED*: (1) "the action of expediting, helping forward, or accomplishing," which apparently died sometime around the middle of the seventeenth century; and (2) "a sending or setting forth with martial intentions," which has been current since the Middle Ages. Interestingly, although the context ("Army," "Martial Discipline," "Muster") points to the second meaning, the phrase "abundance of Expedition" makes it clear that the word is really being used in its first, obsolete sense. This is a good example of Swift's tendency to squeeze every drop of meaning out of a word's etymology.

FASION (p. 76). An ironic use of an older spelling of "Fashion" that the *OED* suggests had not been common since the fifteenth and sixteenth centuries; elsewhere (pp. 80, 81, 84, for example) Swift spells the word in its currently acceptable way. Swift was concerned about the cavalier attitude toward spelling in his day, and in the *Tale* he argues ironically for establishing a Spelling School (p. 41). In a *Proposal for Correcting, Improving and Ascertaining the English Tongue*, he says: "It is sometimes a difficult Matter to read modern Books and Pamphlets; where the Words are so curtailed, and varied from their original Spelling, that whoever hath been used to plain *English*, .will hardly know them by Sight." Cf. Glossary under "annext" and "tho'."

FASTIDIOSITY (p. 124). The word means "disdainfulness" as well as "squeamishness." Guthkelch and Smith say that this is "a humorously pedantic form, not found before Swift." Of course "fastidious" existed before, and in coining "Fastidiosity" Swift followed the transformation of a word like "curious," which had led to "curiosity," or "fastuous," which had recently given birth to "fastuosity." "Fastidiosity" even *sounds* like an extreme fastidiousness.

FLESHT (p. 101). Johnson says "to flesh" means "to initiate: from the sportsman's practice of feeding his hawks and dogs with the first game that they take, or training them to pursuit by giving them the *flesh* of animals." The *OED* adds to this meaning—"to render inveterate; harden (in wrong doing)"—and cites the *Tale* as the last example in this sense. Swift may have been intentionally employing a word that was practically out of vogue. Cf. the probable archaisms "thither" (p. 26), "bequeath" (p. 38), "ye" (pp. 118, 193), and "Arse" (p. 197). But Swift is also playing on another meaning of the word, "to make fleshy, to fatten."

FOOL (p. 174). In the Middle Ages and the Renaissance, the words "fool" and "knave" were often linked, either as synonyms or as opposites. William Empson, *The Structure of Complex Words* (1951; rpt. Ann Arbor, 1967), p. 110, suggests that the modern use of "fool" gets its power from an effect of nausea in the presence of a lunatic; Empson points to Swift's use as the first that has this feeling to it, although "the whole horror of his style was required to fix such an emotion to the word here, because in itself the sentence could carry the amiable complex of Erasmus."

GEAR (p. 195). Partridge identifies "gear" as a slang word for the male or female genitalia. Cf. *Troilus and Cressida*: "And Cupid grant all tongue-tied maidens here/Bed, chamber, Pandar to provide this gear!"

GOOD FOR NOTHING (p. 173). The *OED* cites the *Journal to Stella* as the first use: "We reckon him here a good-for-nothing fellow." Swift uses the phrase also in *Polite Conversation*: "Fye, Miss, you said that once before; and you know, too much of one Thing is good for nothing." Odd as it may seem, the first use of this cliché in literature may be here in the *Tale*; but its inclusion in *Polite Conversation* would suggest that it had earlier currency in speech.

GRUBAEAN (p. 66). The *OED* cites this as the first use of the word in its adjectival form. Grub-street, says Johnson, was "originally the name of a street, near Moorfields in London, much inhabited by writers of small histories, dictionaries, and temporary poems." Swift's delight in awful puns leads him here to play on the italicized word "Worm" at the end of the preceding sentence.

HERD (p. 171). The *OED* points to this as the first use of the verb in the sense "of things: to come together, assemble." But surely this is Swift's figurative use of the word in the older sense of the congregating of animals, here employed derogatorily in reference to ideas. Cf. Wycherley, *The Country Wife* (1675): "Stand off. . . . You herd with the wits, you are obscenity all over." Cf. also Swift's "Ode to the Athenian Society" (1691): "Our good brethren . . . / Must e'en all herd us with their kindred fools."

HERMETICALLY (p. 126). Appearing as early as 1605, this word is found in Bentley's *Folly and Unreasonableness of Atheism* (1692).

"To seal a Glass Hermetically," says Kersey, "is to heat the Neck of it, till it be just ready to melt, and then with a Pair of red-hot Pincers close it together." This is just one of Swift's many ironic uses of mechanical terminology in a nonmechanical context. Cf. Glossary under "Machine."

HISTORI-THEO-PHYSILOGICAL (p. 137). Swift's use is surely a first. He is mocking through exaggeration the new science's penchant for hyphenated terms, as in Boyle's *New Experiments Physico-Mechanical, Touching the Spring of Air and Its Effects* (1661). See Glossary under "Physico-logical."

INCLEMENCIES (p. 56). The first *OED* citation is 1699; but the singular form goes back to 1559. Phillips defines "inclemency" as "rigor, sharpness, a being without pity or compassion." The phrase "inclemency of air" was common in the sixteenth and seventeenth centuries.

INFLATUS (p. 151). Blount defines "inflation" as "a breeding of wind in the body, a puffing up, or a windy swelling." The *OED*'s single citation is 1861. On the same page Swift uses the Latin words *"Spiritus," "Animus," "Afflatus,"* and *"Turgidus."*

INNUENDO (pp. 114, 169, 186). Defined in Blount's *Law Dictionary*: "a Law term, most used in *Declarations* and other pleadings; and the office of this word is onely to declare and design the person or thing which was named uncertain before; as to say, he (*innuendo* the Plaintiff) is a Thief; when as there was mention of another person." On the status of this and other legal terms in Swift's day, see C. R. Kropf, "Libel and Satire in the Eighteenth Century," *Eighteenth-Century Studies* 8 (Winter 1974–75): 153–68. The *OED* says "innuendo" means by extension an "interpolated or appended explanation of, or construction put upon a word, expression, or passage" and cites Defoe, 1701, as the first author to use the word in this sense. Swift draws special attention to this meaning of the word in *Gulliver's Travels*, "A Letter from Captain Gulliver": his plain-speaking narrator complains of his cousin's fear of people in power, who "were apt not only to interpret, but to punish every thing which looked like an *Inuendo* (as I think you called it)." In Swift's usage in the *Tale*, the word seems also to suggest sly, perhaps lewd, hints, as in the "Introduction" to *Polite Conversation*: "I can therefore only allow Innuendoes of this kind to be delivered in Whispers, and only to young Ladies under Twenty, who being in Honour obliged to blush, it may produce a new Subject for Discourse."

INTERCOURSE (p. 60). The primary meaning here is simply that there is a perpetual conversation among orators in pulpits, on ladders, and on stage itinerants. But the context ("Engine," "erected," "Seminary") suggests that Swift is implying also sexual congress, although in the *OED* 1798 is the earliest citation in this sense.

INVESTS (p. 77). The *OED* gives the first use of the verb in this sense—"clothe, cover, adorn"—to Swift. But his intransitive verb is not essentially different from the older transitive one.

JILTED (p. 165). As a verb employed by Wycherley, Congreve, and Locke, this word is described by Blount in the 4th edition of his *Glossographia* (1674) as "a new canting word, signifying to deceive and defeat ones expectation, more especially in the point of Amours."

LANTHORN (pp. 36, 141, 192, 193). Guthkelch and Smith suggest (p. 192) erroneously that this is Swift's coinage. In the *OED* it is listed as an alternate spelling of "lantern"; the spelling "lanthorn" appears in Shakespeare, Bacon, Milton, and Locke. "It is by mistake often written *lanthorn,*" says Johnson. But Swift may be playing again on the composition of a word, for the *OED* comments that "the form *lanthorn* is probably due to popular etymology, lanterns having formerly been almost always made of horn"; after all, the phrases "ocular Conviction" and "Windows of a *Bawdy-house*, or a sordid *Lanthorn*" (p. 36) show that Swift, in at least one of these passages, is talking about the transparency of material. Of course, he may simply be using the older spelling in order to heighten the pomposity of the Modern, as with "Rarieties" (p. 110) and "inclose" (p. 24).

LAYINGS OUT (p. 102). Not recorded in the *OED* or any of the early dictionaries, this noun is apparently Swift's coinage, developed from the verb "to lay out," a common usage in the seventeenth century. Cf. "laid out" (p. 61).

LETTERED (p. 126). Swift's is perhaps a first instance of this word. The first citation in the *OED* of the verb "to letter" in the sense of "to affix a name or title in letters upon" is 1712; 1707 is the first citation of the participle in the sense of a book "having the title, etc. on back in gilt or coloured letters."

LEVITY (pp. 61, 140). A term from physics that signifies an inherent property of a body that causes it to rise. Swift apparently uses it here for the first time in a figurative sense. Cf. Glossary under "Machine."

LIFTINGS (p. 129). Partridge defines "lifting" as a colloquialism for "theft"; cf. "Shop-lifters" (pp. 140, 177). Perhaps Swift also intends something mock-religious here; cf. the various biblical uses of "lifting," as in "lifting up." And perhaps he intends something sexual; recall the double entendres of section 8, and note the words "Turns and Flowings" immediately above. Cf. "Gripings" (pp. 154, 156) and "Loppings" (p. 201).

LOPPINGS (p. 201). Swift must have been aware of the political connotations of this cant term, which had been used, according to the *OED*, by the Rye House conspirators to refer to the killing of the King and the Duke of York.

MACHINE (pp. 56ff., 164). This word was being used in various new senses by the end of the seventeenth century. Swift seems to follow a recent distinction between simple machines such as the ladder (p. 59) and compound machines with two or more moving parts (p. 164). Partridge says that as a low colloquialism "machine" referred to the male or female genitalia, but not until the nineteenth century; Swift in this second instance, however, is clearly making a double entendre: "It was afterward discovered, that the Movement of this whole Machine had been directed by an absent Female, whose Eyes had raised a Protuberancy, and before Emission, she was removed into an Enemy's Country." Cf. Glossary under "gear." Here and elsewhere Swift is parodying rationalist philosophers like Descartes, who often compared men with machines.

MICRO-COAT (p. 78). A humorous neologism. Swift's footnote explains his pun: "Alluding to the Word *Microcosm*, or a little World, as Man hath been called by Philosophers." In reducing the Renaissance "Microcosm" to the Restoration "Micro-Coat," Swift has encompassed a whole century. Cf. "Man's little World" (p. 154).

IN MIGNATURE (p. 38). This spelling of "miniature" was common during the seventeenth century. But the phrase "in miniature"—meaning on a small scale—was apparently new; the *OED* cites Swift and gives the first reference as 1700.

MOBILE (p. 141). An abbreviated form of the Latin *mobile vulgus*, first so shortened by Shadwell in 1676. "Mobile" was subsequently contracted to "mob," one of those words that Swift hated but that was, according to Guthkelch and Smith, fast gaining currency. In the *Tatler*, no. 230, Swift writes: "I have done my utmost for some Years past, to stop the Progress of *Mobb* and *Banter*; but have been plainly born down by Numbers, and betrayed by those who promised to assist me."

MODERNISTS (p. 169). Swift is the first authority in the *OED* for this meaning: "A supporter or follower of modern ways or methods; in the 18th century, a maintainer of superiority of modern over ancient literature." Cf. the word "Modern" itself, which may contain a powerful pun on an apparently obsolete sense (frequent in Shakespeare) meaning everyday, ordinary, or commonplace.

MONSTER-MONGERS (p. 131). Swift's coinage. He has taken an apparently fading sense of "monster," meaning a "prodigy, a marvel" (last *OED* reference, 1710), and combined it with "monger," a very old word meaning "merchant." The construction itself was not new; "fly-monger," "water-monger," "iron-monger," and other such words were available in 1704. The *OED* suggests the tone of these compounds: "In formations dating from the middle of the 16th century onwards '-monger' nearly always implies one who carries on a contemptible or discreditable 'trade' or 'traffic' in what is denoted by the first element of the compound."

NATURALS (p. 29). "In one's [its] naturals" was a common phrase in the seventeenth century; the *OED* defines it as "in a purely natural condition, not altered or improved in any way." In this sense the word was apparently almost dead by 1704. Swift may be punning again: a "natural" was in his day an old word for a half-witted person; as contemporary slang, Partridge says the word also meant "harlot."

NUNCUPATORY (p. 85). This is a rare word extant only during the seventeenth century; and this use is the last cited in the *OED*. Swift exposes his fascination with etymology by incorporating the Spanish and Portuguese "nuncupatorio"—the source word—into the linguistically scrambled phrase that follows. "Nuncupatory" means simply "oral" or "verbal," but Swift's footnote explains his special reference to the Catholic Church: "By this is meant *Tradition*, allowed to have equal Authority with the

Scripture, or rather greater." In his *Law Dictionary*, Blount says "a *Will Nuncupative*, is when the Testator makes his will by word of mouth (not by writing) before sufficient witnesses."

OBSERVANDA (pp. 148, 210). A Latin word meaning "something to be observed or noted." The *OED* cites Swift as the only authority for this term in English.

OCCASION (p. 191). The word means here simply "situation," although in this excremental context Swift perhaps intends also to suggest "occasions," meaning the necessities of nature, a sense first found in 1698. Cf. Glossary under "Bottom," which occurs in the same passage.

OPUS MAGNUM (pp. 127, 187). The *OED* gives Swift credit for the introduction of this Latin term into English. In their "Notes on Dark Authors" Guthkelch and Smith call it "the technical term for the conversion of the baser metals into gold" (p. 356); but the word is used humorously by Swift in reference to the best way to read *A Tale of a Tub*. Cf. Glossary under "*bonae notae*."

OSCITATION (p. 124). One of the polysyllables of the sort Swift objected to in the *Tatler*, no. 230. As early as 1656 Blount gives two primary meanings: "yawning or gaping," and "negligence or idleness." Swift's meaning is the second of these. "Oscitation" appears in Bentley's *Dissertations upon the Epistles of Phalaris* (1697). Cf. Oscitancy" (p. 203).

PAUMED (p. 138). A seventeenth-century spelling of the transitive verb "palm," meaning to impose (a thing) fraudulently upon a person, which had first appeared some twenty years earlier. Originally a low colloquialism, the word is listed in B. E.'s *New Dictionary*; in the *Tatler*, no. 230, Swift refers to it as one of the "modern Terms of Art" and says in *A Letter to a Young Gentleman*: "I suppose the Hearers can be little edified by the Terms of *Palming, Shuffling, Biting, Bamboozling*, and the like, if they have not been sometimes conversant among Pick-pockets and Sharpers." Cf. Glossary under "upon that Score."

PEDERASTICK (p. 41). Although the noun "pederasty"—meaning "sodomy" or "buggery"—goes back to 1613, the *OED* cites this use as the first in the adjectival form.

PERPENSITY (p. 170). The word is defined as "attention" in the *OED*, and Swift's use is the single citation.

PHAENOMENON (pp. 60, 165, 167). Guthkelch and Smith give the word as "Ph*oe*nomenon" in two of the three instances, although there is no authority for this spelling; cf. Glossary under "annext" and "Fasion." In his *Letter to a Young Gentleman* Swift objects to the word "Phaenomenon," as he does to "Atoms" (p. 167) and "Ubiquity" (p. 154). Similarly, "Speculations" (p. 57 and elsewhere) and "Operations" (p. 95 and elsewhere) appear frequently in the *Tale*, although both are criticized in the *Tatler*, no. 230. Swift seems to be ironic in most of these instances.

PHYSICO-LOGICAL (p. 61). This is the same sort of ironic combination as "Histori-theo-physilogical" (p. 137), only more particular. Swift is here poking fun at the many stock "physico-" adjectives of the seventeenth century: "physico-mechanical" (1661), "physico-theosophical" (1668), "physico-mathematical" (1671), "physico-theological" (1675), "physico-medical" (1689), and so forth. Swift's compound is really no more absurd than most of these, although his irony is clear in "Physico-logical Scheme of Oratorical Receptacles." The Modern's overblown, *logical* arguments are repeatedly brought down by Swift's heavy, *physical* imagery.

POINT (pp. 169–70). A good example of Swift's intentional muddling of meaning. The Modern uses the trite "a very delicate Point," then mentions cutting the feather (implying his own quill pen); in the same sentence he refers to "the sole Point of Individuation," suggesting the scholastic process of *individuatio* (Guthkelch and Smith, p. 170 n. 2); and immediately thereafter he promises to "unravel this knotty Point," using a term meaning some problem difficult to solve (see *OED* under "knotty"). As these meanings blur in our minds, we come up with something like a quill pen split in two and tied in a knot—not a bad description of the Modern's writing. Swift's sensitivity to such repetition—in his annotation of Gilbert Burnet's *History of His Own Times*, for example—argues that he repeats himself here in order to create a satiric absurdity. In the allegory of the *Tale*, "Points" refers simultaneously to items of church dogma and laces for attaching the hose to the doublet. As is clear from the following examples, Swift uses the word inconsistently but never neutrally: "reasoning upon such delicate Points" (p. 39); "have recourse to some Points of Weight" (p. 75); and "a loose, flying, circumstantial Point" (p. 85).

Protrusions (p. 202). The *OED* lists two meanings: (1) "the action of protruding," a sense found in Browne and Boyle; and (2) "that which protrudes or juts out," a sense found first in the *Tale*.

Race (p. 80). "This is like Sr W. Temple," wrote Wotton in his copy of the *Tale* (Guthkelch and Smith, p. 314). Johnson defines the term as "a particular strength or taste of wine" and adds that Temple was the first to extend the meaning to "any extraordinary natural force of intellect." See Temple's *Essay upon Ancient and Modern Learning* (1690): "I think the Epistles of Phalaris to have more Race . . . than any others."

Reincrudation (p. 68). The *OED* cites this as a first use. The word means the reduction of a substance that has reached a higher state back into a lower state of existence; see Guthkelch and Smith, "Notes on Dark Authors," p. 354. But the Modern's Latinization of "crud" does not succeed in concealing the corruption at the center of this polysyllable.There may be another irony here: although "Reincarnation" did not appear in English until the nineteenth century, "incarnation" had been extant since the thirteenth, and Swift's "Reincrudation" may be an irreverent allusion to the Incarnation of Christ.

reinfunds (p. 178). The only reference in the *OED*. "To reinfund" means "to pour in again." Cf. "refunding" (p. 160).

Relievo (p. 154). From the Italian "*relievo*," meaning "relief"; or as Florio defines it (Swift owned a copy of the *World of Words*), "raised or embossed worke." The *OED* cites Swift's use as the first in the transferred sense: when he says that internal winds "gave the Eyes a terrible kind of *Relievo*," he means that the Aeolists' eyes were bugged, that they were thrown into grotesque relief.

Remains (p. 70). The word means simply "remainder" here, although in this context ("before I die") Swift may also be implying a corpse, a sense first found in Dryden in 1700.

romage (p. 87). An alternate spelling of "rummage." The *OED* cites this as the first use in the sense of "to scrutinize, examine minutely, investigate"; but Swift's use of the verb is not markedly different from a couple of earlier instances. "To romage" was sometimes used pejoratively in the sense of "to ransack."

Running (pp. 111, 126, 184). This is an interesting example of Swift's varied use of a single word. On p. 111 "Running" could mean, quite literally, too much running, which would indeed harden a bull's feet; but Swift's phrase "ill Pasture and Running" seems to imply that in this context it means "ranging or pasturage," a sense that the *OED* says did not appear until 1695. On p. 126 Swift uses "Running" in the specialized sense of "the flow of liquor during the process of wine-making, brewing, or distillation," a common seventeenth-century meaning. On p. 184 "Running" is used in yet a third way, in the sense of "the flowing or discharge of blood or humours from the body"; Swift's use of the word is listed in the *OED* as the first example of this meaning in a figurative sense. And there may be a pun in any or all of these instances on gonorrhea, which Blount defines as "a disease called the running of the reins, the flux of natural seed of man or woman unwittingly."

UPON THAT SCORE (pp. 23, 26, 94). A vulgar gaming phrase that Swift specifically objects to in his annotations to Gilbert Burnet's *History of His Own Times*. Cf. *A Letter to a Young Gentleman*: "Others, to shew that their Studies have not been confined to Sciences, or ancient Authors, will talk in the Style of a gaming Ordinary." Cf. Glossary under "paumed."

SCRIPTORY (p. 85). Although the word is used by Browne—"Vallatory, Sagittary, Scriptory, and others"—in a somewhat broader way, Swift is credited by the *OED* with the first use in the sense of "expressed in writing, written." "Scriptorian" appears in Blount, Coles, and Phillips.

SEDATEST (p. 138). The *OED* records that "sedate" in reference to a person showed up first in Locke and Dryden; "sedate" also appears in the *Tale* (p. 139). Swift may be the first writer to use the superlative "sedatest." Cf. Glossary under "skilfullest."

SEPARATE MAINTENANCE (p. 121). The term means "support given by a husband to a wife when the parties are separated." The first *OED* reference is to Defoe's *Colonel Jack* (1722); but Swift's words—"In copying the Will, they had met another Precept against Whoring, Divorce, and separate Maintenance"—point to an awareness of the legal significance of the term. Of course, the joke here is that the parties involved are not man and wife but three foppish brothers. Cf. "Yokemate" (p. 38)—meaning marriage partner—used to describe Wotton's relation to Bentley. Cf. Glossary under "Innuendo."

SKILFULLEST (p. 201). This rather awkward form, like "sedatest" (p.

138) and "profoundest" (p. 148), is probably Swift's parody of such difficult-to-pronounce superlatives. Cf. "fruitfullest" in *The Publick Spirit of the Whigs*, "provokingest" in *Polite Conversation*, and the following humorous sentence from a letter to Vanessa: "Well, he is the Courteousest Man, and nothing is so fine in the Quality, as to be courteous."

SPARGEFACTION (p. 110). Meaning "the action of sprinkling or scattering," this Latinate hard word occurs only in the *Tale*.

STATE-ARCANA (p. 68). "*Arcanum*" (pp. 114, 127)—which occurs in Browne and Boyle—refers to the great secrets of nature that the alchemists aimed at discovering. Swift's phrase "the Apocalyps of all State-*Arcana*" exposes his mock reverence for such a thing. This sort of compound was common; cf. "State-Surgeon" (p. 164).

SUBDUING . . . TO (p. 171). Swift's phrase is "without any Thought of subduing Multitudes to his own *Power*, his Reasons or his Visions." In the *OED* the last example of this construction is taken from *Leviathan*: "When a man . . . by Warre subdueth his enemies to his will."

SUPERFICIES (p. 29). Meaning "a plane or level surface." The *OED* gives only two instances of this apparently rare term, Swift's and one earlier. Cf. the quite different uses of the word on pp. 103 and 174.

TAGGED (p. 80). Swift is cited in the *OED* as the first authority in the sense "to append as an addition or afterthought; to fasten, tack on, or add as a tag *to* something." Cf. the different uses on pp. 87, 90, 135, and 136.

THO' (p. 5 and elsewhere). Swift objects to this and other contractions in the *Tatler*, no. 230. It is thus interesting that the form appears in the "Apology," which was published in 1710, the same year as the *Tatler* contribution. Cf. Glossary under "annext."

THOROUGH (p. 6 and elsewhere). "Let this Learned Doctor and his new Academy," says John Oldmixon in his *Reflections on Dr. Swift's Letter to Harley* (1712), "do their utmost to furnish our Language with what the French call *Chevilles*, with his *Thoroughs, Althoughs*, and the whole Army of antiquated Words before-mentioned." Oldmixon likewise criticizes Swift's frequent use of "thereon," "therein," and "thereby." The repeated occurrence of such words in the *Tale* is one of the devices used by Swift to heighten his Modern's pedantic style.

TRANSPOSAL (p. 43). Rare. The first *OED* example is 1695. Johnson mentions Swift and defines the word as "the act of putting things in each other's place"; note the nearly synonymous terms in Swift's phrase "Transposal or Misapplication." Cf. "Disturbance or Transposition" (p. 171).

TROGLODYTE (p. 183). The *OED* cites Swift as the first author to use this word in an adjectival sense. See Phillips: "A people anciently inhabiting the farthest part of Aethiopia, of a fierce salvage nature, dwelling in caves, and feeding on raw flesh." Is Swift referring to one who avoids or ignores sense experience? Or could "Troglodyte Philosopher" be the Modern's crazy malapropism for "Stagyrite Philosopher"?

VEGETABLE (p. 78). Swift's "vegetable Beaux" is a play on the seventeenth-century adjectival use of "vegetable" in the sense of having the living and growing properties of plants, as in "vegetable soul" or other variations such as "vegetable power," "vegetable life," or Marvell's "vegetable love."

VITTLES (p. 118). An alternate spelling of "victuals." But that Swift uses "Vittles" in Peter's *speech* while elsewhere (e.g., pp. 116, 192) using "Victuals" suggests that he acknowledged a difference between the colloquial and proper forms of the word.

YEOMANTRY (p. 181). Guthkelch and Smith explain: "This spelling occurs in edd. 1-5 (*Yeomanry* edd. 1711, 1720, etc.); due to assimilation with *Gentry*, or to false analogy with 'infantry' and similar words." But cf. Glossary under "Bombastry."

Selected Bibliography of Secondary Sources

Allen, Don Cameron. "Style and Certitude." *ELH* 11 (September 1948): 167–75.

Arieti, Silvano. *Interpretation of Schizophrenia*. New York, 1955.

Baker, Sheridan. "Fielding and the Irony of Form," *Eighteenth-Century Studies* 2 (December 1968): 138–54.

Baum, Paull Franklin. *The Other Harmony of Prose: An Essay in English Prose Rhythm*. Durham, N.C., 1952.

Bleuler, Eugen. *Dementia Praecox or the Group of Schizophrenias*. Translated by Joseph Zinkin. New York, 1950.

Bruner, Jerome S. "The Conditions of Creativity." In *Contemporary Approaches to Creative Thinking*, edited by Howard E. Gruber et al., pp. 1–30. New York, 1962.

Christensen, Francis. "A Generative Rhetoric of the Paragraph." Reprinted in *The Sentence and the Paragraph: Articles on Rhetorical Analysis from "College Composition and Communication" and "College English,"* pp. 20–32. Urbana, Ill., 1966.

———. "A Generative Rhetoric of the Sentence." Reprinted in *The Sentence and the Paragraph: Articles on Rhetorical Analysis from "College Composition and Communication" and "College English,"* pp. 199–213. Urbana, Ill., 1966.

Clark, Albert C. *Prose-Rhythm in English*. Oxford, 1913.

Cohen, Murray. "Sensible Words: Linguistic Theory in Late Seventeenth-Century England." In *Studies in Eighteenth-Century Culture*, edited by Ronald C. Rosbottom, 5:229–52. Madison, Wis., 1976.

Colie, Rosalie L. *Paradoxia Epidemica: The Renaissance Tradition of Paradox*. Princeton, 1966.

Croll, Morris W. *Style, Rhetoric and Rhythm: Essays by Morris W. Croll*. Edited by J. Max Patrick and Robert O. Evans. Princeton, 1966.

Davies, Hugh Sykes. "Irony and the English Tongue." In *The World of Jonathan Swift*, edited by Brian Vickers, pp. 129–53. Oxford, 1968.

———. "Milton and the Vocabulary of Verse and Prose." In *Literary English Since Shakespeare*, edited by George Watson, pp. 175–93. Oxford, 1970.

DePorte, Michael V. *Nightmares and Hobbyhorses: Swift, Sterne, and the Augustan Idea of Madness*. San Marino, Calif., 1974.

Edelson, Marshall. *Language and Interpretation in Psychoanalysis*. New Haven, 1975.

Ehrenpreis, Irvin. *Mr. Swift and His Contemporaries. Swift: The Man, His Works, and the Age*, vol. 1. Cambridge, Mass., 1962.

———. *The Personality of Jonathan Swift*. Cambridge, Mass., 1958.

Empson, William. *Seven Types of Ambiguity*. 3rd ed. Norfolk, Conn., 1953.

Foucault, Michel. *Madness and Civilization: A History of Insanity in the Age of Reason*. Translated by Richard Howard. New York, 1965.

———. *The Order of Things: An Archaeology of the Human Sciences*. Translated by Richard Howard. New York, 1970.

Howell, A. C. "*Res et Verba*: Words and Things." *ELH* 13, no. 2 (1946): 131–42.

Howell, Wilbur S. *Logic and Rhetoric in England, 1500–1700*. New York, 1961.

Kasanin, J. S., ed. *Language and Thought in Schizophrenia*. Berkeley, 1955.

Kenner, Hugh. *Flaubert, Joyce, and Beckett: The Stoic Comedians*. Boston, 1962.

Kermode, Frank. *The Sense of an Ending: Studies in the Theory of Fiction*. Oxford, 1967.

Knowlson, James. *Universal Language Schemes in England and France, 1600–1800*. Toronto, 1975.

Laffal, Julius. *Pathological and Normal Language*. New York, 1965.

Laing, R. D. *The Divided Self: An Existential Study in Sanity and Madness*. Reprint. London, 1965.

Lorenz, Maria. "Criticism as Approach to Schizophrenic Language." *Archives of General Psychiatry* 9 (September 1963): 235–45.

Maher, Brendan A. *Principles of Psychopathology: An Experimental Approach*. New York, 1966.

Milic, Louis. *A Quantitative Approach to the Style of Jonathan Swift*. The Hague, 1967.

Neumann, J. H. "Jonathan Swift and the Vocabulary of English." *Modern Language Quarterly* 4 (1943): 191–204.

Nicolson, Marjorie Hope. *The Breaking of the Circle: Studies in the Effect of the "New Science" on Seventeenth-Century Poetry*. Rev. ed. New York, 1960.

O'Donoghue, E. G. *Story of Bethlehem Hospital from Its Foundation in 1247*. London, 1914.

Ohmann, Richard. "Prolegomena to the Analysis of Prose Style." In *Style in Prose Fiction: English Institute Essays*, edited by Harold C. Martin, pp. 1–24. New York, 1959.

Paulson, Ronald. *Theme and Structure in Swift's "Tale of a Tub."* New Haven, 1960.

Price, Martin. *Swift's Rhetorical Art: A Study in Structure and Meaning*. Reprint. London, 1963.

Quinlan, Maurice J. "Swift's Use of Literalization as a Rhetorical Device." *PMLA* 82 (December 1967): 516–21.

Saintsbury, George. *A History of English Prose Rhythm*. Reprint. Bloomington, Ind., 1967.

Scholes, Robert, and Kellogg, Robert. *The Nature of Narrative*. Oxford, 1966.

Scott-Thomas, Lois M. "The Vocabulary of Jonathan Swift." *Dalhousie Review* 25 (1946): 442–47.

Stout, Gardner D., Jr. "Speaker and Satiric Vision in Swift's *Tale of a Tub*." *Eighteenth-Century Studies* 3 (Winter 1969): 175–99.

Strang, Barbara. "Swift and the English Language: A Study in Principles and Practice." In *To Honor Roman Jakobson: Essays on the Occasion of His Seventieth Birthday*, pp. 1947–59. The Hague, 1967.

Tempest, Norton R. *The Rhythm of English Prose: A Manual for Students*. Cambridge, 1930.

Traugott, John. "*A Tale of a Tub*." In *Focus: Swift*, edited by C. J. Rawson, pp. 76–120. London, 1971.

Tufte, Virginia. *Grammar as Style*. New York, 1971.

Ullmann, Stephen. *Language and Style*. New York, 1966.

Watt, Ian. *The Rise of the Novel: Studies in Defoe, Richardson, and Fielding*. Reprint. Berkeley, 1959.

Whorf, Benjamin Lee. *Language, Thought, and Reality: Selected Writings of Benjamin Lee Whorf*. Edited by John B. Carroll. Cambridge, Mass., 1956.

Williams, Kathleen. *Jonathan Swift and the Age of Compromise*. Lawrence, Kans., 1958.

Williamson, George. *The Senecan Amble: Prose from Bacon to Collier*. Chicago, 1951.

Wimsatt, W. K. *Philosophic Words: A Study of Style and Meaning in the "Rambler" and "Dictionary" of Samuel Johnson*. New Haven, 1948.

Index

CPSIA information can be obtained
at www.ICGtesting.com
Printed in the USA
FFOW04n1245290216
21752FF

9 780814 253540